Trails of the Heart ♥ Book Three

# BETTY WOODS

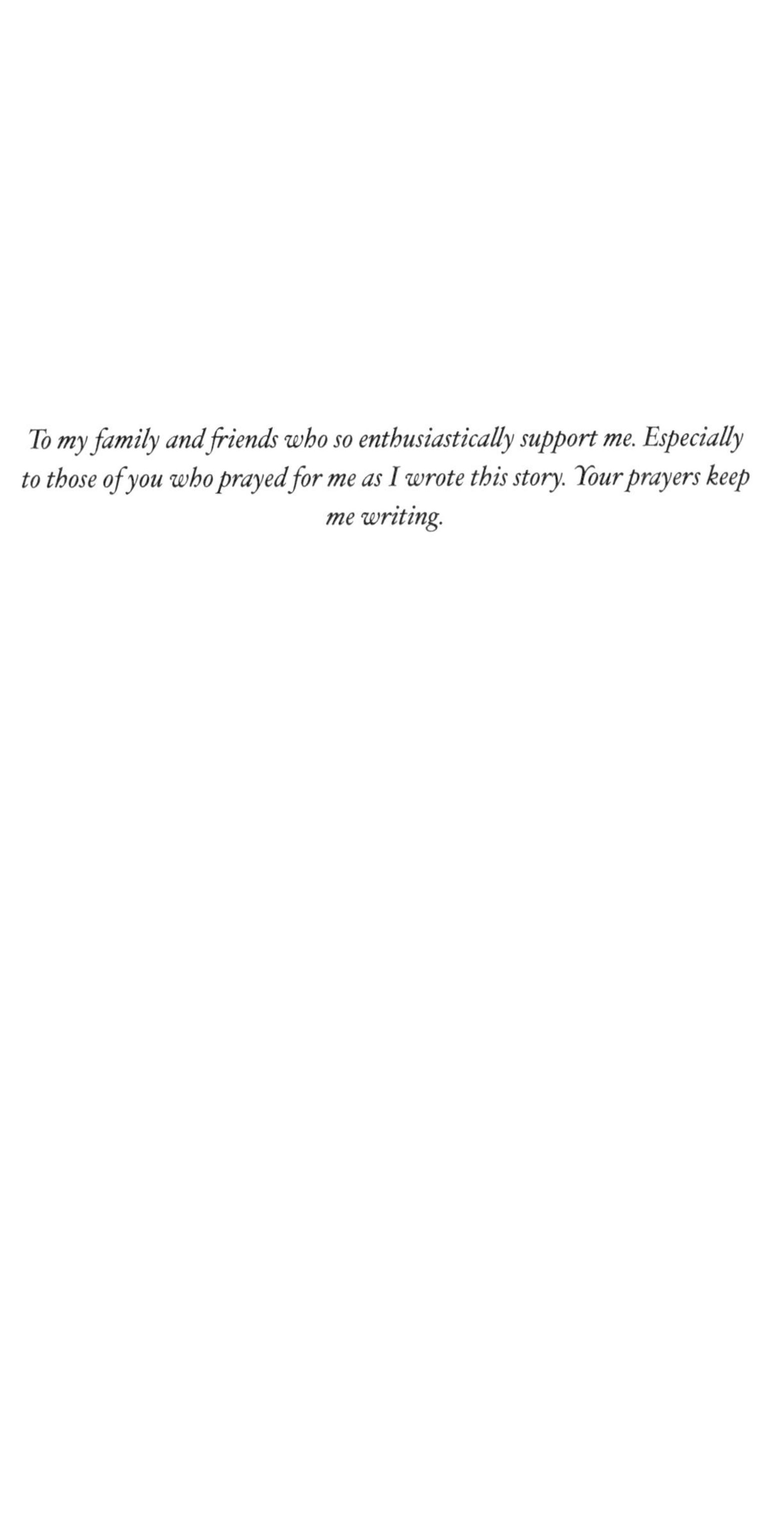

*To my family and friends who so enthusiastically support me. Especially to those of you who prayed for me as I wrote this story. Your prayers keep me writing.*

# ACKNOWLEDGMENTS

Kim Peters, my sweet, artistic friend, who answered my questions about painting. I would have Heidi using the wrong paints and a lot of other things wrong without your help. I hope I did you justice with Heidi's endeavors.

Dr. Eric Herrstrom, my wonderful pastor. His sermon series on forgiveness helped me to help my characters work through their past hurts and not give into bitterness. Lily quotes him while advising Heidi on how to let go of the past.

1

---

*September 1873*
*San Antonio, Texas*

Sucking in another shaky breath, Heidi Schultz stood outside the stage depot, taking her first good look at San Antonio. She'd made her escape. For now.

She scanned the dusty street, busy with wagons, buggies, and people making their way to wherever they were going. If only she could stride somewhere with such purpose. If only she could figure out how to find Suzanne. After that ... God only knew. She had no idea.

A grizzled stage employee set her carpet bag on top of the trunk settled near her feet.

"Sir, could you tell me the best way to find someone who lives around here?"

"I ain't been in town that long myself. The Hawkins over at the general store know everybody. Go there. You're welcome to leave your bags here for a while."

*"Danke."*

The man quirked both white eyebrows.

"Uh—thank you."

"You're welcome."

The instant the man left, she grabbed her carpet bag. She stepped inside the stage depot before digging out her favorite hat. She yanked off the hideous sunbonnet she'd worn to disguise herself from everyone in New Braunfels. With no mirror, she fumbled to pin her hat, ignoring the curious glances of the other people in the room.

After getting directions, she stepped outside. The stage worker hadn't asked her for more information about who she wanted to find. Good. The less people who knew her true business here, the better. In case *Vater* ... no, Father found out where she'd gone. Friends said he had searched for her the day she'd slipped out of the house.

Heidi took in several ragged breaths while staring at the door of the general store. She used the glass window as a mirror to check her hat and hair then brushed as much dust as she could from her wrinkled skirt. Her disheveled appearance screamed she'd been traveling. But under the circumstances, it couldn't be helped. Gripping the door knob, she swallowed hard.

"Afternoon, ma'am." A man with graying dark hair smiled from behind the counter as she stepped inside. "Be with you as soon as I add up this order."

The scents of pickles and crackers from the nearby barrels made her stomach growl in a most unbecoming manner. She'd intended to eat as soon as she got off the stage. But when the man at the depot assured someone could help her find her sister so quickly, food had become something that could wait.

An elderly woman scooped up the needles and thread she'd bought. She smiled at Heidi as she walked past.

"I'll get that for you." Happy for an excuse to help the lady leave the store sooner, Heidi opened the door. She'd rather not have anyone overhear her questions.

"Thank you."

"You're welcome." Heidi waited until the door closed to turn and face the storekeeper, hoping she and the pleasant-looking man would be the only people here for a while.

"May I help you?"

"I hope so."

The storekeeper cocked his head as she walked toward him.

"I'm Heidi Schultz. I'm looking for my sister, uh, my sister … Lily Grimes." The name her sister now used sounded odd to her ears and felt even stranger on her tongue.

The storekeeper stepped from behind the counter. He halted in front of her, looking her up and down. "You're Lily's sister?"

"Yes, sir. I am." Heidi forced herself to look him in the eye and not squirm under his penetrating gaze.

"You've got her blue eyes. Your hair's a little darker blonde than hers. She's thinner and a little shorter."

"You know my sister?"

"Maybe. But beg your pardon, I don't know you."

Heidi's heart pounded as he scrutinized her. She hadn't expected this type of reception. "No, sir. You couldn't know me. I've hardly been out of New Braunfels my entire life."

"I can believe that." His serious blue eyes softened some.

Of course he believed her. Her German accent left no doubt where she was from.

How much to tell this man who was so reluctant to talk about the sister he apparently knew? She'd have to divulge enough to convince him she really was Suzanne's—no Lily's— sister. She took a deep breath. "My sister's first husband was a man named Harvey who died in a tragic accident. She married Mr. Grimes, a local rancher, a couple of years ago."

How she hoped he wouldn't press her for more information. His intense scrutiny had Heidi so rattled she couldn't remember the first husband's last name or the second husband's first name, nor the names of Lily's children from her first marriage.

"Lily and Toby didn't say anything about company coming when they were at church last Sunday."

She licked her dry lips. Toby. She must remember the current husband's first name. "That's because they didn't know I was coming. I should have written them, but there wasn't time. Please, sir, I need to find my sister." Her voice cracked in spite of her efforts at self-control.

"Sorry to upset you, ma'am, but I have to know who's looking for Lily no matter how much you look like her."

"Yes, well, I'd like to see her as soon as possible."

"Why do you keep saying you need to find your own sister as if you don't know where she is?" His eyes narrowed as he continued to study her.

"I haven't seen her since she left home over seven years ago. I-I have the last letter she wrote to me." She shouldn't have said such things to a stranger. Especially since she didn't want to share her private correspondence with Suzanne—no Lily—to anyone. But her desperation to find her sister overcame her need for caution.

"A letter you say?" His piercing gaze softened only a little.

"*Ja*—yes." She rummaged through her reticule to find the letter. She held it out, hoping he wouldn't insist she unfold it so he could read more than the note on the outside of the sheet. "My sister sent it to a trusted friend to give to me, because our parents wouldn't have given me a letter from Lily."

He stared at the letter much longer than necessary. "That's Lily's handwriting. I've read enough of her grocery lists to know." His gaze softened. "How long did you say since you've seen her?"

"A little over seven years."

"From what Lily's told my wife, that'd be about right, so you are Lily's sister." He grinned as he extended his hand. "I'm Owen Hawkins."

"Pleased to meet you, sir."

Relief flooded through her. She'd told this man almost everything she knew about her sister. What she'd have done if he wanted more information, only God knew.

"Sorry to be so rough on you, but I had to be sure. Is it Miss or Mrs. Schultz, if you don't mind me asking?"

"Miss." Since the man didn't recognize Lily's maiden name, he couldn't know too much about her past. Lily must have left more than her family behind a few years ago.

"Lily and Toby aren't expecting you, but God has it all set up."

"He does?" Her squeaky voice sounded childish.

Mr. Hawkins's grin spread ear to ear. "Toby's foreman, Jethro Bannister, should be coming soon to pick up his order. Be glad he drove the wagon instead of riding his horse to town."

"How nice." Her stomach rumbled. Heat rushed up her face.

"Have you eaten lately, young lady?"

"This morning. If you think I have time, I'll walk to a restaurant."

He shook his head. "Best to settle for the crackers and such I can offer you here. Jethro's gentleman enough to wait for you to eat somewhere, but there are enough varmints, animal and human, that it's best not to get home after dark." The gentleman gave her a boyish grin and gestured for her to follow him.

A few minutes later, Heidi sat on a crate next to a makeshift barrel table, enjoying crackers, dried peaches, and water Mr. Hawkins insisted on serving her for free. Her sister must be well thought of considering the way the storekeeper treated Heidi. That is, once he'd assured himself of who she was.

Why someone needed to be so cautious about who asked about Suz—no, Lily—would have to wait for an answer. Heidi had to remember to use the new name her sister had chosen.

If Lily and her husband welcomed Heidi and wanted to answer any of her questions.

The bell over the door jangled as a cowboy who couldn't be more than a few years older than her nineteen years stepped into the general store. He removed his hat as soon as he spotted Heidi perusing dress goods with Mr. Hawkins.

The storekeeper smiled at the man. "You're back at almost the exact time I said."

"Of course. I always like to get home before dark."

"Which is what I told this young lady. Miss Schultz, this is Jethro Bannister."

"My pleasure, Miss."

His formal tone and stiff posture made her wonder how true his words were, especially since he maintained his distance from her and the storekeeper. Which was more than fine, since she had no intentions of needing any man in her life ever again.

"Thank you. I'm Lily's sister. Mr. Hawkins says you can take me to her."

"Sure ..." Both eyebrows went up, almost colliding with the strand of honey-brown hair falling across his tanned forehead. He stared at Mr. Hawkins as if he needed assurance Heidi spoke the truth.

Her habit of being so observant had often helped her assess people. Had probably saved her from *Vater* and Johann's scheming concerning her. But at this moment, she had no business paying such close attention to another man she would gladly ignore if not for needing him to take her to Lily.

"I've got Toby's bill totaled and the supplies ready to load." Mr. Hawkins jarred her from her thoughts.

The two men wasted no time loading the wagon. Mr. Bannister tipped his hat to her as he walked back inside. "We're ready to go."

"Thank you."

"You're welcome. Uh, don't you have a bag or something?"

She nodded. "I left my luggage at the stage depot."

His green eyes widened. Whatever his thoughts, he kept them to himself as he opened the door for her.

Good. She wasn't interested in his ideas or him. An escort who was as uninterested in her would do fine.

"Oh, Mr. Hawkins, could you do me another favor, please?" She halted in the doorway.

"Of course."

"If someone comes in asking questions about me, please don't tell them where I'm at or that I came here at all."

"All right."

"Thank you, sir." Since he'd been so secretive about Lily, she assumed he'd do the same for her. Without asking why. She paused a moment longer to be sure he didn't have any questions for her before following Mr. Bannister out the door.

---

As he helped his unexpected passenger onto the wagon seat, Jethro puzzled over the woman's request to Owen as he walked around, then hopped up next to her. Mrs. Grimes never talked about her family, but if Owen said this woman was his boss's sister-in-law, he'd take the storekeeper's word. Just why she didn't want Owen not to say anything about her or how much luggage she had was none of his concern.

Neither the boss nor Mrs. Grimes had mentioned he'd need to pick up a guest this afternoon. Did they have any idea this woman was coming their way?

"Thank you for doing this." She gave him a thin smile that didn't reach her light blue eyes as he grabbed the reins.

"Nothing to thank me for. Mrs. Grimes would have a fit if I left her sister stranded in San Antonio."

"I hope so." She sighed.

"Well, of course."

Anyone blessed with family left should be happy to see them. Unless they were like his older brother had been the day Jethro left Georgia for good. So glad to see him leave he didn't care what might or might not happen to his own brother.

Willing his unpleasant memories away, he turned his attention to guiding the wagon down the crowded street. The past was done and couldn't be undone. God had helped him find peace in Texas as well as blessings he'd never dreamed about, so he'd be happy with that.

He headed the horses toward the stage depot, hoping he wasn't bringing home trouble disguised as a pretty, but unannounced visitor. Sweet Mrs. Grimes would have met her own sister in person if she'd known the lady was coming. Something didn't seem right about the nervous woman next to him fiddling with her reticule while she sat stiffer than a piece of dried out jerky.

Miss Shultz stared straight ahead the few minutes it took to get to the depot, which was all right with him. He had no idea what to say to this woman. And a gentleman had no business asking all the questions about why she was here but didn't want anyone to know.

"My trunk and carpet bag are the ones closest to the bench."

The large trunk she pointed toward might outweigh a sack of flour. Which meant she could intend to stay quite a while. Her carpet bag bulged, he doubted it could hold another item.

This woman had gall the likes of which he'd rarely seen by imposing on a family who didn't know she was coming. In his two years at the *Tumbling G,* he'd never heard Mrs. Grimes mention a word about her family. But the stranger beside him wasn't his sister, so he'd hold his tongue. More like bite it to keep from saying what he thought.

"Um ... how well do you know Lily?" She waited until the wagon was almost out of town to say another word other than to thank him for hoisting what had to be a very full trunk into the wagon.

"Know her? What do you mean?"

"Just what I said. How well do you know my sister?"

Shaking his head, he studied this strange female. "Since the cook left, I eat most of my meals with them, but she's my boss's wife, not a close friend."

The woman's odd question didn't make sense. If the lady didn't look so much like Mrs. Grimes that he couldn't deny they were sisters, he might turn the wagon around and leave her to Owen.

She sucked in a ragged-sounding breath. "I haven't seen Lily since I was twelve. Under different circumstances, I'd have written first. But I didn't have that luxury."

"Oh."

That little bit of information told him much more than she said. What kind of trouble might this lady be in? Or have caused? He'd leave that for Mrs. Grimes to discover. Any good cowboy knew better than to get too nosy. As did a former Georgia gentleman. So, he'd not ask for any further explanation from the obviously distressed woman.

"Since you're so reluctant to talk about my sister, tell me about the ranch, please."

"The ranch?" He must sound like a tongue-tied boy, but her perceptiveness threw him as off balance as an ornery mustang trying to throw him out of his saddle.

"Yes. I've lived in New Braunfels all my life. I know almost nothing about ranching."

That explained her frilly brown town dress and bustle, neither of which was going to be much at home on the *Tumbling G*. Why had she come?

"There's not much to tell. The longhorns graze and grow big enough to drive to Kansas. We round them up in the spring for the drive and do another roundup this month to brand the new calves and unbranded strays."

"I'd like to know all about a roundup and everything else, please."

Her breathless tone made her sound like an over-eager girl, except her womanly figure said otherwise. When he glanced over in her direction, her eyes shone like a child's at Christmas. Why anyone could be so interested in stories of eating dust behind longhorns was more than he could fathom.

The woman asked him more questions in the next three hours than he'd heard in his entire life. She talked so much she'd worry the horns off a longhorn if the boss let her get within thirty feet of one. If she were this wordy all the time, he'd be learning to cook well enough to eat supper in his own place.

As soon as they topped the first ridge, the ranch came into view. "That's home." Jethro pointed toward the one-story stone house and the wood outbuildings.

"Ohh ..." Her mouth formed a pretty *O* to match her comment as she stared speechless at her first sight of the *Tumbling G*.

His almost sore ears would have thanked her for her silence if ears could talk.

"I'm glad I brought my pencils and paints. The way the evening sun shines on the buildings and the land is breathtaking."

She'd brought her paints too? He clamped his mouth shut to keep from saying something so rude out loud. Someone coming only to visit didn't pack to that extent. The boss and his wife were in for a surprise. Too bad he was the one bringing her in.

But gentle Mrs. Grimes would have his hide if he left her little sister stranded in town. He'd eat whatever he could scrounge in his kitchen tonight. Supper at the main house might be hotter than any Texas summer day he'd seen so far.

**2**

---

A barking, lanky hound interrupted the uncomfortable silence as Mr. Bannister drove the wagon into the yard.

"Ruckus, hush." Mr. Bannister admonished the black dog with white spots as he halted the wagon not far from the house.

"That's an odd name for a dog." Such an inane comment, but she had to say something to keep the man from guessing how nervous she was. If he hadn't already suspected such a thing by the way she'd chattered on and on during the drive here.

Yet she'd been fascinated by cowboys and their ranches for years and couldn't resist the opportunity to satisfy her curiosity. Especially since *Vater* and *Mutter,* for reasons only her parents seemed to know, wouldn't tolerate so much as a mention of cowboys.

"Mrs. Grimes says the name suits the mongrel fine as much noise as he can make." He reached to help her down.

A dark-haired little girl who had to be Lily's daughter bounded out the front door. Thank God she and Lily had exchanged one set of letters the last month or so, giving her some information and a sliver of hope her sister would understand why she'd come. The dog ran to the child, his long tail almost wagging his entire body. The girl stopped midgiggle from petting the hound and gaped at Heidi.

"Ella, go tell your ma and pa y'all have company," Mr. Bannister said.

"Company?" She tilted her head as she continued staring in Heidi's direction.

"Right. Now go tell your ma and pa."

With the dog at her heels, the child trotted toward the house as the front door opened again. "Pa, Mr. Bannister says to tell you and Ma we have company."

The brown-haired man Heidi supposed to be Toby clamped his mouth shut as he paused by the steps and considered her. "Yeah, looks like we do."

His long strides ate up the distance between him and Heidi. He studied her up and down. Not frowning. Not smiling. Much like the reception she'd received at the general store.

She clutched her reticule with trembling hands. "I'm Heidi Schultz."

"Lily's little sister?"

"I can show you Lily's letter in my reticule if you'd like to see it." Heidi licked her parched lips as he continued staring.

Toby shook his head. "One good look at you says you're who you say you are."

The breath she'd been holding in whooshed out quickly as if she were wilting like a dried out flower. "I can explain why I'm here unannounced."

"Why don't you do that inside? Lily will be really unhappy with me if I keep you standing in the yard like this on such a warm day." A slow grin spread across his face. "I'm Toby."

"Pleased to meet you." She hoped her forced smile didn't look as stiff as her lips felt.

He took her arm and guided her toward the porch.

"I'll bring her luggage in the house, boss."

"Thanks." Toby didn't look back at his foreman as he and

Heidi reached the porch steps. "I'll be out soon to help unload the wagon so we can wash up for supper faster."

"Since y'all have company, I can eat at my place."

Toby turned just enough to look at Mr. Bannister. "Lily's planning on you eating with us." He opened the door for Heidi and allowed her to precede him inside. "Darlin', I've got one more surprise for you in the parlor."

"What?"

Heidi's whole being thrilled to hear her sister's still-recognizable voice coming from the back of the house.

"Just get in here, darlin'."

A little boy toddled in ahead of Lily. She gasped as she halted inside the doorway. "Oh, my ... Heidi?" Both hands covered her heart as she shook her head. Her slow smile grew into an ear-to-ear grin that lit up her entire face.

Heidi could only nod.

Lily closed the distance between them and enveloped Heidi in a fierce, smothering hug. She stepped back, her hands resting lightly on Heidi's shoulders "Let me look at you." Her eyes glistened with tears. "So grown up now."

"*Ja.*" A torrent of German questions rushed out as she peered into Lily's shining eyes.

Lily shook her head. "I only speak English now."

"You do? Why?"

"We'll talk about that later." Lily beamed as she patted Heidi's shoulder. "First, that wonderful surprise letter from you and now seeing you here in person. You're the answer to years of prayers."

Heidi hoped her sister still felt the same after she found out her uninvited guest had come to stay, at least long enough to figure out what to do and where to go next. They had more to talk about than her sister realized.

Mr. Bannister walked through the door, carrying her carpet bag. Ella followed behind him. "Where should I set this?"

"Um, in Harvey's room. I'll make him a pallet in our room

tonight." Lily let her arms go slack at her side as she glanced at her husband.

Toby nodded as he scooped the little boy in his arms and motioned for a staring Ella to come to his side.

"I'll get your trunk in next, Miss Schultz." Mr. Bannister paused long enough to look in Heidi's direction.

"*Dan*—thank you." Despite her nerves, she must remember not to speak German. Why not, she'd dearly love to know. So many questions she must ask as soon as she could.

The shocked looks Lily and Toby had exchanged as soon as the foreman said the word trunk told her she needed to think of a way to explain things quickly. She swallowed hard, as she tried to decide how to accomplish such a feat.

"*Vater*—uh—Papa intended to force me to wed. Mama too. I can't imagine spending the rest of my life with … with someone like Johann. He's not interested in God. And Papa and Mama didn't believe me when I told them and …" She bit her trembling lip as she stared into her silent sister's eyes. "Your letter. It was so warm and loving. I … I came here." The words tumbled out. How she prayed they made sense to Lily and Toby.

"You poor dear. You have no idea how well I understand." Lily patted her cheek.

JETHRO PUSHED through the front door with the trunk hoisted on his shoulder. Miss Schultz had packed a lot more than paints, but neither the boss nor Mrs. Grimes acted surprised to see the good-sized trunk.

"Better set that in Ella's room so you don't have to move it again." Mr. Grimes tipped his head toward the bedrooms. "Then we'll tend to the supplies."

"Sure."

He took care of the trunk as quickly as possible. The sooner Jethro could get outside, the happier he'd be. The boss and missus had matching furrowed brows. And one glance at their guest's tear-filled eyes assured him he didn't want to end up in the middle of whatever the woman was involved in. He'd had more than enough of his share of uncomfortable family situations after the war.

Mr. Grimes followed him outside. He glanced at Jethro after slinging a flour sack over his shoulder. "Good thing you went to town today."

"Glad to hear that. I wasn't the least bit sure about bringing Miss Schultz here." Jethro grabbed the coffee tin and lard.

"Her father planned to force her to marry. She balked and ran to us." Mr. Grimes shook his head. "Doesn't sound like my stubborn father-in-law has changed. His wife either." He turned toward the house. "I might tell you that story another day if Lily doesn't mind."

"Sure, boss." Jethro answered out of habit as he followed Mr. Grimes. What he was sure of, he needed to figure a way to fix his own supper. "I found a cook and enough men to start roundup next week, except I told one of them to ride out and talk to you first."

Mr. Grimes halted a few feet from the porch steps. "Why?"

"I ran across a Ben Tyler who said he rode with you on your first drive. I didn't promise him a job because he already smelled of whisky just after noon."

"I'll talk to him if he shows up." As if that settled everything, the boss headed inside.

Jethro's mind worked harder than his body did carrying in groceries as he tried his best to think of some way to eat at his house. "I don't mind fending for myself tonight since your wife wasn't expecting her sister."

Mr. Grimes shook his head as they carried the last of the supplies toward the house. "Lily's got plenty fixed, and I wouldn't want to hurt Heidi's feelings if she thought you stayed away because of her."

"I hadn't thought of that. I'll be back in as soon as I tend to the horse and wagon."

"I'll help you." The boss grinned.

Jethro couldn't smile back.

He'd left Georgia to forget family difficulties and misunderstandings. Sitting at the table listening to whatever the Grimes needed to talk about would probably ruin his appetite since he didn't want to be so much as a silent listener to any kind of family discussion.

Sooner than Jethro liked, Mr. Grimes took his usual spot at the end of the table while Jethro seated himself across from Miss Schultz and Ella. He forced a stiff smile at the pair. Miss Schultz's pretty lips twitched up slightly. As quickly as the sparkle left her light blue eyes, she might not be any happier to see him than he was to be looking at her. What she thought about him shouldn't be the least bit worrisome, except he'd done nothing but assist her all afternoon. She should at least have the decency to like him.

No, she didn't have to do that. And he didn't have to like her no matter how pleasant-looking she was right now. He'd be better off not taking a liking to such a talkative woman, especially one who could be bringing all sorts of trouble with her.

He welcomed closing his eyes and bowing his head as the boss thanked God for the food and sending Miss Schultz to them. Jethro hoped the Grimes family could stay so grateful for acquiring their unannounced guest and whatever difficulties she may have brought with her.

"I have another aunt." Ella beamed at him as Mr. Grimes passed the cornbread to Miss Schultz.

"Yes, you do." He concentrated on the bowl of stew in front of him.

"You have to finish telling me how Frieda and her husband managed to get you out of New Braunfels." Mrs. Grimes grinned as she set small pieces of beef on the highchair tray for Harvey to grab.

"I hid under a tarp in the wagon bed all the way to their house while Papa and Mama were at a concert Tuesday night. I stayed away from the windows while inside Frieda's house."

"But how did you get on the stage without being recognized?" Mrs. Grimes paused with her spoon in the air as she waited for an answer.

"I waited until today to leave, because we all assumed Papa would be checking the stage depot. Erich bought my ticket and walked the back streets to the stage with me as if he were the one leaving. I wore the most awful sunbonnet to hide my face. I intend to burn it."

The boss cleared his throat as Jethro continued to stare down at his food. A sunbonnet wasn't considered awful around here. Mrs. Grimes almost always wore hers when doing chores outside.

"I'll gladly take another bonnet to use while weeding the garden." Only Mrs. Grimes could still smile so sweetly at someone who'd pretty much insulted her, no matter how unintended the slight had been.

"Oh, uh, I'll be happy to give it to you."

"Thank you."

Miss Schultz shook her head. "No, thank you both for taking me in. I don't want to even think about living the rest of my life with someone like Johann Merkle only because Papa thinks the man can one day take over the wagon works for him."

The lady's exaggerated shudder made Jethro wonder how she kept from spilling the water sloshing in the glass she'd just picked up. Good thing she had sense enough to steady it with both hands. She should consider becoming an actress on a stage somewhere.

"He sounds as bad as the man Papa and Mama chose for me years ago."

The somber look on Mrs. Grimes's face almost made Jethro

shudder. The boss hadn't sounded as if he cared much for his in-laws. Like him, Jethro couldn't think much of someone who treated their daughters the way these ladies were talking about.

"Worse, at least *I* think he is. He's only been in town about three months, so he's still more like a stranger to me even though he saved Papa's life from a runaway horse and buggy. No matter how decent a man he may be, he's already thirty years old."

Jethro almost choked to keep from laughing at the long-winded, wide-eyed woman. She would make a superb actress. His father had been twelve years older than his mother, but they'd had a very happy life. Until his father was murdered.

Mr. Grimes chuckled.

His wife gave him her usual adoring smile before returning her attention to her sister. "Toby will be thirty in a few months."

"But you'll be going on twenty-six by then. And I ... Oh my. I sound awful, don't I?" She turned her huge woeful eyes on her brother-in-law.

He shook his head, smiling as indulgently as he did when Ella said something amiss. "I wouldn't be interested in a young thing like you even if I were looking. Lily's the only woman I'll ever want."

Miss Schultz straightened up dried out-jerky-stiff the way she'd done when riding in the wagon. "I'm nineteen and long past a child." Her eyes got even bigger as she clapped her hand over her mouth. "I'm so sorry. I shouldn't have said it like that. I—"

"Heidi, dear. Let's change the subject." Mrs. Grimes grinned as she placed pieces of cooked carrots on her son's tray.

Miss Schultz nodded before finally taking a sip of her water.

A woman who could out talk a politician had no business looking so serenely fetching once she was quiet. Sometimes Jethro wished for a loving woman who could make him as happy as Mrs. Grimes made the boss, but the lady sitting across the table from him was not that kind.

"I'm looking forward to learning as much as I can about your ranch. Mr. Bannister was kind enough to tell me all sorts of things on the drive here."

The sparkle returned to her eyes as she tossed a becoming smile first in Mrs. Grimes's direction and then toward the boss.

Jethro finished his stew as quickly as he could without gobbling it like a starving man. "Mrs. Grimes, that was delicious as usual. I need to get back to my place and finish putting away my own supplies." He scooted his chair back. "You still plan to start fixing the roof on the cook shack in the morning?" He paused for Mr. Grimes's answer.

"Yeah."

"Then I'll see y'all tomorrow."

He forced his boots to saunter out the back door instead of doing a fast trot. Whatever family problems the Grimes needed to talk about, he thanked God he hadn't ended up in the middle of any such discussion. He'd been fortunate to only have to listen to Miss Schultz's ramblings on sunbonnets and older men.

But he couldn't help feeling sorry for a lady having to leave home and everything else familiar the way she had done. The Yankees had forced plenty of hard changes on a boy who'd had to become the man of the house at fifteen when they killed his father.

Jethro shook his head, willing the bad memories to leave him alone, as he shoved open the door to his house. He could sympathize with Miss Schultz, but his sympathies were all he'd give such a talkative woman. She was the complete opposite of what he'd pray for if he seriously wanted a wife one day.

# 3

Heidi slipped out of the bed she'd shared with Ella as soon as the first rays of dawn filtered through the curtain. Her niece didn't stir. How the wiggly little girl slept so soundly was beyond Heidi's understanding. She'd lost track of how many times the child had rolled over almost on top of her or kicked her without ever waking. Sleeping on the hard wooden floor might have afforded her more rest.

She tiptoed to her trunk, glad she'd laid out clean clothes last night. She'd unpack later before every dress she owned had to be ironed. The dim room made it hard for her to dress quickly. Not wearing her bustle saved some time. Judging from the way Lily dressed, she wouldn't need a bustle until she went to town. She settled for tying her hair back with one of Ella's ribbons lying on the dresser. Properly pinning her hair would have to wait for better light.

Soft voices drifted down the hall. Good. Lily and Toby were awake. She made her way to the kitchen. Lily had left the lamp on the worktable. She lit it. If she could locate the coffee tin on the shelf next to the stove, she could grind the coffee and do something mature and useful. Which she desperately needed to do after yesterday.

Talking with Lily and Toby in the parlor last night had gone much better than the conversation at the dinner table had. Thank God they felt too sorry for her to be worried she had no idea how long she might be imposing on them.

But Mr. Bannister probably wondered if she had any more sense than her six year-old niece. He could think whatever he wanted. She wasn't interested in him or any other man who might come along. Heidi refused to become dependent on a man. After what *Vater* and *Mutter* had tried, she'd take care of herself and never rely on anyone ever again.

That is as soon as she could figure out how to keep her promise to herself. She'd have to find work in town soon as well as a decent boarding house. She owed Erich and Frieda for her stage ticket and didn't want to be a burden to Lily and Toby any longer than she could help. Surely, San Antonio had suitable jobs for a young woman.

Once she decided what kind of job she'd be suited for. Her father had grudgingly let her help with his ledgers after her brother's recent death. But how many other businessmen were like *Vater* and frowned on a woman working with ledgers or anything else that didn't concern caring for a household?

After locating the coffee grinder, Heidi sat at the worktable and took her frustrations out on the beans.

"Good morning."

Heidi jumped at the sound of Lily's voice.

"I didn't mean to scare you."

"I was thinking about jobs I might look for in San Antonio."

Lily smiled as she laid her hand on Heidi's arm. "Don't rush. I'd love some time for us to get to know each other again."

"So would I, but I need to pay Frieda back and—"

"We'll take care of that." Toby's boots clumped on the floor as he entered.

"But I never intended for you to do such a thing."

He grinned. "We know. This way you can take your time finding a good job and not settle for the first thing you find."

"*Danke.* Thank you." She gripped the handle on the grinder. She was truly grateful for such unexpected generosity, but taking care of herself meant not owing anyone anything ever again. "I'll repay you as soon as I can."

"Only after you have money saved back for what you need." Lily patted Heidi's shoulder, then walked over and slipped her apron over her head as if everything were settled.

Except Heidi had never felt so unsettled. The more she puzzled over her future, the more her stomach churned. The coffee would be like dust if she kept this up.

Lily got the wood burning in the stove. "I'll get the children up while this warms up."

"What else can I do to help?" Heidi set the coffee pot on the stove.

"You don't know how to make biscuits, do you?"

Heidi shook her head. Her sister had stopped doing more than speaking German when she'd run off with Harvey seven years ago. Something else Heidi would like to understand.

"I'll show you how when I get back."

Toby seated himself in his chair at the table. "You look as bumfuzzled as if Lily had grown wings and flown out of the room."

"She's so different than I remember. But somehow, she's still the same."

"Everyone changes over the years, especially people who've been hurt by loved ones."

"What do you mean?"

If not for wanting to help Lily with breakfast, Heidi would have gladly taken a chair next to Toby and let him explain about the sister she did and didn't know any more. Instead, she remained standing by the worktable.

His expression sobered. "I'll let Lily tell you everything when she's ready."

"I hope that's soon. I have so many questions." She kept her voice low. She wasn't sure if Lily would be upset or not to hear their discussion.

"Don't rush her." He spoke just above a whisper.

His tone was gentle in spite of his serious words. This man must love Lily dearly, judging from what she'd seen the short time she'd been here. If only someone cared so deeply for her.

No. She'd take care of herself. She'd thought *Vater* and *Mutter* loved her no matter what, but they'd proved otherwise. Since her brother's death, they cared more about finding a good man to take over the wagon works than looking for someone to cherish her. So, she'd guard her heart from dangerous longings that would only obligate her to another person.

Toby interrupted her musings. "You must be thinking some deep thoughts. You haven't said two words in the last minute or so."

"I do have a lot to think about."

"You can think out loud with Lily or me any time you'd like. We're praying for you."

"*Danke*—thank you."

Her worrisome thoughts made her forget not to speak German, but Toby didn't look upset. She walked over to check the coffee pot that didn't need checking. Her brother-in-law's kind words warmed her through and through, but independent people didn't make it a habit to think out loud with others. No matter how talkative she'd always been and preferred to be. Another change she simply had to make.

Her comfortable yet uncomfortable silence lasted until Lily and the children came in the room. Ella headed straight for Heidi as Lily carried in a still sleepy-looking Harvey.

"I like having an aunt who stays here." Ella wrapped her arms around Heidi's waist in a fierce embrace.

Heidi bent to return her niece's hug. "Thank you." If only everything were as simple about this visit as the little girl thought.

Ella stepped back to grin up at her. "I already told Ruckus you're staying longer than Aunt Charlotte and Uncle David do."

"Charlotte's my sister. David's her husband. Since she's got two boys to keep up with now, you won't see her riding over here wearing her trousers, boots, and spurs." Toby's eyes twinkled.

"Oh." Heidi had no idea how to reply to such remarks.

Lily set Harvey on the floor by Toby's chair. "Ready for your first try at biscuits?"

"Yes." She took the other apron from the nearby hook and slipped it over her head. Her simple day dress was much nicer than Lily's calico one. But if Lily or Toby noticed, they didn't say anything.

"Biscuits are Toby's favorite part of breakfast, but they're not hard to make." Lily set a bowl on the worktable. "And Charlotte only wears trousers while riding on their ranch. Toby is teasing you."

Heidi nodded, still not sure how to respond to any mention of a woman who wore trousers anywhere. Yet Toby teasing her the way her brothers had warmed her heart. Lily and Toby had already accepted her. More importantly, neither had tried to talk her out of eventually living in San Antonio alone.

Lily showed her how to mix the flour, baking powder, and salt in the bowl while Ella set the table.

"Lily and I were talking about your problems after you went to bed." Toby watched Heidi's first efforts with biscuits more closely than she wished.

Simple, or not, she didn't want to ruin one of his favorites. But, her curiosity over what he might say next took her attention away from watching Lily making a well in the flour mixture before adding milk in the middle. Lily handed Heidi the spoon.

Toby picked up his cup of coffee. "We think you should stay here a little while before looking for a job in town in case your pa finds out which stage you took."

"You do?" She shuddered at the thought of Papa finding her.

"We do. Knead the dough with your fingers. It's messy but makes delicious biscuits." Lily demonstrated before letting Heidi finish.

"Owen and Doris Hawkins know some of Lily's story and are the only ones who know you're with us. They won't tell anyone. So, if your pa comes to town looking for you, he'll think you've gone on somewhere else when no one has seen you or knows who you are." Toby's brown eyes looked as serious as his words sounded.

"How long should I wait?" What a terrible time for her nose to itch. She swiped at it with the top of her hand.

"We'll think and pray about it." Lily floured a spot on the worktable. "Roll the dough out about half an inch thick and cut it with the biscuit cutter."

The back door opened as Lily wiped her sticky hands on a damp rag. "Good morning, Jethro."

"Good morning." Mr. Bannister walked inside and hung his hat on a hook by the door but remained standing as she and Lily finished breakfast.

Strange. Did this man take all his meals with the family? Did she have a big flour spot on her nose from scratching it? She could feel a loose strand of hair on her left cheek. If only she'd known she needed to properly pin her hair. *Stop it.* She didn't care what kind of impression she made on this man or any other.

"Mornin', Jethro. Whoa, son." Toby rose to snag Harvey as the little boy toddled toward the hot stove.

Ella guided her brother over to the corner. "Play with your blocks."

After Heidi put the biscuits in the oven, she tucked her loose hair behind her ears. Ella's hair ribbon was not serving its purpose well. She hadn't worn her hair down in front of anyone but family since her sixteenth birthday. Not impressing Mr. Bannister was fine, but she didn't want him to think ill of her. A woman living alone in San Antonio would still need to guard her reputation.

The men discussed the roundup next week. Heidi tried her best to listen to Lily's instructions about how Toby liked his fried eggs while catching what the men were saying.

She helped Lily put the food on the table then took the chair next to Ella. Mr. Bannister gave her a perfunctory nod as he seated himself. Good. She didn't want him paying attention to her. But did she look so disheveled he'd ignore her?

Toby blessed the food. Lily passed the platter of eggs and bacon after taking small portions to put on Harvey's highchair tray.

"How many cowboys do you need for a roundup?" Heidi peered over at Toby after filling her plate.

"About a half dozen, plus a cook. Then we get together with other ranchers and help each other."

"It all sounds so intriguing."

"That's one way to describe it." Toby gave her the same indulgent-looking smile she'd seen from him last night.

---

INTRIGUING WAS A BETTER description for the woman sitting across from him than for the roundup she was asking about. The flour on her turned-up nose drew his attention to her lively blue eyes. She ducked her head as she forked her eggs. A loose strand of medium blonde hair fell across her face. Whatever she'd used to tie it back wasn't working too well. Quite a contrast from the fashionable-looking woman he'd brought here yesterday. Although her apron couldn't hide the dress that resembled one of Mrs. Grimes's Sunday best.

He quickly studied his own plate when Miss Schultz raised her head. Maybe she hadn't noticed him watching her. Something he couldn't make a habit of doing. He had no interest in her and didn't want her to get any wrong ideas.

"Mr. Bannister told me a roundup can last three weeks or more."

"That's about right." Mr. Grimes grinned as he buttered a biscuit. "You did a good job with your first biscuits. Your coffee's good too."

"Thank you."

Her first biscuits? The woman couldn't cook? Even he could make decent biscuits. Surely, her mother had seen to teaching her housekeeping and cooking. But all she'd talked about yesterday was painting and drawing. This woman must be pampered and spoiled beyond words or reason.

"I brought my pencils and oil paints. The evening sun yesterday was gorgeous. I'd like to capture that in a drawing or on a canvas."

"I always thought you had talent. I'm glad you're still drawing." Mrs. Grimes gave her sister an adoring smile.

"My seventh-grade teacher insisted Papa and Mama see I had lessons."

"Good. I want to see what you can do."

"Thank you."

The conversation about drawing and painting continued. If anyone noticed Jethro didn't contribute a word, they didn't say anything.

"Can you draw a picture of Ruckus?" Ella turned her full attention to her aunt.

"Of course. Animals make wonderful subjects. I'd like very much to draw or paint longhorns too." Heidi glanced at Mr. Grimes.

"Only from a good distance. They can be cantankerous. A charging bull would tear up more than your picture."

"I hadn't thought of that. But I'd like to find a way to paint them." She took the last bite of her eggs.

Mr. Grimes set his empty coffee cup down. "I'll have to think how." He turned his attention to his wife as he scooted his chair back. "Jethro and I'll fix the roof on the cook shack this morning. Jethro says Josiah, the new cook, should be here this afternoon, so we'll load the chuck wagon after lunch."

"All right." Mrs. Grimes finished washing Harvey's sticky hands with a damp rag.

"Thanks for a good breakfast." Jethro rose to follow his boss out the back door, glad he had a full day's work to do. So far, he'd been lucky not to be a party to any discussion of Miss Schultz's problems. He'd like to keep it that way.

Plus keep his distance from a woman he considered too pretty for his own good. Her bright blue dress emphasized her clear blue eyes, making her look as nice as the pictures she'd talked about painting. Even with flour spots on her nose and her hair coming loose. But if he ever married, he wouldn't want a spoiled wife who didn't know how to cook. A man couldn't live on pictures alone, no matter how attractive the painter might be.

# 4

Heidi hoped she didn't look too happy to see the men leave. Mr. Bannister had watched her much too carefully, especially since she was so disarrayed. Whatever his reasons, he could keep them to himself. Lily was the person she wanted to speak with alone.

So many questions swirled through her mind that only her sister could answer. "I'll be happy to help you with whatever you need to do today." She took a dish towel from the hook by the shelf holding the dishes. She *did* know how to wash and dry dishes.

"We'll get you settled in after I pick beans and corn from the garden. I want to do that this morning in case it gets hot this afternoon." Lily poured hot water from the kettle into the dish pan. "You can hang your dresses in the wardrobe in Ella's room after we finish in the garden."

"I'll help you pick vegetables."

Lily's eyes widened. "Does Mother have a garden now?"

Heidi shook her head.

"I'll show you how to tell what to pick. I've got carrots about ready too." Lily smiled.

"I need to properly pin my hair first. I didn't want to wake Ella this morning, so I didn't linger in her room."

Lily handed her a dish to dry. "She sleeps through almost anything."

"Even if Harvey cries." Ella laid the rag she'd used to wipe the table on the counter. "He doesn't cry much anymore, so he usually doesn't bother anybody."

"He does seem to be a happy little boy." Heidi knew little about babies, but her nephew sat quite content in a corner putting blocks in a pan, them dumping them out to start again.

Ella was listening to the conversation between Heidi and Lily more closely than Heidi had thought. She'd best save her questions for a time when she could truly be alone with Lily. "Toby says they'll start the roundup on Monday?" A question she could safely voice.

"Yes. We'll all rest on the Lord's Day tomorrow. You probably shouldn't be seen in town yet, so we'll have our own small service here. We don't get to church in San Antonio every Sunday."

"I've got a lot of things to adjust to, but I'm enjoying this new adventure." She stacked a dry plate on the shelf near her head.

Their conversation about mundane things continued as they worked together to clean the kitchen. How nice to talk to someone who wasn't trying to force her to be with a man she didn't love. She and Mama hadn't got along well since Papa had decided he wanted Johann to take over his business one day. The last dish soon sat in its spot. Heidi slipped her apron off and hung it on a hook.

"You might want to keep an apron on to protect such a pretty dress. I suggest you wear the sunbonnet you mentioned last night so your face doesn't burn while we're outside."

Heidi brushed flour from one of her sleeves. "I suppose that would be a good idea." She reached for the apron.

After properly fixing her hair, Heidi put on the bonnet she'd rather burn. She grimaced at her reflection in the mirror before returning to the kitchen to follow Lily, Ella, and Harvey to the garden behind the house. Mama had never had a garden that she could remember, but picking vegetables couldn't be a difficult task no matter how skeptical her sister's tone of voice had implied when Heidi offered to help.

The dog bounded up to them, wagging his tail.

"He likes you, Aunt Heidi." Ella patted her hound's head as he sidled up to her. "Harvey, you can play with me and Ruckus so you won't be in Ma's way."

"Stay where I can see both of you." Lily called to her children as they scampered off with the dog.

Heidi stepped into the garden with Lily. She recognized the corn but wasn't sure about the other plants. "It seems strange not to hear wagons going down the street and listening to the birds instead of other people's voices."

"The quiet takes getting used to, but now, I'd rather have this." Lily walked between the rows of corn.

"As happy as you look, you must like ranch life. Why did you leave New Braunfels? No one would ever tell me." Her words slipped out before she realized it. So much for waiting for Lily to tell her story as Toby had suggested this morning. She had to get better at not talking so much.

"For love. Like you, Father and Mother wanted me to pair me off with someone else. I chose Harvey instead."

"That's why you understand so well what I've done."

"Yes." She pulled a husk back on an ear of corn. "Put a little pressure on the kernel with your finger. If it's moist, it's ready to pick."

They went through the rows, checking for ripe ears of corn. Then Lily showed her how she decided which carrots to pull up and which green beans to pick. Lily's short explanation for leaving New Braunfels probably meant she didn't want to talk about eloping with Harvey, but Heidi's questions burned inside her warmer than the sun heating her shoulders as she walked the garden.

"I realize you might not like talking about such things, but why give up our native language? Why don't you have kraut or sausages in your house?"

Lily almost dropped the green beans in her hands before putting them into the basket by her feet. "After I left, I wrote Mother and Father more than once to tell them I was safe and well with Harvey. To try to explain he was a good man, the man who made me truly happy."

"I never saw those letters." What Heidi did see was her sister's eyes full of pain all these years later. So much pain that she couldn't miss Lily's cool references to Mother and Father instead of any endearing terms. No wonder Toby had told her not to rush Lily.

"Frieda wrote me. They burned my letters without opening them." Lily turned to pick more beans, but not before Heidi saw the tears in her sister's eyes. "When Ella was born, I wrote Frieda. I wrote her when Harvey died. She told them about those times, about Toby and when little Harvey came. She wrote me that she forced them to listen to her."

"If I hadn't become friends with Frieda a few months ago, I wouldn't have known you were still alive. Mama and Papa got so angry with me when I asked where you were and why you left I was afraid to ask again."

Lily kept her back to Heidi. "Exactly. Frieda said they refused to so much as mention my name. If Frieda hadn't written to me about Otto's death in February, I wouldn't have known my own brother died. My old life is as dead to me as I am to them. I refuse to acknowledge anything German in my home." Lily sucked in a shuddering breath.

"Not even your name."

"That too. Suzanne means Lily. That's who I am." She squared her shoulders.

"How did you learn to make biscuits and everything else?" If only she could take back more words she said without thinking first. Her sister's distress was obvious. Lily's voice now had a steely edge Heidi couldn't recall ever hearing.

"Harvey's late mother taught me. She took me in as if I were hers by blood." Lily jerked the beans with so much force the plant leaves shook. "She also helped me see I needed to forgive them."

"Have you been able to do that?" Heidi would appreciate any advice on how to not hold a grudge against their parents.

"Yes. With God's help and strength. Forgotten everything? No." Lily's voice trembled.

"I'm sorry I hurt you with my questions. I shouldn't have asked."

"None of it's your fault." Lily turned and enveloped Heidi in a fierce hug. "I'm so glad you could go to Frieda and get away too."

Heidi sniffed away tears. Lily's quivering voice sounded as if she were close to crying too. "So am I."

Ella and a whining little boy interrupted whatever else Lily might have intended to say. "Ma, is it time to start lunch?"

Shading her eyes from the sun, Lily checked the sky. "It looks close enough to time."

Heidi checked the watch pinned to her dress beneath her apron. "It's almost eleven o'clock."

Ella gasped. "You got a little watch like Pa?"

"Yes, I do. I'll show it to you after we go inside." Heidi marveled at Ella's reaction to a simple lady's watch. Ranch life was different in ways she hadn't imagined.

She helped Lily fix a simple lunch of bread, dried beef, and potatoes. Toby and Mr. Bannister came in to eat about noon. To Heidi's delight, the busy men didn't linger long over their meal.

"I'll put Harvey down for a nap, then we'll get your dresses in Ella's wardrobe before they're so wrinkled you have to iron them all."

"That would be good. I'll start unpacking while you tend to Harvey."

"Can I help you, Aunt Heidi?"

"I'm sure I can find something for you to do." Ella's broad grin made Heidi sure she'd keep her promise even though she wasn't sure what the little girl might help her do.

When Lily walked into the bedroom, Heidi sat on the bed with Ella explaining what she did with her pencils. "These are special. Not like the ones you'd use in school."

"I don't go to school. Ma and Pa are teaching me."

"Oh. That's good." Heidi hadn't thought until now the child wouldn't have access to a school.

"I know my letters and some words. I can do sums too." Ella's brown eyes sparkled.

"You can show Heidi what you know later. I'm sure she wants to finish unpacking." Lily interrupted whatever else the girl might have intended to say.

Heidi lifted her favorite Sunday dress from the trunk.

"Ohhh. It's beautiful." Lily's gaze went up and down the moss green silk as if taking in every inch of the outfit.

"If I'm here long enough, you can borrow it to wear to church the next time you go." She held the dress out toward her sister.

Lily lightly fingered the soft fabric. "Thank you, but dresses like that will be fitting a little tight soon."

"They will?"

"They will." Lily beamed. "This baby should be here in February."

"How wonderful."

By the time Harvey awoke, Heidi had finished unpacking. Her brush, comb, and hand mirror lay on the dresser. Her underclothes were tucked into what had been empty drawers. Yet no matter how much at home Lily wanted her to be, this was all temporary. A month should be enough time to be sure Papa didn't find her if he came to San Antonio to look for her.

―――――

JETHRO WIPED the sweat off his face with his bandana. "I should be used to how hot Texas Septembers can be."

"They're hot for someone raised here too." Mr. Grimes tossed another sack of flour into the chuck wagon. "Josiah, you almost through loading your pots?"

"Almost, boss." The new cook's gap-tooth grin made him look older than the man probably was.

"I see a rider heading this way." Jethro squinted to get a better look at whoever was approaching.

"Afternoon, Mr. Grimes. Boys." A man halted his horse a few feet from them.

"Tyler? Ben Tyler?" The boss looked the rider over as he dismounted.

"That's right. Guess I still look about the same. Can't say that for you. Your wife sittin' on the porch with the other pretty lady said I'd find you here. Never thought you'd have a wife." The man extended his hand.

"I do. The best in Texas." Mr. Grimes continued studying Tyler as they shook hands.

"Your foreman said to ride out here and see if you still need another hand."

The boss nodded. The way Mr. Grimes so carefully eyed Tyler told Jethro he'd been right to have the man come talk to Mr. Grimes first. The gleam in the stranger's eyes when he mentioned two pretty ladies didn't sit well with Jethro. Every hand would respect the boss's wife, but no one needed to get too curious about Miss Schultz. Especially a man with a questionable reputation.

"I could use another man." Mr. Grimes must have finished his assessment of Tyler.

"I'd be happy to help you out."

"All right. Put your gear in the bunkhouse." Mr. Grimes pointed to the building about thirty feet away.

"Bannister said you aren't leaving until Monday, but I came

today in case you changed your mind and want to leave tomorrow."

"We won't leave on the Lord's Day."

Tyler's eyes widened. "Whatever you say."

Instead of reacting to Tyler's look of surprise, Mr. Grimes turned his attention to the cook. "Josiah, can you scrounge something for you and Tyler to eat for supper?"

"Sure, boss."

Jethro spent the rest of his time trying to think of a way to invite himself to eat with Tyler and the cook. But since Mr. Grimes had specifically not mentioned him eating with the other men, the boss must assume Jethro would still eat supper with the family. So far he'd been lucky not to be part of any family discussion. He'd like to keep it that way. Too bad he couldn't think of a way to eat with the other men without being rude.

So he went home a while later to clean up and make himself presentable enough to sit at the Grimes's table. Something smelled good as soon as he got close to the door. His stomach growled as he knocked.

Mr. Grimes let him into the parlor. "Lily's got supper about ready." He headed to the kitchen with Jethro not far behind as usual.

By the time he'd filled his plate with ham, potato cakes, and corn, he was glad he could enjoy Mrs. Grimes's good cooking. He doubted the grizzled cook he hired could fix anything as good as what he'd feast on.

"Heidi is a quick learner." Mrs. Grimes showered her sister with a loving smile. "She made the cornbread and the potato cakes with very little help."

Mr. Grimes finished chewing his first bite of corn bread. "Very good."

"Thank you. I have a good teacher." Her eyes went down as she cut up her ham.

To Jethro's relief, the conversation centered on what

everyone had done for the day without any mention of why Miss Schultz had come here. She looked and sounded relaxed, almost as if she'd lived on a ranch all her life. Except a rancher's wife could cook.

"Delicious, ladies." Mr. Grimes scooted his chair back after cleaning his plate.

Miss Schultz glowed at the words of praise. "I'll finish this wonderful day by walking up the east rise with my pencils and draw a picture of the evening sun shining on the house."

"Not alone." Mrs. Grimes glanced at her husband as if for confirmation. "You're not used to this rugged country."

"I've been painting the countryside outside of New Braunfels by myself. I can easily carry my satchel and camp stool."

"Can you draw and keep an eye out for snakes or bobcats at the same time?" Mr. Grimes's tone was gentle but firm.

She sighed. "I hadn't thought about that. Could I bother you to accompany me?"

"Maybe after roundup. I'm fixin' to be gone for a while, so I'll stay close tonight."

"I understand." Her downturned mouth signaled her disappointment. Her art must mean a lot to her.

"I can come with you." Jethro's words popped out of his mouth before he had time to stop them, before he turned from looking into her woeful eyes that reminded him of Louisa, his late younger sister. His only sister. Who still held a special place in his heart.

"You'd do that for me?"

"Yes." *No.* But he'd already saddled himself with a problem he'd never intended.

Her bright smile warmed him inside much more than it should. "Could I ask you to hitch up the buggy so I can take what I need to use my oil paints?"

"I can do that." Do this woman one small favor and she'd ask for how many more? But he'd dug his own hole. He scooted his chair back. "I'll get the buggy ready while you help clean the kitchen."

"Thank you so much more than I can say."

Jethro rose, sure she'd find a way to say more if he didn't take this opportunity to head outside. "You're welcome." *Hypocrite.* His words almost choked him. But he'd soon be gone for a good two weeks or more. After that, Mr. Grimes could accompany his sister-in-law.

Stepping into the barn, Jethro paused to let his eyes adjust to the dim light. What had come over him to volunteer to go with Miss Schultz so she could safely draw or paint? She'd talked his ears sore the entire drive here. Yet he'd agreed to let her do it again.

The lady was heading his way before Jethro finished hitching the horse to the buggy. Mr. Grimes, carrying two folding stools and his canteen, walked beside her. She had some sort of satchel in one hand and a small bag in the other. This woman must be planning an expedition instead of painting a picture. How could she have thought she could manage all that alone? Her imagination must be as boundless as her vocabulary.

Sooner than he wished, she sat next to him in the buggy.

"Could we go east, please? I'd like to paint the scene as I saw it when you showed it to me."

"Any direction is fine with me." *Liar.* The only direction he wanted to go was toward his own place. He headed the horse out of the yard, bracing himself for what could be a very long evening.

"Would you hand me the reins, please? I won't know the best place to stop until I see it, so it would be easier if I drive the buggy."

He clamped his mouth shut as he turned to stare at her. Most of the rancher's wives could handle a buggy with no trouble, but he doubted this city-raised woman could. "Even if you can drive a buggy, I'm not sure Mr. Grimes would like that since he and the missus were so happy for me to take you out here." Most especially since they'd bought this new bigger buggy with a back seat.

"I often took my parents' buggy outside of town to paint landscapes. I enjoyed the solitude. They enjoyed me not making a public spectacle of myself by setting up my easel and paints on the front porch where the light was best."

"I don't understand." And he didn't but wished he hadn't spoken as soon as the words slipped out. He doubted her explanation would be short.

"Mama and Papa have never understood my love for doing something that's not useful."

"Most people think nice pictures to decorate a wall are useful." More words that came out on their own. But he couldn't help but sympathize with anyone misunderstood by their family.

"Yes, a lot of people like paintings in their homes. I've been told I'm talented." She sighed.

Why she sounded so unhappy about compliments didn't make sense, but he'd already said more than he intended. Best to count himself lucky she'd said so little for a change.

"Could I please take the reins? I hope to buy my own buggy someday after I'm established in San Antonio."

He admired her spunk and determination to live her own life apart from her parents' dictates. They had more in common than she knew or he'd thought. But he wouldn't tell her that, or she'd probably never quit talking to him. He handed her the reins.

"Thank you. I do appreciate you inconveniencing yourself for me, but I'd rather have come alone."

"I understand."

"Perhaps you do, since you live a somewhat solitary life in your own house." Another exaggerated sigh floated out. "I wish Mama and Papa understood me, or at least tried to."

He forced himself not to look her way. He knew better than she realized what it was like to be misunderstood by family.

Unlike Heidi, he didn't like talking about it. Not Heidi. Miss Schultz. He barely knew the woman.

"My other older sister, Greta, and her husband moved to Minnesota four years ago. I fear my parents indulged me, letting me take lessons only because I was the only daughter still at home. Lily left when I was twelve."

"Could be." Her parents must be hard to get along with if all three daughters had left home.

Squaring her shoulders, she tossed him a radiant smile. "But that's all done with now. I'm building a new life. I'm going to enjoy painting much more often."

Not too often. He'd rather enjoy a quiet evening on his own porch or sitting by his fire than listening to Miss Schultz's endless chattering, especially when it might involve her family problems.

She halted the buggy as they topped the nearest rise. "Perfect. The sun is illuminating the house the way it did yesterday."

While Miss Schultz wrapped the reins around the brake, he got out then walked around the buggy to help her down.

"Thank you, but I'd rather not have help. Once I have my own buggy, no one will be around to assist me on my drives outside of town to paint."

"Mr. and Mrs. Grimes wouldn't be happy with me if I let you lose your balance."

"I'll allow you to only this once. If I trip over my skirts the next time, I'll be sure to tell them I insisted you not help me."

*Next time?* Sympathizing with her family problems that too closely mirrored his would cause him problems if he weren't more careful with his words than he'd been so far. Not talking was the best way to deal with what he didn't like thinking about or being reminded of. He had no intentions of being roped into this situation again for however long she stayed.

She pulled a stool from behind the seat. He reached for the other one.

"Please don't think I'm being rude, but I'd rather not have your help with anything."

"A gentleman always assists a lady."

"No one helped me set up my paints when I drove outside of New Braunfels. And, too, if I'm to take care of myself, I should start doing so now."

He put the stool he'd carried next to the one she opened up then stepped aside. "If that's what you want."

Standing idly by watching her retrieve everything without his help, took considerable restraint. As a Georgia gentleman, he'd been taking care of ladies since he was old enough to do so. His mother and sister had never entered a carriage without male assistance. He'd never met a woman anything like the independent, fashionably dressed one he was watching now. After she seated herself on the stool next to the one holding her paints, he found a soft grassy spot for his own chair.

"This view is perfect." She situated a canvas in her lap and picked up a paint brush, all while surveying the ranch house and buildings from their perch on the ridge.

She alternated between painting and stopping to stare off toward the house. Without saying a word, the entire time. Amazing. With nothing else to do, Jethro studied the painter sitting a few feet away. The evening sun illuminated her sandy blond hair and fair skin as well as her bright blue dress with ruffles at the top of the sleeves. The almost angelic glow of her face belied the determined spirit he'd witnessed as she insisted he shouldn't help her in any way.

No. He had to think of something else. Focus on the sun getting lower in the sky. Be sure no snakes or scorpions came too close. If the Lord ever blessed him with a wife, he wouldn't fuss if she were as pretty as the lady in front of him. But he didn't want any woman with family problems or one who could talk the way this one could if not occupied with her paints.

"I've done what I can for now. I'll finish this landscape

another day." She rose then carefully laid her canvas on the other stool.

He stayed put and watched her load her things behind the front buggy seat. This had to be the first time in his life he'd remained seated when a lady stood. His manners got the best of him. He got to his feet and then wandered over to the painting still setting on the stool.

Even unfinished, her talent was obvious. She'd captured the evening sun shining on the main house to perfection. The breeze kicked up enough to make the dirt swirl, threatening to blow dust onto the canvas. He snatched the painting, turning his back to block the canvas from the wind.

"Oh, my!" She rushed toward him.

"Good thing it wasn't finished. I grabbed the edges with no paint."

She let out her breath as she studied the canvas in his hands. "Thank you. Thank you so much. Would you mind holding onto it in the buggy when we head back?"

"I can do that."

She folded the last stool and stowed it with the other one. Since he held her treasured painting, he couldn't assist her up onto the buggy seat. He laid the canvas on the seat between them before climbing inside.

"Thank you so much. Also for respecting my wishes and not picking up a thing." Her ear-to-ear grin emphasized her happiness. She snapped the reins and headed the horse toward the barn. "I hope to convince Lily and Toby I can come up here alone, so I don't have to bother you again."

"Unless you've got a good enough aim to take care of a rattler or copperhead, I doubt they'll listen to you." Why couldn't he keep his mouth shut around this woman he didn't want to be with?

"One thing I haven't learned is how to shoot. Perhaps I should since I might need to protect myself one day. Should I plan to buy a small gun to put in my reticule?"

He chuckled. "A little derringer might work for snakes if you're close and a really good shot. But it won't scare off a stray Comanche or bobcat." Once more, he spoke when he shouldn't. If she thought she would be in danger, she might insist he come with her instead of trying to come alone.

Her lips formed a pretty *O* as she jerked her head his direction to stare wide-eyed at him. Just as quickly, she returned her attention to the horse ahead of her. "As much as I might need an escort in this rugged country, you'd rather not be here with me at all, would you?"

Not really, but no gentleman would be rude enough to speak so plainly to a lady. Nor would a true cowboy. Good manners had never been as bad to him as they had today. "I *am* more used to my own company. The way you want to be by yourself soon."

She nodded. "I do understand. But Lily and Toby will probably insist you accompany me."

Not probably. Would. Especially since he'd volunteered to go with her tonight. He'd put himself in a predicament he had no idea how to extract himself from. Entangling himself with anyone, male or female, who was tangled in their own family problems would be something he'd never do. Except he may have done just that.

**5**

———

For the first time since she'd come, Heidi awoke on Sunday morning without wondering where she was. So wonderful to feel secure. She stretched, careful not to disturb Ella. Lily had said Sundays were different on the *Tumbling G,* but surely, everyone would still want breakfast.

After dressing and putting up her hair, Heidi went to the kitchen to get the fire going in the stove. She couldn't recall starting any meal alone while home in New Braunfels. No. Home would never be there again.

She squared her shoulders while blinking away the burning moisture in her eyes. Just where home would be in San Antonio, she didn't yet know, but she'd be home somewhere again. She'd prefer renting a small house instead of boarding with someone. Living totally on her own. Deciding who would be her friends and who wouldn't. Being in total control of her life.

Not long after she'd set the coffee pot on the stove, Lily and Toby joined her.

"You'll spoil me by starting the coffee every morning." Lily patted Heidi's arm. "I'll get the children up. Then we'll make pancakes. Breakfast is the one meal I cook on Sundays. The others are whatever is left from Saturday."

Heidi smiled her reply, hoping Lily didn't get too accustomed to having Heidi here no matter how pleasant her stay was so far. Being so welcome helped ease the pain of completely cutting ties with her parents. The way they'd treated her like a tradeable commodity to ensure the wagon works remained in the family hurt more than she wanted to think about.

But she couldn't allow herself the luxury of getting too comfortable staying with Lily and Toby. Like her sister, she'd start a new life of her choosing.

Her new adventure learning to make pancakes went well. Toby complimented her efforts. Mr. Bannister ate more than she thought such a slender man could manage. The children ate well too. The men did chores while Lily and Heidi cleaned up the kitchen. Then they all gathered in the parlor for what Heidi was sure would be the smallest worship service she'd ever attended. Plus, one in English instead of German.

Lily and Ella settled on the couch on either side of Toby, leaving the chairs near the couch for Heidi and Mr. Bannister to claim. Harvey sat on the floor with his wooden horses and cows.

"Looks like Josiah and Tyler aren't going to join us for our Bible reading and prayer." Toby picked up the Bible lying in his lap. "I didn't set the best example when Ben and I rode together on that first drive."

"But you do now." Lily patted Toby's arm.

The intense way they gazed into each other's eyes signaled something only the two of them understood.

"Darlin', I like what you said last night when we were reading together. Tell everyone else too." Toby handed the Bible to Lily.

"We were reading Psalm 104. It's about blessing God and how wonderful everything is He made." She went on to talk about God stretching out the heavens like a curtain, how He made the mountains, rivers, and cattle. "Then we read verse twenty-four. 'O Lord, how manifold are thy works! In wisdom hast thou made them all: the earth is full of thy riches.'" Lily turned to Heidi. "The beautiful picture you started Friday night reminded me of all God's wonders."

"It did?" Heidi's eyes misted. Never had anyone appreciated her paintings like this.

"Yes, it did. I'm glad you brought your paints and pencils. We'll have to order an easel for you the next time we're in town since you said you couldn't bring yours."

"Thank you." Heidi doubted she'd ever said so little when expressing herself, but Lily's praise left her speechless for probably one of the first times in her life.

Lily and Toby went on to talk more about the Psalm. Mr. Bannister added a few comments. They prayed together. The men asked for safety during the roundup. Ella thanked God for her new aunt. Heidi thanked God she could come to Lily and Toby's house. Lily led them all in singing a hymn.

Mr. Bannister rose after the last verse. "I'm going back to my place. I need to finish getting ready to leave tomorrow and watch for the other men I hired to ride in this afternoon."

"We'll see you later for supper." Toby stood. "I'd better be sure my gear is ready too."

"Let's go outside and enjoy this nice day since it's not as hot as yesterday." Lily winked at her grinning daughter.

Ella hopped to the floor. "Aunt Heidi, do you want to play with me and Ruckus?"

Running through the yard the way she'd seen Ella do wasn't Heidi's idea of fun. "What if I get my pencils and draw a picture of Ruckus for you while you're playing?"

"Oh, yes!" Ella giggled as she clapped her hands together.

A short time later, Heidi carried a chair from the porch and set it in the yard. "Play close by. Then I can see you and your dog."

Heidi spent the next hour or so watching her niece and Ruckus romp. Harvey toddled after the two as best he could while Lily sat on the porch step observing the entire scene. Toby joined Lily on the steps after he finished gathering up whatever he needed for roundup.

"What are you drawing?" Toby called to Heidi.

"Ruckus. The children too."

"You'll have to show us when you're done. Lily never said anything about you drawing or painting."

"She's always drawn pictures, but I left before she took lessons. I'm enjoying getting to know my little sister again."

Lily's words swelled Heidi's heart with happiness. "I'm glad to get to know all of you."

She returned her attention to the sketch pad propped in her lap. Running to Lily had advantages she'd never thought about.

As well as what perhaps only she considered to be disadvantages. She must not depend on Lily and Toby too much no matter how nice or how accepting they were. She would never be beholden to anyone. Never allow someone to get close enough to betray her again.

By the time Ella plopped down next to her mother to catch her breath, Heidi was satisfied with rough sketches of Ruckus, plus one of the children playing with their dog. "Tell me what you think." She handed her drawing of Ruckus to Ella.

"Ohhh. You draw so good." Ella's ear-to-ear grin emphasized her words.

"This is wonderful." Lily leaned toward Ella. She slid the sketch into her lap for Toby to see.

"I did one of the children playing too." Heidi gave the drawing to her sister.

Toby sidled closer to Lily. "It looks like Ella's braids could bounce right off the paper. You're very good."

"Thank you. I'd still like very much to draw cattle and cowboys if you can think of a way for me to do that."

"Maybe you could find a way for Heidi to draw some of the roundup while y'all are still close to home?" Lily asked Toby.

Heidi held her breath, waiting for his response. How she'd

like to satisfy her curiosity about cowboys by watching a roundup.

"I'll think about it." Toby's eyes darted from Lily to Heidi standing in front of him. "I'd have to see you're safe, plus not in the way."

"I understand." Her spirit soared up past the few fluffy white clouds floating in the sky. The way Toby had stared in awe at her drawings gave her hope for sketching real life ranch events.

***

MONDAY MORNING, Jethro scooted his chair back from the kitchen table as soon as Mr. Grimes pushed away. "Ladies, thank you for a delicious breakfast. If I eat any more, my horse might not be able to carry me."

"Thank you." Miss Schultz's sparkling eyes told him his compliment might have been received better than he'd intended. No matter. He'd be gone the next three weeks, maybe more.

Mr. Grimes soon followed Jethro out the back door. "You take charge this morning. I'll ride out after a while."

"Sure, boss." He wasn't sure why Mr. Grimes wasn't heading out with everyone the way he usually did, but the owner could join the roundup whenever he liked. As foreman, his job was to do whatever the boss wanted, just the way he wanted. So Jethro would start the roundup without Mr. Grimes.

By late morning, Jethro squinted into the sun as he and the couple of men working with him settled the cows they'd found downwind from the chuck wagon. From what he could see in the distance, other groups of hands from the other two outfits had found good bunches of beeves too. "Boys, looks like we'll have plenty of moss heads to brand this afternoon." He dismounted, ready to eat whatever Josiah was cooking for their noon meal.

Tyler shifted in his saddle. "Is that a buggy heading this way?"

"Sure is." And as best as Jethro could tell, his boss was driving the Grimes buggy with a female passenger. "You boys help the others coming in to bunch these cows together." He'd take full advantage of being foreman to walk off and satisfy his curiosity.

As the buggy rolled closer to camp, Mr. Grimes waved. Miss Schultz was the woman he'd spied. Jethro closed his mouth before he choked on the dust or his shock. Not the kind of reason he'd have ever thought of for the boss not to come with the men as usual. What was she doing here? And how had she convinced Mr. Grimes to bring her?

The buggy halted on the other side of the chuck wagon. Jethro trotted over to the passenger side. Sure the boss wouldn't have it any other way, he'd help Miss Schultz down. She could protest later. Except if Mr. Grimes was happy to drive her today, he wouldn't have to worry about any kind of later with her.

"Thank you." She smiled straight into his eyes the instant both feet were on the ground.

"You're welcome." What a change from the way she'd insisted on doing things the other night. Why? He might not ever find out since he hoped not to have to escort her for her painting efforts again.

Mr. Grimes grabbed a stool from behind the front seat. "Heidi, where do you want to sit?"

"The best place for me to observe and sketch." She pulled her satchel from the buggy.

"There won't be much to look at or draw for a while since everyone's fixin' to eat soon." Mr. Grimes set her stool a short distance from the fire. But far enough away to not bother the cook or get in the way of the men who would soon be sitting down for their meal.

"It's so exciting to see a real roundup." She sounded like a delighted child as she gazed at the camp. "Thank you for letting me do this."

"You're welcome." Mr. Grimes turned his attention to Jethro while not straying too far from his sister-in-law. "Looks like you're getting a good start."

"Yes, sir. Tyler, Santos, and I drove in some nice-looking calves."

While Jethro and Mr. Grimes talked cows, he kept an eye on Miss Schultz. She settled onto her stool then took out her pencils. Hopefully she'd soon be concentrating quietly on her art the way she'd done Saturday night. The more men who came in, the worse the language would get. Except for a few men like his boss and Mr. Shepherd, the boss's brother-in-law.

David Shepherd and some of his hands soon rode in, herding a good group of longhorns. After dismounting, the man wasted no time heading over to Mr. Grimes. The two shook hands.

"Heidi, this is David Shepherd." Mr. Grimes turned his attention to his guest. "David, this is Lily's sister, Heidi Schultz. She's staying with us a while."

"Pleased to meet you, Miss Schultz." Shepherd tipped his hat. "You'll have to come see us and meet my wife, Charlotte."

"I'd like that. I've already heard about both of you." She stood then shook Shepherd's hand.

In a short time, every man in the *Tumbling G* crew not left watching the herd gathered by the fire, all of them paying more attention to Miss Schultz than their upcoming meal. A few openly gawked in her direction. Jethro gave those men what he hoped was the sternest glare they'd ever seen. Stern enough to make them duck their heads or look away. Good thing the other outfits had their own cooks so he didn't have to keep an eye on more than *Tumbling G* men.

"Fellas, this is my sister-in-law, Miss Schultz. She's never been on a ranch until she came here, and she wanted to see what a roundup looks like." Mr. Grimes's easy smile seemed to say he was fine with the whole idea of Miss Schultz being here.

Every man tipped his hat toward her.

"This is as ready to eat as it'll ever be, gents." Josiah dusted the coals off the Dutch oven. "The lady goes first today."

The men soon turned their attention to the food. No matter how many of them might wish they could pay more mind to the pretty blonde perched on her campstool. With a lady present, talk around the fire was much tamer than usual.

A lady who shouldn't be here. She wore the brown dress, minus the bustle, she'd had on when Jethro picked her up in town. But she couldn't be missed if she were dressed in sewn-together horse blankets. So good she had sense enough not to wear the pretty blue dress that brought out her eyes. Not good he'd paid such close attention to what she'd been wearing.

After they ate, Mr. Grimes moved his sister-in-law to a slight rise a safe distance from the fire where they'd soon be heating branding irons. Why a city-raised woman was so fascinated with ranching didn't make sense.

Every time he glanced her direction, she was focused on her drawing. He'd assumed the dirt and dust caused by wrangling longhorns, plus the stench of burning cowhide from the branding irons, would have driven her away. But she stayed put on her stool most of the afternoon. The Grimes's buggy didn't leave for home until the sun showed it to be around three o'clock.

"I'm glad to see them go." Tyler wiped the sweat off his face with his bandana after they released a branded calf.

"Really?" Jethro doubted many of the men felt that way.

"Yeah. I ain't never had anybody watch me that close unless it was a buzzard."

Jethro chuckled at the comparison. "She's an artist. Pretty good one too. We might all show up in one of her drawings."

"Is that so?" Tyler swung up in his saddle, ready to help cut another calf from the group of cattle.

Since Tyler didn't seem too interested in Miss Schultz, Jethro hoped the other men hadn't paid too much attention to her either. Most of them probably agreed with him she shouldn't have been here. Whatever their opinions, he heard no mention of the woman the rest of the afternoon as they finished branding the cows they'd rounded up in the morning. He hoped that continued as he made his way toward the fire and dinner.

"First time I've seen any boss bring a lady to watch a roundup." Santos, plate in hand, seated himself on the ground to eat. "Too bad I was so busy I couldn't get a better look at such a pretty woman."

Tyler balanced his plate in his lap as he sat. "She was watching us only so she could draw pictures. Right, Bannister?"

"Right. And she's Mrs. Grimes's sister. After today, we'll be too far off for the boss to bring her again. Everyone saw all of her you'll see." Jethro took a bite of cornbread, hoping his words would turn the conversation away from Miss Schultz. Why that mattered so much to him, he'd have to figure out later.

"Except for you?" Tyler pointed his fork toward Jethro. "You've seen her enough to know she's good at drawing. You got another reason you didn't like anyone looking at such a pretty lady too much?"

The cornbread in Jethro's mouth turned to almost choking dust. He washed it down with a big swig of coffee. "No."

Santos shook his head as he aimed a mischievous grin toward Jethro. "Say whatever you want, but every time I tried to watch the lady, you gave me some powerful strong looks. The kind I've only seen from a man sweet on a woman who doesn't want anyone else looking at her."

"I met her Friday, so I barely know her." Jethro gulped down more coffee, glad his tanned face wouldn't give away the heat rushing up from his collar. "Besides, I didn't work my way up to foreman without learning a few things. One of those is not to mess with any of the boss's family." Paying too much attention to the owner's daughter had cost him one job. A hard lesson he didn't care to discuss or repeat.

"Right." Tyler didn't look convinced by Jethro's explanation. But unlike Santos, he kept his thoughts to himself.

Talk finally turned to other women the men had known. Jethro finished his meal in silence, glad no one had asked why he insisted they leave a boss's family member alone. Miranda's lilting laugh and kissable lips still haunted him if he weren't careful. As did her father's threats about what would happen to Jethro if he dared to set one toe on the man's ranch again.

He wouldn't repeat that mistake any more than he'd ever get involved in family squabbles like the ones he'd left behind in Georgia. He'd been betrayed by enough people to last him a lifetime.

Jethro rose and slung the last of the coffee from his cup into the fire. "I hear my quilts calling me. See you in the mornin', boys."

"Bet he'll be dreamin' about a pretty little artist calling for him."

Whether on purpose or not, Santos didn't lower his voice enough to keep Jethro from overhearing. The other men chuckled. Denying the hands' assumptions again would only confirm they were right about Miss Schultz.

He had no intention of explaining why he wouldn't be dreaming about her. Not talking about his past heartaches helped him keep his bad memories tamped down. Deep enough to stop the nightmares from waking him the way they'd used to.

**6**

---

"Thank you so much for allowing me to watch the branding this afternoon." Heidi glanced over at Toby as he drove the buggy toward the house.

"You're welcome." He tossed her a quick grin before returning his attention back to the horse.

"I've wanted to see cowboys working for so long. But Papa tolerates the ranchers who order wagons only because they make him money. Mama is no better. I've never been able to get them to tell me why."

Toby's expression sobered. "Lily can tell you why. But again, don't rush her."

"Something else that's painful for her?"

"Yeah."

His one-word answer spoke so much more than he said. Papa and Mama had to have hurt Lily more than she'd admitted in the garden the other day. Toby was probably the only person who knew how deep her pain must still go.

"I've got enough sketches to finish or turn into paintings to keep me busy for quite a while." She changed the subject since Toby's grimace grew as they discussed Lily's hurts.

Despite the sketches tucked into her satchel, she still had a hard time believing she'd actually witnessed something she'd only dreamed of seeing. Toby had inconvenienced himself considerably for her sake. More than any other man in her life had ever done.

Her parents merely tolerated her art and would never put themselves out to help her the way Toby had. Their lack of interest had bothered her for years. But voicing those thoughts caused her heart to ache, so like Lily, she'd keep silent about what hurt too much to talk about.

"I'll look forward to seeing the finished pictures when I get home."

"Thank you." Toby's genuine interest helped ease the tightness in her chest thoughts of Papa and Mama now caused whenever they came to mind. So sad how the very people she'd trusted all her life to watch over her had betrayed her and her sister.

By the time they got back to the house, Lily was working on supper. Toby helped Heidi carry her art supplies to her and Ella's room. No. Ella's room. No matter how pleasant this place was, Heidi was here only temporarily.

Heidi walked into the kitchen then slipped her apron over her head. "What can I do to help?"

"Make the cornbread after the stew finishes simmering. Since I wasn't sure how long y'all would stay, I planned something I could keep warm if necessary."

Toby walked into the kitchen and kissed Lily's cheek as she stirred the stew. "You'll have to see Heidi's drawings after supper. I'll go tend to the horse and buggy."

"I want to see every one of them." Lily set the lid back on the pot.

Once again, Toby's words of praise warmed Heidi's heart. Lily wouldn't be the only one who missed him these next two to three weeks while he was gone for roundup. None of her brothers had praised her the way her brother-in-law did.

No. She wouldn't dwell on how disappointed she'd become

with her New Braunfels family. These last few days with Lily and Toby had too many pleasant things to think about. Especially since this was the first step toward the new life she intended to make for herself in San Antonio soon.

After Heidi and Lily finished cleaning up from dinner, they joined Toby in the parlor. Lily seated herself on the couch next to her husband and perused each sketch Heidi had made during her afternoon adventure.

"These are good. We'll have to show them to Jethro and the others when they come back." Lily held a sketch of Mr. Bannister roping a calf.

"By then, I should have a painting or two finished." The first one she'd do would be one without Mr. Bannister. She hadn't realized how many drawings included the foreman until Lily and Toby started looking them over.

"This one is so real-looking," Toby handed the page to Lily. "Look. It's David cutting out a calf."

Lily looked straight at Heidi sitting in the chair by the couch. "It looks just like David. I plan for us to go see Charlotte soon, maybe tomorrow. Could we take this one with us?"

"Of course." Heidi's spirits soared at such high praise. Mama and Papa had never wanted to show off her drawings to others. "I've heard so much about Charlotte. I'd like to meet her."

"She'll be happy to see you too." Lily returned to Heidi's drawings.

———

HEIDI AWOKE the next morning from the best sleep she'd had in the last month, maybe two. Lily's and Toby's praise for her art had wrapped around her bruised heart like a warm comforting quilt on a cold night. Plus, Ella had stayed mostly on her side of the bed.

The smell of coffee drifted in from the kitchen as she dressed. Judging from the dim light, she hadn't overslept. With

Mr. Bannister working the roundup, she didn't have to pin her hair up by feel in a dark room and could tie it back until later. So much was right with her new world, especially since she could now look forward to a future of her choosing.

Lily and Toby were already in the kitchen when she walked in. "Good morning."

"Mornin' to you." Toby grinned from his spot at the table.

"You look like you slept well." Lily glanced in Heidi's direction as she put a pan of biscuits into the oven. "Toby wants an early start so he can catch up to the men this morning."

"Thank you again for inconveniencing yourself for me yesterday." Heidi returned Toby's smile as she slipped her apron over her head.

"My pleasure."

Lily got the children up after the adults had eaten. Ella went straight to Toby's chair where he sat finishing his last cup of coffee.

"I'll miss you, Pa."

"I'll miss you too." Toby scooted his chair back.

Ella crawled in his lap, pressing her head against his chest. Toby wrapped his arms around her. Heidi concentrated on stacking dirty plates then carried them to the dishpan as quickly as she could manage without dropping anything. Such a tender scene made her heart ached so much she had to turn her back. She had once trusted her papa like that. Never again.

A few minutes later, Toby headed toward the front door. Lily and the children followed. Heidi lagged behind them. She'd rather miss the family goodbye but couldn't think of how to do that.

After another hug from Ella, Toby took Lily in his arms and kissed her full on the lips. Papa and Mama cared for each other, but they never displayed their affection in front of family or anyone else.

After releasing Lily, he made eye contact with Heidi. "I'll

look forward to seeing your paintings when I get home. I'm glad you're here."

"Thank you." Somehow, she kept her voice from cracking as she choked out the words. How she wished she could have escaped the family goodbye that only reminded her she hadn't had what she'd thought in New Braunfels.

After giving a wiggly Harvey a quick hug, Toby slung his saddle bags over his shoulder and stepped off the porch. He gave his family one last glance before walking toward the barn.

"Let's get you two some breakfast, and then we should go see Aunt Charlotte." Lily smiled as she ushered the children inside.

"Yes!" Ella skipped her way to the kitchen.

While Lily fed her children, Heidi cleared the table. Ella wasted no time finishing her eggs and bacon. She carried her plate to Heidi. "Harvey *never* hurries. I'm ready to have fun."

Heidi couldn't help but grin at Ella's extra emphasis on never, followed by an exaggerated sigh. "Since you're in such a rush, help me clean up. Then I can braid your hair while your mother gets Harvey ready to go."

"Thank you, thank you, thank you."

"You're very welcome." Heidi handed Ella a plate to dry.

A few minutes later, Heidi sat on the bed with her niece standing in front of her. She brushed Ella's thick brown curls. "You have such pretty hair. Mine doesn't curl like yours."

"I'm being very still like Ma always says so you can braid it better. And faster."

"Yes, faster." Heidi suppressed a chuckle. "I'll be fast pinning up my hair so I can help hitch the horse to the buggy sooner." Good thing she'd chosen her dark blue dress instead of a lighter-colored one that wouldn't work as well for a dusty drive. Ella would not have wanted her aunt to delay things by changing clothes.

An hour or so later, Heidi helped Ella, doll in hand, into the back seat of the buggy while Lily settled Harvey next to his sister. Then set her satchel on the floor behind the front seat.

Lily insisted Charlotte and her housekeeper, Francisca, would enjoy seeing all of Heidi's drawings. "I can drive and free you up to tend to the children if needed."

"I'd appreciate that." Lily climbed into the buggy as Heidi took the reins.

"Ooo, another yellow butterfly. Those are my favorites, 'cause I like yellow so much." With Ella's almost constant chatter, the two-hour drive was not boring.

"I'll have to paint you a picture with yellow butterflies." Heidi kept her focus on the rolling terrain in front of her as she talked to Ella.

"I would so, so like that."

From the sound of Ella's voice, the little girl must almost be bouncing in the back seat. As was Heidi's happy heart. Frieda had been so right to insist Heidi run to Lily before going somewhere else to start over.

"Charlotte and David's house is over the next ridge. No matter how much Toby likes to tease, Charlotte won't be dressed in trousers, boots, and spurs. Unless Zeke, their hired hand, needs her help."

Heidi glanced into her sister's twinkling eyes. "I'm looking forward to meeting her." Lily had told her how Charlotte had disguised herself as a teenage boy to go up the trail with Toby and then fallen in love with David on the way. Such an independent woman should be quite sympathetic to Heidi and understand her need to live her own life.

A pair of barking hounds greeted them as the buggy rolled into the yard. Two women, followed by two small boys, stepped onto the porch before Heidi or Lily set foot on the ground. The instant Heidi helped Ella down, the little girl ran to the porch.

"We brought my Aunt Heidi for y'all to meet." Ella hugged the red-haired woman who had to be Charlotte and then went into the arms of the older woman, Francisca.

Ella grinned as she stepped back from Francisca. "*Abuela*, Annie wore the dress you made her." She held up her doll. "And look how pretty my braids are. Aunt Heidi did them and tied the bows 'cause she said I should look nice for a special trip to see you and Aunt Charlotte."

An older man came up from the direction of the outbuildings as Lily set Harvey on the ground. "I'll tend to your horse and buggy, Mrs. Grimes."

"Thank you, Zeke."

Carrying her satchel, Heidi followed Lily and Harvey onto the porch.

"Charlotte, Francisca, this is Heidi Schultz, the little sister I've told you about. Our father wanted to force her into a bad marriage, so she came to Toby and me to get away."

"We're so happy to see you here and safe." Charlotte beamed at Heidi. "Let's go inside and visit. We still have time before lunch."

Lily smiled as she and Harvey stepped into the parlor.

After settling Harvey and his cousins, Jeremiah and Matthew, in a corner to play with blocks and wooden horses, the women got their chance to chat. Heidi couldn't recall Lily ever being so talkative. Heidi smiled and nodded at the comments concerning gardens and children. She doubted she'd ever said so little. Her satchel lay propped against her leg. The sisters-in-law had so much visiting to do Heidi's sketches were forgotten.

Francisca rose a while later. "I start lunch. Ella, would you like to help?"

"I always like to help you." Ella set her doll on Francisca's chair.

Lily glanced toward Heidi. "Oh, your sketches. Francisca, you should see them too."

"Toby let me watch the roundup yesterday." Heidi pulled her satchel onto her lap then took out her drawing of David.

"He did?"

Heidi nodded. "He drove me out there in the buggy then helped me find the perfect place to sketch everything."

Charlotte laughed. "Thank your sister he's changed so much. He wasn't happy when I helped with roundups.

"Heidi wore a proper dress not men's trousers." Lily's eyes twinkled as she and Charlotte exchanged amused looks. "And she rides sidesaddle."

Still smiling, Charlotte shook her head in mock despair. "I can ride sidesaddle if I choose to. Let me see your sketches."

Heidi walked over to hand the drawing to Charlotte.

Charlotte gasped. "Oh, my. David."

"You can keep it if you'd like." Heidi thrilled at the look of awe on Charlotte's face.

"I'd like that very much. Thank you."

Charlotte and Francisca exclaimed over each sketch before Francisca and Ella went to the kitchen. The simple meal of cold ham, bread, and carrots tasted delicious since the warm conversation begun in the parlor continued throughout the meal.

Not long after the kitchen was cleaned, Charlotte put her two little boys down for naps. Lily decided they should leave for home. "You know y'all are welcome to come see us any time."

"Yes, we do." Charlotte and Francisca followed them out to the buggy Zeke had waiting.

"I want Aunt Heidi to help me in again." Ella's adoring smile emphasized her words.

"Up you go then." Heidi helped her niece onto the seat.

Lily settled a yawning Harvey next to his sister. "Let your brother stretch out for a nap."

"Yes, ma'am."

Heidi soon snapped the reins to head toward home. No. Lily and Toby's house. She had no home of her own at this time. But she would soon. One of her own choosing.

"Ella, calls Francisca *abuela*. What does that mean?" She'd rather satisfy her curiosity than think too much about why she needed to start a new life.

"*Abuela* is grandmother in Spanish. Francisca and her husband, Eduardo, are family to all of us and the closest thing to grandparents our children or Charlotte's and David's children have. Eduardo is with David, or you'd have met him today too."

"Oh." Her simple one-word answer was all Heidi felt she should voice, since Lily didn't like talking about their parents, Ella and Harvey's true grandparents. How sad Mama and Papa chose to act as if Lily and her entire family didn't exist. Were they doing the same with her now? Or actively trying to find her? Which one she preferred, Heidi wasn't sure.

"Look. A bunny over on Ma's side. Two bunnies."

"I see them." Heidi glanced in the bunnies' direction.

"Ma and Pa say bunnies are fine out here but not in the garden. "'Cause they eat gardens."

"Yes, but that's the way God made bunnies." Heidi returned her attention to the horse and the gently rolling hills.

Heidi, Ella, and Lily chatted the rest of the way back to the house. Amazing how well a six-year-old girl could carry on a conversation. Lily and Toby allowed Ella to express herself much more than Mama or Papa allowed in their house. When the buggy rolled into the yard, Ella insisted Heidi help her out of the buggy. Ella soon trotted off with Ruckus, telling him all about her time at the *Double S*. Heidi took care of unhitching the horse, leaving Lily free to get Harvey in the house.

That evening, Heidi helped Lily fix a simple dinner of cold beef and potatoes. They cleaned the kitchen together then went to the parlor.

"I'm so glad you're here." Lily smiled as she seated herself in her rocking chair by the fireplace. "I don't usually try to go anywhere when Toby isn't home. Traveling alone isn't easy with two children."

"We've had a wonderful day." Heidi took a spot on the couch.

"A wonderful, wonderful day." Ella, doll in hand, crawled onto the couch next to Heidi.

Harvey started fussing before they finished going over their day. Lily rose.

"Time for bed, little one." She picked up her son. "Ella, you should get ready for bed, too, since we've had such a busy day."

"Yes, ma'am. Aunt Heidi too?"

"No, she can go to sleep when she's ready."

"Since Pa isn't here, will you help Ma pray with me before I go to sleep?" Ella paused in the doorway.

"Of course."

Lily left to tend to Harvey. Heidi picked up the newspaper Mr. Bannister had bought the day he'd driven her to the *Tumbling G.* So much had happened these last few days she hadn't had time to look at the news.

After Heidi and Lily prayed with Ella, they returned to the parlor. Lily pulled a basket over to her chair. "I'll mend a tear in Ella's other petticoat while you finish reading the paper." She glanced up from threading her needle. "You'll make a wonderful mother one day when God blesses you with children."

Heidi shook her head. "I have no plans to become a wife much less become a mother." Her voice cracked. Why had Lily brought up such a thorny subject to end what had been a perfect day?

"Oh?" Lily peered across the room, straight into Heidi's eyes. "Judging from your sad expression, you don't want to talk about why you feel this way. I hope we can talk about it later."

A nod was the only reply Heidi could manage. Papa and Johann weren't the only men she'd encountered who considered marriage as a business proposition. She'd trusted her childhood friend, Karl, with her heart only to have him bend to his father's wishes and marry the banker's daughter instead.

Heidi would never allow herself to be vulnerable like that again.

**7**

---

Jethro squinted toward the afternoon sun, glad the last three and a half weeks were over. He was always bone tired after finishing roundup, but this time, his mind was more exhausted than his body. He rode as close to Mr. Grimes as possible. As far away from Ben Tyler and the other men as he could. The sooner they got to the house and the boss could pay the hands off, the happier Jethro would be.

The men had mentioned Miss Schultz more often than he cared to hear whenever the boss wasn't nearby. Worse, Tyler had joined in with Santos and decided Jethro thought much more of the lady than he did. Protesting he'd only met her a few days before the roundup started hadn't helped. He didn't want to think how bad their teasing would have been if they knew he'd driven her from San Antonio or escorted her the next evening so she could paint. He'd managed to keep that information to himself.

When they topped the next ridge, the weathered barn came into view. He'd never been so happy to see a barn. "I'll ride on to my place. I can fix my own supper tonight since the missus has no idea when we might come in."

Mr. Grimes shook his head. "We're coming home in time for

her to fix a little something for us. Especially since she's got Heidi to help."

Jethro was past tired of hearing that name but couldn't say such a thing to his boss. "I don't mind fending for myself."

"I'm glad you don't, but Lily will expect you for supper as usual."

"I'll be there."

A short time later, Jethro rode toward the barn. He tended to his horse, giving the boss plenty of time to pay the hands. Then went to his place. He didn't rush putting away his gear before shaving and cleaning up. He'd missed the complete silence and solitude of having four walls to himself. Where he could think his own thoughts without being interrupted or teased about a woman he knew next to nothing about.

Except now he wasn't too busy to think about things he'd avoided figuring out during roundup. He stared at his reflection in the washstand mirror as he shaved. Why were the men so sure he already thought so highly of Miss Schultz? He didn't.

Yes, he did. In some ways. He flicked soap off his razor into the basin, wishing he could rid his mind of such thoughts as easily as he could get rid of the soap. He understood her wish to sever ties with her parents. As well as admired her plucky spirit for being so determined to live her own life despite how much harder that was for a woman to do.

But admiring her didn't mean he had designs on her the way Santos and Tyler had hinted repeatedly the last few weeks. She wasn't his kind of woman for so many reasons.

Sooner than he wished, he had to leave his sanctuary. Mrs. Grimes served supper about five since it got dark earlier this time of year. He'd best be in her parlor early and waiting instead of being late.

He'd barely had time to greet Mr. Grimes when Ella came to tell them it was time to eat. Since the boss had to be as worn out as Jethro was, he hoped this meal wouldn't be a long one. After the ladies were seated, he took his usual chair. Miss

Schultz was much too fetching in a dark green dress. Still too fancy for a ranch. Whatever business her father owned must be successful.

The boss blessed the food and thanked the Lord for a good roundup and keeping everyone safe. "I'm always glad to get home to good food and even better company." He grinned at his wife while he took a thick slice of ham off the platter she passed him. "Josiah's a good man, but no one cooks as good as you, darlin'."

"Thank you, dear." Mrs. Grimes beamed at her husband before turning to put food on Harvey's highchair tray.

"I'm glad the roundup went so well." Miss Schultz sounded as happy as if she'd heard the best news ever as she took the ham platter from Mr. Grimes.

Why ranching fascinated the woman still didn't make sense to Jethro. Maybe he'd ask her why the next time he went with her while she painted. No. Mr. Grimes could have that chore.

While Jethro wrestled with his wayward thoughts, the conversation turned to the ladies and Ella talking about how their time had gone the last three weeks. Interspersed with as many questions about the roundup as Miss Schultz could squeeze in.

"Charlotte was thrilled when Heidi gave her the drawing she did of David." Mrs. Grimes gave her sister a glowing smile.

The boss buttered his last piece of cornbread. "I'm sure she was. Did you finish the others while we were gone?"

"Yes. I'd like to paint more longhorns. A different view of the sunset too. I have so many ideas." Miss Schultz's eyes sparkled the way they had while painting that Friday evening he escorted her.

"Sometime soon we'll see you can do that. But I'm worn out from head to toe tonight. Jethro probably is too." Mr. Grimes scooted his chair back.

"If you're not too tired, I'll show you my latest drawings after Lily and I clean the kitchen."

"That would be fine. Jethro and I can handle that for a little while tonight. Right?"

"Right." *Wrong.* Jethro had planned to use his exhaustion as the way to leave as soon as they finished eating. But his perfectly true excuse would do him no good. He'd enjoyed the almost family relationship with the Grimes without the entanglements he didn't want until tonight.

With two ladies cleaning the kitchen, they soon joined Jethro and Mr. Grimes in the parlor. Miss Schultz carried her satchel and a couple of canvases with her. She glowed with sheer happiness as she handed a painting to Mr. Grimes, sitting next to his wife on the couch.

"The chuck wagon and cook fire look almost real in this painting." Mr. Grimes carefully held the canvas by the edges as he stared at it.

"Thank you." She took the painting over to Jethro after Mr. Grimes finished looking at it.

Jethro's fingers brushed hers as she gave him the canvas. She jerked her hand back the instant he had a good grip on it. Good. He didn't want her to want to touch him. "You're a very talented lady."

Talented enough he might not have the heart to tell her no the next time she needed an escort to paint. No. He had to listen to his head. Keeping his distance from her and her problems was best.

Her radiant smile lit up her entire face. "Thank you."

Jethro halfway expected her to twirl in a circle the way his sister, Louisa, had done as a little girl. Yes, think of her like a little sister not a talented woman who was pretty enough to be dangerous for any man, especially him.

Miss Schultz showed them a few more sketches and then slipped them back into her satchel. "Since I saw Mr. Bannister trying to hide more than one yawn, I assume both of you men are too tired for more."

The boss nodded. "Bone tired."

"I so appreciate everyone's compliments." She hugged her satchel close. "I'll look forward to going out to paint again."

She peered straight at Jethro. So did Mr. and Mrs. Grimes. Like it or not, Jethro would be her escort. He hunted through his mind for a polite way to say he couldn't do that.

Several of her drawings had been of him alone or him with another cowboy. If she were interested in him, he needed to let her know his true intentions. He couldn't afford to lose another job getting too close to the boss's family. He'd never put himself in that situation again.

Harvey walked away from his blocks to grab at Ella's doll.

"No!" Ella jerked Annie away.

The little boy howled.

Everyone turned their attention to Harvey. Jethro doubted he'd ever been so happy to hear a child fuss.

Mrs. Grimes picked up her son. "Time for bed. Ella, you need to get ready too."

"That's a good idea. The boss stood. "Good night, everyone."

"Good night." Miss Schultz returned her attention to Jethro. "I'll see you at breakfast tomorrow, Mr. Bannister."

Jethro rose. "Till tomorrow." He covered another yawn while stepping toward the front door as quickly as possible without being rude. The sooner he left, the less time she'd have to ask when he could go with her to draw.

---

AFTER BREAKFAST THE NEXT MORNING, Mr. Grimes scooted his chair back as usual.

"What are we doing today?" Jethro hoped the boss stuck to his usual routine of an easy day after coming home from roundup.

"Last week's storms damaged the chicken coop, we'll fix that first. Maybe clean the barn after lunch unless I decide I'd rather rest some more."

"Sounds good to me." Jethro rose to follow the boss out the back door.

They spent the morning working on the roof of the chicken coop, finishing up not long before lunch time. Thanks to a nice breeze and pleasant fall weather, they had barely broken a sweat. Jethro picked up the ladder to take it back to the barn.

Mr. Grimes grabbed the bucket of nails and the hammer. "Glad we could spend the morning working in the sun in October instead of August."

They cleaned up and headed to the kitchen. Jethro inhaled the smell of fresh bread as they walked inside. Despite sharing meals with a woman who'd done too many drawings of him during roundup, he liked the definite advantage of eating at the Grimes's table.

After the boss said the blessing, Miss Schultz grinned as she passed a platter of bread. "Finally a recipe I was familiar with since I've been baking bread with Mama for years."

Mr. Grimes took two slices then passed the platter to Jethro. He helped himself to what appeared to be perfectly baked bread. Mrs. Schultz must have taught her daughter some things in the kitchen.

"I'm going to show Heidi how to make molasses pies this afternoon." Mrs. Grimes buttered a piece of bread before handing a small piece to Harvey.

Mr. Grimes licked his lips. "I'll take one of those any time."

So would Jethro.

"I'll need to go to town tomorrow. We'll be low on flour and molasses after today." Mrs. Grimes picked up her water glass.

"Can we get ice cream?" Ella glanced from one parent to the other.

"We'll see." Mr. Grimes's eyes twinkled. They usually stopped for ice cream, and Ella knew it.

"A trip to town would be wonderful. I can start looking for a job." Miss Schultz's face had lit up the instant her sister mentioned going to San Antonio.

Mrs. Grimes's expression sobered. "I don't think you should be seen in San Antonio this soon."

"But I've been here almost a month."

"Yes, but we both know how stubborn and persistent Father can be. I can't imagine he's given up looking for you yet."

"Did he look for you after you eloped with Harvey?"

Shaking her head, Mrs. Grimes swallowed hard. "No. I left a note we were getting married, so he left us alone." She averted her eyes and busied herself with putting more food on her son's highchair tray.

"I see. I'll stay here tomorrow." Her tone sounded as if she were being condemned to jail.

Such a dramatic woman should look for a job as an actress. Yet her downcast expression and sad eyes made Jethro wish he could make her feel better the way he'd done when Louisa was disappointed. No. She wanted to take care of herself. She might as well start by handling frustrating situations.

------

HEIDI WORKED to hide her disappointment as everyone ate. Lily was probably right about Papa. Her cherished dream would have to wait a while longer. How much longer, she didn't want to think about.

"We could order an easel for you tomorrow." Lily smiled at Heidi.

"I don't have money for that. I had to sell a locket, or I'd be penniless."

"You can pay us back later and for anything else you need us to pick up." Toby laid his fork on his empty plate.

"Thank you. I appreciate all you're doing for me."

"You're welcome." Toby scooted his chair back. "I'm going to take it easy this afternoon and clean my gun while you ladies bake pies." His eyes twinkled. "At least I hope you make more than one."

"We will." Lily wiped Harvey's hands with a damp rag.

"I'll sweep floors and do some other cleaning at my place." Mr. Bannister rose. "I'll look forward to pie later." He glanced from Lily to Heidi before walking to the back door.

Heidi spent a pleasant afternoon in the kitchen with Lily. She'd come to enjoy their time together, getting reacquainted with each other. A bonus she hadn't expected.

"We should bring back a couple of dress lengths of calico for you tomorrow." Lily took the pies out of the oven. "You should save your pretty dresses for when you're working in town."

Heidi shook her head as she set the lard on the shelf. "That's not necessary. I'll be safe in San Antonio soon. Especially after people see all of you there tomorrow without me."

"Maybe. But I want to be absolutely sure you're safe first."

"Thank you, but don't buy fabric for me. I *will* be leaving soon."

The way Lily's eyes clouded concerned Heidi. If she couldn't safely stay in San Antonio, she'd go somewhere else. The longer she stayed here in Lily's loving home, the harder it would be to leave. Especially if she went farther away and had to live completely alone somewhere.

Thoughts of her uncertain future vanished that evening as Toby and Mr. Bannister complimented her first efforts at baking molasses pies.

"Very good." Toby licked his lips after finishing a generous slice of pie.

Mr. Bannister laid his fork on his empty plate. "Yes, delicious."

"Thank you. I've got an excellent teacher." She rose and started stacking dirty plates.

"I'd like very much to do more sketches tonight." She'd take full advantage of the men's easy afternoon and their full stomachs.

"I told Ella she could have a short ride on Smoky. Jethro, would you go with Heidi?"

Mr. Bannister set his water glass on the table. "I can do that."

Heidi didn't mind the way he hesitated a moment before answering. She didn't want him to escort her either.

"I'll clean the kitchen so Heidi and Ella can enjoy themselves a little longer before dark." Lily carried the remainder of the dirty dishes to the dish pan.

"I don't mind helping you first."

"I did dishes alone for years. Go draw a nice picture for me." Lily patted Heidi's arm.

"Thank you." Heidi gathered her supplies and stools while Mr. Bannister left to hitch the horse to the buggy.

A short time later, Mr. Bannister handed the reins to Heidi and allowed her to drive the buggy out of the yard. "Thank you for not helping me load anything."

"If Mr. Grimes and Ella hadn't already left, I'd had to have at least carried the stools for you."

"Yes, I suppose so. Toby insisted on helping me at the roundup." She let the silence between them go on as she decided where she'd like to paint. "I think I want a better view of the barn today. A weathered building in the distance instead of a stone house will give me a different perspective."

He shrugged. "Whatever you'd like."

"I'd like something else too." She tightened her grip on the reins. "Would you think me too forward if I asked you to call me Heidi instead of Miss Schultz? And may I call you Jethro? We take our meals together. My family thinks enough of you they don't mind you coming with me." She glanced at him. He didn't look upset at her idea.

"I guess that would be all right."

She returned her attention to the horse and her driving. "I must be completely honest with you."

"About what?"

"I am thankful for your friendship, but I want nothing more, even though we're on a first-name basis."

"Please don't be offended if I agree with you. You're a talented lady, but I only desire friendship."

"I'm not the least bit offended. In fact, I'm happy to hear you concur. Riding in a buggy with a man who isn't scheming to gain my hand or my family's business is refreshing."

"Thank you. I appreciate your honesty."

"You're welcome." And he was. Unlike the twinge of regret in her heart that he so easily agreed they'd be nothing more than friends. No. She couldn't and wouldn't entertain any romantic notions about any man. Watching Lily and Toby together must be what had caused such a wayward idea. The sooner she left to start her own life, the better.

8

─────────

The late afternoon breeze swirled around them while Heidi and Lily sat on the porch. Lily tossed a corn husk past the steps. Ruckus barked as he and Ella ran to try to catch the husk. Harvey toddled after them, failing at his efforts to keep up with his sister and her dog.

On days like this, the noisy dog lived up to his name. Yet the combination of children's laughter blended with the hound's raucous barking created a pleasant scene while she snapped the green beans they'd soon fix for supper. Not dinner. She'd already picked up Toby's way of referring to meals.

She hadn't intended to be sitting on Toby and Lily's porch the last week of October, but she was. Wearing one of the calico dresses Lily had helped her sew. They'd be going to town for supplies soon. She'd go with them this time to look for a job.

Heidi bent to grab another handful of unsnapped beans from the basket at her feet. Ruckus's bark changed to something more forceful. He growled, staring to the east.

"Ma, I see a buggy coming and a man on horseback too." Ella shaded her eyes with her hand.

Lily rose, dumping the husked corn from her lap, as she

77

hurried to reach the porch steps. Heidi followed. She'd pick up the scattered beans later.

"I don't recognize that buggy." Lily peered toward whomever was coming. "I only see one man in the buggy, so I don't know why the other one is on a horse."

Ruckus planted himself in front of the children, his growl sounding more ominous as the strangers came closer.

"*Gutentag.*" The buggy driver waved as he yelled.

"No!" Lily's face blanched at the sound of Papa's voice.

Heidi shuddered. All the color had probably drained from her cheeks too.

"Ella, you and Ruckus run and see if Pa and Jethro are still at the smokehouse. Heidi, get in the house. Take Harvey." Lily stepped in front of Heidi and Harvey, not shifting her gaze from the approaching buggy.

The man on horseback turned his mount, urging the horse into a canter. He must be in a hurry to get back to wherever he came from.

"But what about you? Dealing with Papa alone?" Heidi hoped the men hadn't left the smokehouse yet.

"I'll be fine. Get inside. Now." Lily kept her back to them.

Taking Harvey into her arms, Heidi rushed up the steps. Then halted by the door with the knob in easy reach. She couldn't leave the sister who had done so much for her to face Papa alone.

"Get in the house." Lily gave her a sidelong glance.

Heidi shook her head. "I can't desert you."

By the time Papa drove into the yard, Toby and Jethro were running to Lily. Toby pushed his wife behind him. Jethro took the porch steps two at a time to stand beside her and Harvey, squirming in her arms.

"*Gutentag,* Suzanne." Papa's mouth drew into a thin line as he wrapped the reins around the brake while addressing Lily by the name she'd discarded years ago.

"Lily. Lily Grimes, Father." Lily's voice had an edge to it

Heidi had never heard. Even when she was correcting Ella for doing something terribly wrong.

Ella ran up with Ruckus. She paused not far from the buggy then gawked from her parents to the grandfather she didn't know as if trying to figure out what was happening.

"Ella, you and Ruckus go up on the porch with Heidi and Harvey." Lily motioned to her daughter. Despite the quizzical look on the little girl's face, she obeyed.

Papa climbed out of the buggy. The cold look in his eyes sent shivers up and down Heidi's spine. As if sensing the tension hanging in the air, Harvey stilled and stared in the direction of his mother.

Toby stepped toward Papa, stopping a couple of feet in front of him. "You must be Mr. Schultz. I'm Toby Grimes." The usually welcoming man didn't extend his hand to his father-in-law.

"*Ja.*" Papa continued speaking in German, telling Toby he'd come only to talk sense into Heidi and would be taking her back to New Braunfels.

"Speak English so I can understand you." Toby folded his arms across his chest as he glared down at the shorter man. "Otherwise, don't say another word."

Papa looked past Toby toward Lily. "Suzanne—"

"As my wife said, her name is Lily. Don't ever call her by any other name."

"That is not the name her mother and I gave her." Papa glared at Toby.

"What you gave her was pain and heartache she left behind. Unlike you, I love her and want her. Hurt my sweet Lily again, and I'll pick you up and toss you back in that buggy before you know what happened." Toby moved closer to Papa. His icy tone sounded colder than Papa's eyes looked.

Scowling back at the tall muscular man, Papa flinched ever so slightly. The only acknowledgment he'd probably give that he realized Toby wasn't making an idle threat. "Heidi, you will come home with me where you belong." Papa shifted his gaze to the porch.

Jethro took a step in front of her.

"No, Papa. My home is here now." As badly as she was shaking on the inside, Heidi marveled at how calm her words sounded.

Papa ignored Toby's request for English and told her in German how mistaken she was to leave New Braunfels.

"English, Mr. Schultz, or nothing at all." Toby reached out as if he'd take Papa's arm and carry out his threat to throw him into the buggy.

Papa swallowed hard but didn't back away.

"Father, it will be dark before you get back to San Antonio, and you're not familiar with this country. If you will be civil and do as Toby says, you may have supper with us and stay the night." Lily's firm, matter-of-fact tone left no doubt her invitation wasn't an offer for a warm, hospitable visit.

Her sister's compassion was amazing. Heidi instead prayed Papa would turn down the offer. If not for Toby and Lily, he'd drag her to New Braunfels and think nothing of such behavior. A harrowing drive alone back to San Antonio would serve him right. Hopefully also ensure he wouldn't return to threaten her again. She'd pray about her attitude later. For now, she wanted her father gone, never to return.

"What'll it be, Mr. Schultz?" Toby's stern expression matched Heidi's distrust rather than Lily's tender-hearted gaze.

Papa shook his head as he glanced toward the direction he'd come from. The rider who had accompanied him was out of sight. Papa squared his shoulders, looking Toby in the eyes. "I will stay the night since I didn't know Gunther would ride off and leave me here to find my way back to San Antonio alone."

"Gunther Eichmann?" Toby's words sounded like a growl.

"*Ja.*" Papa shook his head as if he realized he shouldn't have replied in German. "Yes."

"That man knows he's not welcome here. I'll help you see to your horse and buggy, Mr. Schultz." Toby took the horse's reins.

Heidi remembered the blacksmith who'd left New Braunfels two years ago but didn't know why Toby disliked Gunther so. She would ask later.

As Papa followed Toby, Lily walked up onto the porch. "Let's go inside."

"If you ladies don't need anything, I'll head to my place and clean up." Jethro turned to Lily. "Mrs. Grimes, I can eat there since you'll have company tonight."

"No. Eat with us as usual." Lily took her son from Heidi's arms.

Jethro tipped his hat. "Yes, ma'am. Thank you." He wasted no time going down the stairs and then trotted toward his house. He probably hadn't enjoyed the last few minutes any more than Heidi had.

She needed time alone to gather her rattled thoughts swirling through her mind. "I'll finish snapping the beans and husking the corn out here."

Her hand gripping the doorknob, Lily studied Heidi. "Since Father is with Toby, you should be all right."

"I'll hurry and take these to the kitchen soon."

Lily nodded before quickly ushering her children into the house. Heidi didn't mind not being around to help Lily explain to a six-year-old girl about her stranger grandfather who had never shown a moment's interest in her. Knowing Ella, the little girl had to be full of questions about the scene she'd witnessed.

Her niece wasn't the only one confused about what had happened. Recalling her own responses troubled Heidi. She'd told Papa the *Tumbling G* was home now. It wasn't and wouldn't be.

Also, what to make of Jethro's actions? He'd rushed to her side then stepped in front of her when Papa insisted she should come with him. She'd welcomed his protection more than she should. A truly independent woman didn't need a man or anyone else to watch over her. She would take care of herself. Face her troubles without relying on anyone.

She snatched the beans that had fallen from her lap as she and Lily had hurried to see who was coming. Snapping beans and husking the few ears of corn left should help her calm down. How would she deal with Papa since her tender-hearted sister had asked him to stay? Heidi had feared he'd find her. But how? She'd ask him tonight. The more she knew, the better she could keep this from happening again. Perhaps she should go somewhere farther away.

Some of Papa's customers talked of traveling all the way to Dallas. She'd be a total stranger there. Dallas might be the perfect place to start the kind of life she wanted. As long as she could control the rebellious ache welling up in her heart at the thought of being so far from Lily and her sweet family.

While finishing her task, Heidi pushed such thoughts aside. She would become self-sufficient and not allow her emotions to deter her dream. By the time she walked into the kitchen, she'd collected her wayward feelings enough to dream about her own rented house in San Antonio, or Dallas if need be.

"Are you all right?" Lily studied Heidi from head to toe as she emptied the corn and green beans onto the worktable.

"Yes, but I do wish Papa didn't need to stay the night."

"So do I. Honoring him the way the Bible says is not easy." Lily sliced her knife through a potato with more force than necessary to cut it.

By the time a pot of green beans and potatoes simmered on the stove, Toby walked into the kitchen. How he'd managed to keep Papa occupied so long, Heidi didn't care to ask. He gave Lily a quick kiss on her cheek as she lifted the lid to stir the vegetables.

"I told your father to sit in the parlor while he waits for supper. I'll keep him out of your way until you call us to eat." He spoke softly in his wife's ear.

Lily leaned her head against him. "Supper will take a little longer." She darted a glance toward their daughter. "I'll tell you later what I told Ella."

"Don't worry. I made sure he understands not to bring up any of the past in front of our girl unless he wants to go back to San Antonio in the dark."

"Thank you, dear."

He nodded before heading out of the room.

Sooner than Heidi wished, Lily sent Ella to the parlor to tell the men dinner was ready. She'd never planned to sit at any table across from Papa again. Thank God for Lily and Toby standing by her. And for Jethro who had the unfortunate task of sitting next to Papa. She'd have to thank him later for all he'd done too.

---

JETHRO BOWED his head as Mr. Grimes blessed the meal. Other than the delicious-smelling food on the table, Jethro could think of nothing else to be thankful for at the moment. He'd rather walk barefoot to San Antonio on the hottest day in August with an empty canteen than to be where he was. Taking the platter of dried beef from dour-looking Mr. Schultz while a silent Heidi passed the bowl of vegetables to Ella reminded him of the last meal he'd endured the night before he'd left home. He'd promised himself he'd never end up in a situation like that again.

But here he was. And here he'd have to stay until he could gracefully take his leave.

"I'm glad we got the door fixed on the smoke house today." Mr. Grimes glanced at his wife sitting at the other end of the table.

Mrs. Grimes didn't look up from placing green beans and bites of potatoes on the tray of Harvey's highchair. "So am I. We need to butcher another hog soon."

"We'll get that done. Then Jethro and I'll go deer hunting."

"I'd like some venison." Mrs. Grimes's thin smile wasn't the bright one she usually had for her husband.

The boss grinned. "I don't mind leaving you here with Heidi around." He turned his attention to Mr. Schultz, staring at him until the man peered up from his plate to look Mr. Grimes in the eyes. "Heidi's been a great help since she came. Especially since Lily's in the family way. She's happy to stay with us until after the baby is born in February."

Heidi clamped her mouth shut as she grabbed for her glass. Mrs. Grimes's wide eyes signaled she and her husband hadn't discussed any such thing about Heidi staying. Heidi looked just as surprised at the idea. But Mr. Shultz's steely gaze was so focused on the son-in-law he appeared to despise that he didn't notice how his daughters reacted to what appeared to be an unexpected announcement. Jethro looked down at his food, hoping he didn't look as shocked as the ladies did.

"That we will discuss later." Mr. Schultz stabbed a potato with his fork hard enough to make his plate clatter.

"No, sir. You're at our table because of how early it gets dark this time of year, not so you can argue about anything."

Mr. Schultz swallowed hard as if his bite of potato might stick in his throat but said nothing. Not a single word of congratulations about the coming baby. A man so uninterested in his own grandchildren had to be one of the coldest people Jethro had ever met. Yet Jethro's brother had been so relieved to see him go he wondered how happy anyone in Georgia would be to know Jethro was doing so well.

He shoved such unsettling thoughts away while listening to Mr. and Mrs. Grimes talk about the weather then Heidi's drawings.

"Your daughter is very talented." Jethro's words slipped out before he realized. No matter how he still wished he wasn't the one to watch over her while she painted, he couldn't help praising her to the man who didn't appear to care one whit about her abilities.

Their visitor finished his meal in silence.

As soon as Mr. Grimes pushed his chair away from the table,

Jethro scooted his back. Too many things about tonight made for painful reminders of Georgia. The sooner he could get out of here, the better. "Ladies, thank you for a delicious meal. I'll bid all of you good night." He rose.

"Could I walk out to the porch with you, Jethro?" Heidi turned her pleading eyes his direction.

Eyes that once more reminded him of Louisa, who he could never say no to. His sister would be about the same age as Heidi if she had lived. "Of course."

He followed her out of the room and through the parlor instead of taking the quicker route out the kitchen back door. Why she wanted to be with him on the porch or anywhere else didn't make sense. Especially for a woman who had plainly stated she would rather be alone.

She turned to face him as soon as he closed the front door behind them. "Thank you for all you've done today."

"What?" With only a sliver of a moon and a few stars, he couldn't see her face well.

"I appreciate the way you stood beside me when Papa got out of the buggy. You didn't have to do that. I didn't expect you to do it. Thank you."

He shrugged. "Guess since I've been guarding you from snakes and critters, it's become a habit. Even with the human variety."

"I never thought I'd speak about my own father in such a manner, but it's come to that." She sighed, then squared her narrow shoulders. "I can't allow Papa's dictates to ruin my life, but it pains me to think I may never see him or Mama again. Never go back to New Braunfels."

"Doing what's right or best isn't always without some heartache." The words tumbled out before he could stop them. He'd never come so close to being so honest with anyone since he'd left Georgia.

She cocked her head as she stared up at him. "You're speaking from experience?"

"Yeah." His one-word answer was all he could force from his tight throat.

"And you'd rather not talk about it. Good night, Jethro. And thank you. Again."

He tipped his hat to her. "You're welcome."

She nodded before opening the door and disappearing inside.

His heavy steps were much slower than they'd been when he'd run onto the porch to Heidi's side. He'd rushed to her defense without questioning or thinking about what he was doing. But he'd have done the same thing for a good friend. Or for Louisa.

Thinking of Heidi like a sister was all right. Allowing her to become more was not. Not just because she usually talked too much. But a woman with so many family problems that reminded him of his own past troubles would never be more than a friend.

## 9

**W**hen Heidi stepped back into the parlor, Toby sat on the couch. Papa occupied the chair next to the other end of the couch. Each man's stiff posture indicated their discomfort with the other. "I'll help Lily clean up." If her father wanted to protest, he kept silent as she walked past him. Toby's threat to send him back to town in the dark must be working.

Too soon, the dishes were all stacked on the shelf. Very little conversation had drifted from the parlor into the kitchen. With Ella helping clean up, Heidi and Lily were careful how they discussed Papa.

"Ella, go play with Annie in your room. Pa, Heidi, and I need to talk to our guest in the parlor."

"Yes, ma'am."

Lily seated herself beside Toby. Heidi chose Lily's rocker by the fireplace, as far away from Papa as she could manage. His gaze had followed her every move since she'd walked into the room. Toby openly kept his eyes on Papa. Probably the reason her father remained quiet.

"How did you find me?" Heidi voiced the question she must have answered, glad her steady voice didn't betray the turmoil in her heart.

"Old *Frau* Merkle finally remembered seeing Erich's wagon parked behind our house the night you left. After I started asking, other friends said they'd seen you with Frieda. Since she'd insisted we know where Suzan—"

"Lily. Her name is Lily. This is your last warning." Toby's blazing brown eyes left no doubt he'd follow through with everything he'd threatened if Papa didn't do as Toby said.

"Since I knew where your *sister* was, I wondered. I took the stage to San Antonio yesterday. A worker at the depot recalled seeing a woman matching your description about a month ago." He looked down at his feet, never making eye contact. "Gunther was nice enough to guide me out here today."

"That's another name you're not to say in my house." Lily's unusually harsh tone signaled Papa had best be careful with his words with her and Toby. "He had the gall to suggest I should leave Toby for him. Was that your doing?" Lily hurled her words at Papa.

"*Nein*. No." The way Papa sputtered suggested he might be telling the truth.

"However you found out about Heidi, or whatever you did or didn't do concerning Gunther doesn't matter." Toby paused to look Papa in the eyes. "What does matter is I will escort you to town tomorrow and personally see you get on the stage to New Braunfels. You're not to bother Heidi again."

Heidi had never seen her brother-in-law glare at anyone the way he did at Papa just now. Papa swallowed hard, looking as if it took every ounce of his willpower to remain seated. The man who gave all the orders at his wagon works was not accustomed to having anyone tell him what to do.

An uncomfortable silence hung over the room as Toby and Papa stared each other down.

Lily got to her feet. "Time for bed, Harvey." She picked up her son. "Father, you may come back only if the Lord softens your heart first." She walked out of the room without another word or glance in Papa's direction.

"Mr. Shultz, I'll show you to Harvey's room. Lily will make him a pallet in our room tonight."

"I'll help Ella get ready." Heidi stood. "Goodbye, Papa."

Saying such words made her heart ache. But thank God for the courage to speak calmly without bursting into tears. Her parents' betrayal hurt more than she could put into words, even if talking about her pain would have helped solve anything.

---

AFTER A NEAR-SILENT BREAKFAST, Toby left with Papa to go to San Antonio to be sure Papa took the stage to New Braunfels. As quickly as Jethro had left the table to hitch up the horse to Papa's rented buggy, the foreman must have been as eager to see Papa depart as everyone else. Neither Heidi nor Lily bid their father goodbye.

Heidi exhaled in relief, relaxing the rest of the knots in her shoulders as Lily handed her the last plate to dry. "Thank you doesn't sound adequate. Do you think we've truly seen the last of Papa?" Heidi stacked the plate on the shelf near her head.

Lily shrugged. "I hope so."

"Allowing Papa to think I'm staying here until after your baby comes might help." Heidi slipped her apron over her head then leaned back against the countertop. "But we need to talk about how long I'll really be here."

"Yes, we do after Toby gets home. Let's go out to the porch and watch the children play. The dusting I intended to do will wait. I'm not in the mood for housework today"

"I agree." Heidi followed Lily, Ella, and Harvey outside. The morning sunshine was already warming up the fall air.

Heidi and Lily seated themselves in the wooden chairs on the porch while Ella romped with Ruckus, followed by Harvey valiantly working to keep his balance as he chased after his sister and her dog.

The children's laughter brought the first smile to Lily's face since Papa had driven into the yard yesterday. "Ella and Harvey are truly gifts from God."

"They are." She hoped Lily wasn't about to again suggest how much Heidi would enjoy her own children one day. "Judging by the shocked look on your face last night, Toby hadn't talked to you about me staying to help you until February." She deliberately changed the subject, rather than risk Lily bringing up something she didn't want to talk about.

"No, he hadn't. That's why we'll talk about that after he comes home this afternoon."

"All right. I'll wait until then to insist I should be safe on my own in San Antonio now." She carefully chose her words when what she wanted to say was she didn't intend to postpone her dream until February or March.

"Ella, be sure Ruckus doesn't accidently knock Harvey down." Lily called to her daughter in time to prevent a collision between the hound and the little boy.

Toby came home around two o'clock. Since Harvey was napping, Lily sat on the porch mending socks while Heidi sketched a landscape. Ella sat nearby playing with her doll.

"Afternoon, ladies." Toby bent to kiss Lily's hair. "Your father got on the stage. I followed it through town a ways to be sure he didn't get off. I also mailed the letter you wrote Frieda last night."

"Thank you. I don't want her or Erich thinking it was their fault Papa found Heidi here."

"Good idea."

"Could we talk now about how long I'll be here?" Heidi didn't want to be rude, but she had to get them to understand she wouldn't be staying as long as Toby had led Papa to think. She laid her paper and pencils in her lap.

"I guess now's as good a time as any." Toby pulled a chair over next to his wife and then turned it around to where he could straddle it with his arms resting on the back and see Heidi and Lily. "Did y'all talk about it while I was gone?"

"No." Lily tied a knot in her thread. "I wanted you to be here."

"Yeah, I'm sure you do." He grinned in his wife's direction. "I hadn't thought about Heidi staying to help you until I mentioned it to your father. You know when I get a good idea like that, I can't hold it in."

"No. You can't and don't." Lily's twinkling eyes signaled she wasn't upset with Toby. "But I'm doing fine without help. Heidi is anxious to find a good job and start over."

"I understand. I really do." His expression sobered as he stared straight at Heidi. "Did Lily tell you she had problems with Harvey and he came so early he's alive only by the grace of God?"

"No. She didn't."

"That's what I figured." He reached over and placed his hand on Lily's arm. "Darlin', I can tell Heidi every word you're fixin' to say about how good you feel."

Lily shook her head.

"And every word would be true." Toby returned his gaze to Heidi. "But I'm not as good at trusting God as Lily is. Would you stay, Heidi? Please."

The desperate look in Toby's eyes melted Heidi's resolve to leave. Plus, not helping the sister who'd done so much for her was unthinkable. "I'll stay."

An ear-to-ear grin spread across his face. "Thank you. When you do go to San Antonio, we'll be sure you have enough money to make a good new start."

"Thank you." Having Lily and Toby understand her wishes made her feel warm inside again.

***

JETHRO WAITED to walk toward the porch until after Mr. and Mrs. Grimes finished talking with Heidi about whatever they were discussing. He'd come closer to witnessing their family squabble than he cared for. Never mind he'd probably missed the worst of it by spending as much time at his place as he could manage since yesterday afternoon.

"Boss, since you're back, I'm going for a ride. I made good progress cleaning the barn."

"I appreciate that. I didn't expect you to do it alone."

"I don't mind." Throwing himself into cleaning stalls had been a good way for Jethro to keep his mind off the bad memories that had come back to haunt him. Enough that he'd dreamt about Georgia last night for the first time in several years.

"Jethro, could I please ride with you? I'd like to look for more places to sketch." Heidi's hopeful expression again reminded him of his sister.

*No.* He wanted to shout his answer, but Mr. and Mrs. Grimes wouldn't understand how badly he needed time alone to think and pray. No one but God knew the entire truth of why he'd left Georgia. Not talking about his past. Not thinking about it more than he could help was how he'd learned to handle it all.

"Sure." He choked out the one-word reply.

Mr. Grimes stood. "I'll saddle Lily's horse while you get yours.'"

The boss walked with him to the barn. Mr. Grimes was a quiet man and left Jethro to his own thoughts. Unlike Heidi. He wouldn't get much praying done. Even less with her riding next to him.

As they stepped inside, they paused to let their eyes adjust to the dim barn. "Just because Heidi is Lily's sister doesn't mean you have to say yes every time she asks you for a favor. Want me to tell her you changed your mind?"

The offer was more tempting than he dared say even to his sympathetic boss. Until a picture of Heidi's expectant blue eyes that reminded him of Louisa forced its way into his mind. How her father ignored her the way he'd done was hard to figure out.

"She can come. Crazy as it sounds, she kind of grows on you." Where had that ridiculous idea come from?

Mr. Grimes chuckled. "Yeah, she does in her own way."

After saddling the horses, they led them to the yard. Toby helped Heidi to mount her horse. Jethro swung up in his saddle.

"Where would you like to go?" Heidi tossed him a radiant smile.

"My favorite ridge is to the south of here. One of the first places Mr. Grimes showed me because it's his favorite."

Jethro led the way, trying not to think too much about the last time he'd had a lady riding sidesaddle with him. His former boss had not been happy to learn his daughter had gone for an unchaperoned ride with Jethro. He'd had to look for another job not long after.

Mr. and Mrs. Grimes didn't seem to mind him spending time with Heidi. But that was probably only as long as he remembered he was the hired man and nothing more. The Lord had led him to the *Tumbling G*. He had no plans to lose this blessing.

"Thank you for allowing me to intrude on your plans." Heidi interrupted their silent ride not long after the outbuildings were no longer in sight.

"You're welcome." And he'd thought she should be the one who should go into acting.

"I saw your hesitation when I asked to come with you, but I didn't want to make you look bad to Toby if you said no." Her eyes twinkled. "So, I'll be quieter than I've ever been during a ride."

He couldn't help but grin. Moments later, the sparkle in her eyes disappeared as her entire countenance sobered.

"After I apologize to you for what you've endured since Papa came yesterday."

"No apology needed. None of it was your fault."

"No, but because you were still expected to eat with us, you were put into a terrible situation just sitting through meals."

"It's all right. I survived." *Barely*.

The last day or so had brought back too many vivid reminders of his past problems. The heated arguments. The way his brother had turned on him and turned their mother against him. He'd been awake since three this morning. Reading his Bible and crying out to the Lord the way he'd done after leaving Georgia seven years ago.

"I see the sadness in your eyes. You're not doing as well as you'd like me to think. But since you're a quiet, private man, I'll not press you to say more. I'll even do my best not to ask you ranching questions."

*You will?* He bit his tongue to keep from saying the words out loud. She was quiet only when concentrating on her art. If she kept silent the next five minutes, he'd be shocked.

Yet her perceptiveness and sensitivity to his feelings amazed him. So unlike some of the self-centered, almost inane comments she'd made at supper the night he'd brought her from San Antonio. Hard to believe such contradictory statements could come from the same woman. Maybe he'd misjudged her that first night.

True to her promise, Heidi didn't say another word the entire time it took to ride to his favorite spot. Whenever he glanced in her direction, she was studying the scenery as she'd said she wanted to do. Until they reached the top of the ridge.

"Ohhh. The view from here is so pretty it makes it hard to breathe." She stared in awe of the scenic country visible for several miles. "The rolling hills, scattered trees, and brush will make a beautiful landscape. I'm so glad we shouldn't have frost until next month and everything is still green. It all contrasts beautifully with the intense blue of a cloudless sky."

He helped her dismount. "Soak it all in. That's why I come here."

A look of sheer delight shone on her face and into her eyes as soon as her feet touched the ground. He hoped she didn't notice he'd held onto her a little longer than he should have. She quickly turned her attention back to the view she'd been exclaiming over, leaving him to wonder if she'd noticed he'd touched her at all. Which was fine since both of them wanted nothing but friendship.

"Longhorns!" She pointed toward the valley. "I can see cattle from here."

"We are on a ranch." His sarcastic words slipped out before he could stop them.

"Yes but as I've said before, I so want to sketch or paint longhorns. How close could I get to them and still be safe while I'm drawing?" She continued staring toward the horizon.

At least he hadn't offended her. "I'm not sure. I've never tried to just watch them unless we're herding them up a trail."

"I suppose so."

"Why are you so interested in ranches and cowboys?"

Her smiled faded. "Probably because my parents wouldn't allow any talk of cowboys no matter how much they fascinated me. I've long been intrigued by the way they dress and act so differently than the townspeople I'm accustomed to. Toby told me Lily could tell me why ..." She closed her eyes and took a deep breath, letting whatever else she intended to say almost literally hang in the air between them.

He let her silence go on, not sure he wanted an answer to his question if it had anything to do with her family troubles.

"I think I've deciphered why by myself." She turned to face him. "My parents disowned Lily when she eloped with her late husband, Harvey. He was a cowboy. They have despised ranchers since then. I was only twelve, so I didn't understand why."

"That makes sense. At least to them."

She sighed. "Yes, to them. As does forcing a union between me and a man of their choosing so Papa's wagon works can remain in the family." Her voice cracked. She turned to stare straight ahead.

Swallowing hard, Jethro tried to focus on the beautiful, rugged country God had made. Focus on God's blessings. Not his past pain threatening to rear up like a hungry mountain lion tearing into a rabbit and tear apart the peace he'd struggled so hard to find.

"Jethro?"

"What?"

"Lily said a while back that hard as it's been, she's forgiven Mama and Papa. Not forgotten everything, but forgiven them." She took in a shuddering breath. "I'm trying. But ... what if I can't forgive them?"

"God tells us to forgive. Doing it takes strength from Him, especially if someone isn't sorry for what they've done. But it's the only way to find peace."

She peered into his eyes. "You have personal experience with what you're talking about. Don't you?"

He nodded. "Several years' worth."

"I'm sorry."

A hawk screeched as it circled overhead, diverting her attention as she shaded her eyes with her hand to watch it. A cotton tail scurried under a clump of brush a few feet from her skirt. Some days he'd like to run away like that rabbit. Except his past would always go with him. Like Mrs. Grimes, he'd managed to forgive his family but not forget. Being betrayed still hurt. He'd bury the hurt deep inside himself again.

## 10

Heidi barely took time to stretch when she awoke early Sunday morning. Lily and Toby had decided yesterday they all needed to go to church in San Antonio. Papa's departure on Friday morning still had everyone feeling out of sorts no matter how routine Saturday had been. The one good thing about his visit meant she could now go to town and not worry about who might see her there. She'd laid out her favorite moss green silk dress, bustle and all, last night to help her get ready more quickly this morning.

By the time Lily and Toby walked into the kitchen, Heidi had the fire going in the stove and coffee in the pot. "Good morning."

"Good morning to you." Lily smiled in her direction. "Looks like I'm not the only one eager to go to church this morning."

"No. You're not."

The entire family rushed to be able to leave on time. A sunny October day that promised such pleasant weather for a drive couldn't be wasted. Jethro's shining green eyes signaled he must be as happy as she felt as he helped her into the back seat of the buggy. Lily settled Harvey on one side of Heidi while Toby set Ella on the other side.

97

With the entire family along, the conversation was lively as Toby drove. Ella made her usual observations about butterflies while cautioning Harvey not to touch them if they flew close enough. Lily talked of friends she hoped would be at church.

Jethro rode his horse alongside them but said little. Perhaps he was still thinking about their talk on their ride Friday afternoon. She had finally kept her promise to be quiet after his wise comments on forgiving people and allowed him his own thoughts. Even managing to say little as they rode back to the house.

His few words had stirred her curiosity about him. He must have suffered through someone doing something wrong, hurting him deeply. Yet he gave her hope she, too, could build a new life and leave the old one behind without becoming hardened or bitter.

When the buggy rolled into the church yard, Heidi's heart thrilled at the site of the steepled white building. How she'd missed going to church and worshiping with someone other than family.

Ella skipped beside Heidi as they walked toward the door. "I want to sit by you, please."

"I'd like that."

Toby chose a pew close to the back. Since Lily and Toby wanted to sit by the aisle with their wiggly son, Heidi ended up seated on the other side of Toby with Ella between her and Jethro. Her niece had no idea how much Heidi liked having the little girl sitting next to her, reinforcing the idea she and Jethro were only friends.

When they rose to sing *What a Friend We Have in Jesus,* Heidi's heart drank in every lovely note from the piano and every word of the hymn. No matter who had betrayed her, she still had Jesus as the one true friend who would protect and shield her. Jethro's enthusiastic singing left no doubt the words touched him too.

The pastor stood to begin his sermon. "I appreciate

everyone's heartfelt singing of one of my favorite hymns. The Lord impressed me today to talk about one of the hardest things for us to pray about and to do. Look in your Bibles at Matthew chapter six, verses nine through thirteen."

Heidi had heard the verses since childhood and could recite them from memory. After reading all the verses of Jesus's prayer, the pastor focused on His words about forgiving others. "We're to forgive others the way God forgives us."

The pain she'd tried to stuff deep down inside welled up, making her heart ache so she could feel her chest tightening. The parents she'd loved and trusted all her life wanted to trade her off in marriage as if she were a horse. They'd secure her financial future, see she'd always have what she needed and more. But wasn't her heart, her feelings, worth more than money and the things a successful business could buy?

She closed her eyes, wishing she could close her ears. Better yet, find an excuse to leave. The pastor went on to talk about Jesus telling Peter to forgive over and over again. But Papa and Mama weren't the least bit sorry for hurting her. They were so wrapped up in carrying out their plans for her they didn't even see how much pain they'd caused her. Or care about it if they did realize how they'd hurt her.

Papa's visit had proved as much. He'd offered no apology. Only demanded she come back with him. If not for Lily and Toby, perhaps Jethro too, he'd have hauled her to New Braunfels. Condemning her to a loveless marriage didn't seem to bother him at all.

How did someone forgive such an awful, deliberate betrayal?

After the service, Lily and Toby paused to greet the pastor before walking outside. Heidi stared past them to the church yard, wishing she could run out the door to the buggy.

"Brother Bridges, this is my sister, Heidi Schultz. She's staying with us a while." Lily beamed as she introduced Heidi.

"We're glad you're here." The balding man extended his hand.

"Thank you."

Several people stopped to talk to Lily and Toby as they started toward the buggy. Lily made sure they met Heidi, especially every young man who came up to them. Heidi cringed on the inside while smiling on the outside. The unsettling sermon had given her more than enough to think about without dealing with too friendly men. Once she settled in San Antonio, she might have to explain to more than one of them she had no intentions of being more than a friend with any male.

More than once, she glanced to where Jethro stood talking with a couple of cowboys under a shade tree. She hoped he wasn't the only man willing to accept her wishes. He might be the only one who understood her struggle to forgive Papa and Mama.

"Lily, Toby." A woman with graying hair hurried up to them. "Are y'all coming to our house as usual?"

"We planned on a picnic on the way home since we have Heidi and Jethro with us too."

Lily tightened her hold on Harvey's hand as he tried to pull away from her.

"So nice to see you, Heidi. I'm Doris Hawkins. Owen told me all about meeting you at our store." She extended her hand.

"Nice to meet you." Heidi couldn't help contrasting the woman's warm greeting with the cool way her husband had assessed Heidi at first. But after what she and Lily had been through, she appreciated the man's caution.

"There's not room for all of us at your table." Lily's words brought Heidi's thoughts back to the present.

"No, but a picnic on our back porch would be lovely." The lady's smile was as warm and inviting as her hospitable offer.

"What do you think?" Lily deferred to Toby.

He grinned. "Doris wouldn't hear to us saying no. And you've never turned her down. So why ask me?"

Lily laughed. "All right. We'll picnic on your porch."

"I'll tell Jethro." Toby headed toward his foreman.

Before they got to the buggy, Lily introduced Heidi to the pastor's son and another man. Lily obviously hadn't taken Heidi seriously when she'd said she intended to remain single. Heidi hoped their difference of opinion didn't cause problems between them now or later after she left.

Jethro walked up in time to help Heidi into the buggy. The mischievous twinkle in his eyes made her wonder if he was silently teasing her about assisting her. Unlike allowing her to do things herself when he was with her while she painted. He then swung up in his saddle, ready to go with them to the Hawkins's house.

Doris stepped outside to greet them when the buggy rolled up. "I'm so glad you came. Pastor Bridges and his family should be here any moment too. We'll have such a wonderful afternoon."

"Are you sure you have room for all of us?" Lily's doubtful tone was evident from Heidi's spot in the back seat.

"Of course."

Pastor and Mrs. Bridges, along with their son, walked up as Toby helped Lily out of the buggy. Jethro quickly dismounted to assist Heidi after she handed Harvey to his mother. She hoped it was her own imagining he held on to her a little longer than necessary.

"Allow me to introduce my family, Miss Schultz." The pastor gestured toward the lady beside him. "My lovely wife, Judith, and our son, Andrew."

"So nice to meet you." Judith's warm smile emphasized her words.

"Nice to meet you too." Heidi meant her reply to Mrs. Bridges. What to say to her son might be another matter.

"We met after the service." Andrew's gaze was more welcoming than Heidi wished.

A few minutes later, Heidi helped the other ladies set the food on the kitchen table while they talked. The picnic lunch Lily had brought was soon combined with what Doris had fixed along with the pies Mrs. Bridges had made. The men carried chairs to the porch.

Lily explained why Heidi had come to her and Toby. "The reason she's here is sad, but we're so happy she found us."

"Thank God you did." Doris handed Heidi a small stack of plates.

"Yes, thank God." Heidi set the plates next to another stack.

For a woman who'd said her family consisted only of her husband and adopted sixteen year-old nephew, she had a lot of plates. Enough that the lady must be as accustomed to entertaining as Mama was in New Braunfels.

No. She wouldn't think of the place that would never be home again. Instead, she'd focus on a nice afternoon with loved ones who wanted her and making their friends her friends too. Much more pleasant things to think about than her struggles during the sermon earlier.

After Owen thanked God for Brother Bridges's fine sermon and blessed the food, everyone filled their plates then went out to the porch. Plate in hand, Heidi took the last empty chair. Next to Jethro. She wasn't sure how it happened, but she strongly suspected Lily had done her best to help the situation come about. If so, Heidi needed to find a way to remind Lily she had no intentions of hunting for a man.

"So nice to have such a pleasant breeze today." She smiled at Jethro.

Since he'd taken a bite of cornbread, he nodded.

From her spot on the nearby step, Ella twisted to look Heidi's way. "Aunt Heidi, did you bring your pictures? I wanted to show Mrs. Hawkins how pretty they are."

"No. I left them at home." The word home slipped out before she realized it. Lily and Toby's house wasn't home. She'd find a job and fend for herself as soon as she could. Staying too long after the baby was born might make her a burden instead of a help. She doubted she was doing enough to earn the easel and new paints they'd ordered for her the last time they'd come to town.

Ella cocked her head. "You should bring them next time. By then, you and Mr. Bannister will have time to go look for places where you can paint more."

"We'll have to see what the weather does this time of year as quickly as it can change."

"I hope you get to draw more soon."

"So do I." Which she did. She didn't want everyone thinking she and Jethro were more than friends. Except for Andrew Bridges. His almost constant gazing at her was unnerving. As was how comfortable she felt sitting next to Jethro.

---

JETHRO HAD NEVER THOUGHT he'd be happy to hear anyone mention him escorting Heidi anywhere. But the pastor's son had watched her every move since she'd stepped onto the porch. He didn't blame him. The woman was stunning in her light green dress. Every time Jethro had glanced in her direction in the church yard, some man was introducing himself to her. Or staring at her from a distance. He wasn't the only one who couldn't help watching her. As much as he shouldn't mind the attention she'd received, he did.

"The cornbread you made is delicious as usual." He hoped his inane compliment signaled to Andrew he and Heidi did more together than look for places for her to paint pictures. His friend probably didn't need his help fending off unwanted male attention, but Jethro didn't mind assisting her. Friends did that for each other.

"Thank you."

Andrew barely disguised a glare in Jethro's direction, looking as if he'd like to shove the rest of the cornbread down Jethro's throat to give him an even better taste of it. His banal words must have accomplished what he wanted. Heidi bit into her carrots without taking the slightest notice of the pastor's son. Good.

The instant Heidi took the last bite of her food, Andrew stood and then made his way to her. "If you'd like dessert, Miss Schultz, I'll be happy to bring you a piece of my mother's apple pie."

"Thank you, but you don't need to go to so much trouble for me."

"It's no trouble at all." His smooth smile and nice suit gave him the look of the perfect gentleman he was portraying. The opposite of what Jethro was in his trousers and boots.

Jethro couldn't help hoping the serious expression on Heidi's face indicated a different sort of trouble for Andrew. The usually plain-spoken woman had to be thinking of a polite way to let the man know she didn't welcome his attention. She'd wasted no time telling Jethro she had no plans of matrimony.

"I would like a piece of pie. Thank you."

Andrew took her plate and then disappeared into the house. He returned much too soon. "Would you mind if I bring my chair over here by you and Jethro?"

"Um ..." She glanced around at the others, trying to pretend they weren't watching the unfolding scene. "Jethro and I don't mind if you do. Neither of us get much of a chance to socialize with people our age."

If Heidi noticed Andrew's barely disguised frown at her use of Jethro's first name, she didn't let it show. The man had no idea she wasn't here to hunt a husband. Jethro knew it. Which meant he really shouldn't care what Andrew or any other man thought of Heidi. Especially since he wouldn't consider her for a wife any more than she'd consider him for a husband.

As soon as the other ladies started gathering up dirty plates, Heidi got to her feet and took Jethro and Andrew's dishes. She wasted no time carrying them inside. The way Andrew watched her, Jethro wondered if the man might seriously think of donning an apron and helping the women in the kitchen. He almost choked on a swallowed chuckle as he pictured such a ridiculous idea in his mind.

"The Hawkins have a nice horseshoe pit at the end of the yard. Would you like to play?" Andrew focused his attention on Jethro only after the back door closed behind Heidi.

"All right. No use wasting such a nice day." Jethro stood. He could think of a lot of other things he'd rather do on a Sunday afternoon. Such as getting caught in a hail storm on the trail.

Andrew took off his suitcoat and draped it over the back of his chair. While Mr. Grimes, Owen, and the pastor continued talking on the porch, Jethro played the most competitive and intense couple of games of horseshoes he'd played in his life. Andrew was good and did his best to beat every throw Jethro made.

"I'll allow you to challenge me to a rematch another day." Andrew wiped his damp forehead after winning the second game.

"I might do that." If there were a next time, which Jethro hoped there wouldn't be.

The ladies returned to the porch after cleaning the dishes. Mrs. Grimes held a whining Harvey by the hand. "As much as we've enjoyed everyone's company, we need to head home."

After everyone said goodbye, Jethro maneuvered himself to the right spot to help Heidi into the Grimes's buggy before Andrew could get near her. Cowboys were used to making quick moves. Much more so than any town-bred man.

The ride home was quietly routine, almost dull. He'd take that after the way his day had gone once church ended. Since the Grimes family nor Heidi expected him to say much, he spent the time mulling over Brother Bridges's excellent sermon.

As he'd told Heidi, he hadn't found peace until God had given him the strength to forgive his family. But watching Heidi struggle through her problems the last few days had caused his past hurts to resurface. Any time that happened, the remembered shouted arguments with his brother or the woeful looks from his mother threatened to undo the tranquility he'd worked so hard to find.

When the buggy rolled to a stop in the yard, Jethro dismounted. He helped Ella down. Then assisted Heidi. Reminding himself to let go of her the instant her feet touched the ground.

This time, she stopped to look at him. "Could we talk on the porch after you tend to your horse and help Toby with evening chores?"

"Sure. I'll let you know when I'm finished if I don't see you outside."

"I'd like that."

But would he? Jethro spent the entire time wondering what Heidi wanted to tell him. Had she noticed the extra attention he'd paid her while they were at the Hawkins' house? If so, he might not want to hear what she wanted to say.

When he headed toward the front porch, Heidi sat with her pencils and paper propped in her lap. Still wearing the green dress that looked so nice on her. Ella and Ruckus, followed by Harvey, trotted past him as he reached the steps. Mr. Grimes had taken his usual chair by his wife where they had a good view of their children.

Heidi set her pencils and paper by her chair. "I'd like to stretch my limbs a little and ask you for suggestions of other places to paint if you don't mind."

She would? "I'll help you if I can." Her words sounded as ridiculous as some of what he'd said at the Hawkins's house. She'd never asked him for suggestions for her paintings. Ignoring the smiles Mr. and Mrs. Grimes aimed at him and Heidi, he turned to allow her to walk past him and down the steps. Waiting until they were out of earshot to satisfy his curiosity about her real intent took every bit of willpower he could muster.

"The only true words I spoke on the porch concerned stretching my limbs. Please don't be offended I don't want suggestions about where to paint." She halted on the other side of the barn where they were out of sight. "I said what I did so Lily and Toby don't think we're going for a walk because we're becoming fond of each other."

"No offense taken. I suspected as much." He braced himself for what she might really want to talk about.

"I'd like to thank you for keeping Andrew Bridges at bay and allowing me to sit by you and talk as if we know each other better than we do."

He hoped his mouth hadn't opened too wide. Instead of aggravating her, he'd made her happy by keeping another man away from her? Not what he'd expected, but maybe what he liked. Or shouldn't like since she'd never be more than a friend. "Uh, I didn't mind."

"You didn't?" She tilted her head as if studying him, perhaps trying to understand what his too quick reply might mean.

He searched through his scrambled thoughts for a good way to explain himself without her thinking he had similar intentions to the ones Andrew had. "I know your future plans do not include marriage. I helped you fend off Andrew the way I'd help any other friend who needs a little assistance."

The breath she let out sounded like a huge sigh of relief. Perhaps she had suspected what his motives were.

"Thank you. I appreciate your honesty."

"You're welcome." He meant what he said. Except he'd enjoyed making Andrew jealous. As long as she didn't realize how dishonest he was being now, he'd be all right.

"But I'm afraid some people now think you and I might be more interested in each other than we are. Lily and Mrs. Hawkins were much too happy when they saw me sit next to you."

He shrugged, hoping to look less upset than he was to hear her pronouncement. He'd been concentrating on Andrew so much he'd failed to see how anyone else reacted to Heidi sitting so near him. No one needed to start assuming he had designs on her or she cared for him. "We aren't in San Antonio much, so the townspeople will have plenty of time to forget whatever they were thinking."

"And we can easily convince Lily and Toby we're only friends." She grinned. "Since we have all that settled, we should go back to the house. The less time we spend alone, the less time we give my family to think we like each other more than we do."

Dusk was falling, and the porch was empty by the time they walked up. A lamp shone from the window in the parlor.

She paused by the steps. "Good night, Jethro. Thank you for being such a good friend."

"You're welcome." He tipped his hat before turning toward his own place.

Good thing no one had heard their short conversation. Anyone thinking clearly would probably conclude he was crazy to consider a woman like Heidi as only a friend. Trouble was, he was also beginning to think he'd sounded a little crazy.

No. He couldn't let those thoughts go on. Even if she were the kind of woman he wanted, he doubted Mr. and Mrs. Grimes would be happy if he started thinking too highly of Heidi. She was a beautiful, talented lady. He was a cowboy foreman with little to offer her if she did want him.

Which she didn't.

## 11

The brisk fall breeze whipped at Heidi's skirt as she pinned a sheet to the clothesline "I'm glad yesterday was warmer."

"So am I. We all needed a trip to church. Being with friends was good too." Lily beamed as she hung one of Ella's petticoats.

Heidi stooped to grab another wet sheet. Since Ella and Harvey were busy playing with Ruckus, this might be the best time to explain again Heidi's plans did not include marriage. "Not everything was good yesterday."

Lily paused, clothespin in hand, to look straight at Heidi. "It wasn't?"

"No." Heidi stared straight at the sheet in front of her. How to say what needed said without hurting her sweet sister who was doing so much for her? "I shouldn't have allowed Mr. Bridges to bring me a piece of pie."

Lily's eyes widened. "Oh? Why not?"

"Since I have no plans for matrimony, I shouldn't be letting him or any other man do things for me." Heidi shook out the sheet with more force than necessary before pinning it to the clothesline. "It's wrong to mislead him."

"I see." The puzzled look in Lily's eyes meant she probably didn't see. "What about allowing Jethro to go with you to paint?"

"I told him my plans the first time he went with me. He's been through some kind of family difficulty a few years ago and understands why. He accepts my ideas."

"The Lord had blessed me with two loving men. I don't understand why you won't so much as look for a good man." The tender look in Lily's eyes caused a lump to form in Heidi's throat.

"Because I will never be beholden to a man again." Heidi jabbed a clothespin over the last sheet. "Once I'm settled in San Antonio, I'll live my own life, make my own decisions, and never be dictated to by anyone."

Lily picked up the empty laundry basket. "Come. Sit with me. We need to talk." Her firm, gentle tone signaled she wouldn't be put off. "Ella, Heidi and I are going to rest on the porch a little while. You and Harvey come play in the front yard." She pulled a chair close enough to the railing to watch her children. Heidi placed her chair beside her sister's. "Heidi, dear, you'd have to become a hermit living in the wilderness to be that self-sufficient."

"No, I can live in town wherever I'd like. Choose the job I want. Decide how to spend my money." Thinking about the dream she wanted so badly made her ache inside with longing.

"Maybe one day. But why are you so set on this?"

"Choosing my own path is the only way to keep someone from hurting me again the way Papa and Mama have. The way Karl Muller hurt me too." Heidi blinked away the tears threatening to spill onto her cheeks. Now was not the time to cry over what had happened no matter how much she still hurt. Nor the time to tell her sister how her childhood friend Karl had hurt her by bending to his parents' choice for a bride. She'd brought up enough painful things for now.

"Have you prayed about the kind of life you want?" Lily turned toward Heidi.

"Many times. I prayed for a way not to be paired off with Johann. For a safe escape." She took a deep breath. Recalling her last few days in New Braunfels still unnerved her. "God helped me find you. He protected me when Papa found me."

Lily patted Heidi's arm. "Have you prayed about what God wants once you're in San Antonio or if He wants you there?"

"Of course. How can God not want me in San Antonio when He's answered every prayer to get me here?" How could her sister not see what Heidi saw so clearly?

"I'm not saying He doesn't want you in town." Lily sighed. "But are you sure what He'd have you do there, how He'd have you live? Have you asked God about remaining single?" Lily turned her chair to face Heidi, close enough for their knees to touch. She took Heidi's hands in hers. "I'm sorry you're hurting so badly."

"I can't ever have someone who can tell me what I have to do. Who could betray me and ruin my life."

"And break your heart ... again." Her sister's soft voice sounded like a caress.

Heidi squeezed her eyes shut, wishing she could shut out the truth Lily had spoken. Her heart was more broken than she'd like to discuss at the moment. But not considering the solution she'd decided on to prevent further pain hurt too. Especially since spinsterhood was the only option she could see that wouldn't leave her vulnerable to being wounded again.

"Look at me, my sweet Heidi." Lily patted Heidi's cheek.

Lily's gentle voice and loving touch compelled Heidi to do as her sister asked.

"Not everyone will hurt you. There are so many good people. Good men. Like Toby, David. Eduardo, too, if you knew him."

"But people change. Papa and Mama did."

Lily sucked in a deep breath. "Yes, they can. But we can't live in fear, always afraid of being hurt, too afraid to risk or reach out. What kind of life is that? Is that really living?"

"I ... I haven't thought about it like that."

"That's all right. Think. And pray. Maybe God brought you here to show you what He really wants for you and not what you think He wants."

"Maybe so." *Maybe not.* But letting Lily think Heidi might reconsider the promises she'd made to herself would bring on more talk from her sister of why Heidi should not want total independence.

"Toby and I know what it's like to be hurt. Healing takes time. It takes God's help and strength."

"Ma, look. A big fuzzy caterpillar." Ella trotted toward the steps. She held her hand out to show off her catch.

"I see." Lily leaned back instead of forward toward her daughter. "Why don't you set it in the grass. It probably has a family."

"Yes, ma'am." Ella skipped off to do her mother's bidding.

"A family?" Heidi shook her head.

"It's Toby's idea from when she was little and bringing me horned toads. She put them down when he told her they had families too." Lily grinned. 'You *do* have a family. We're happy to talk to you or help any way we can."

"Thank you."

Heidi spent the rest of the day thinking about her talk with Lily. As she'd told her sister, God had answered too many prayers for help and protection for Him to not want her to make a new life in San Antonio. For herself without someone else to interfere. Looking to God and God alone for her future couldn't be wrong.

---

As Jethro took the last bite of his bread at noon, Mr. Grimes scooted his chair back from the table. "Jethro and I were talking this morning about going deer hunting soon. He's already cleaned his rifle, so I'll clean mine this afternoon and let Jethro see if he can catch some fish for supper.

"Fish sounds fine." Mrs. Grimes nodded toward her sister. "Heidi, you should go too. You might find some pretty spots by the creek for drawing pictures."

"I'd be pitiful help if I leave you with all the ironing."

"I only have one ironing board. You used to go fishing with Otto whenever you could."

"Yes, I did." She ducked her head.

Was she avoiding eye contact? He hoped so. Mrs. Grimes's idea for Heidi to go along with him was much too obvious.

"Have you been fishing since Otto died last year?"

Heidi shook her head.

"Then you should definitely go with Jethro. Find a nice place to draw later. Make a good fishing memory." Mrs. Grimes wiped Harvey's hands with a rag as if her pronouncement settled everything.

"I've imposed on Jethro enough lately. Plus, I'll not have you ironing my clothes."

"I'll save your clothes for you to do later. New memories can help us deal with the sad ones."

While Heidi appeared to weigh her sister's words or hunt for another excuse to stay home, Jethro waited for the boss to say something about not expecting his foreman to entertain Heidi for them. But he didn't. Whoever Otto was, he must have meant a lot to Heidi. Maybe Mrs. Grimes's motives weren't what he'd assumed.

"Two people fishing can catch more fish so we'll have plenty." Words Jethro shouldn't be saying slipped out. Again.

"If you truly don't mind me coming along ..." Heidi glanced up at him.

"I don't." But he should. He shouldn't want to help her as often as he had lately.

While the ladies cleaned the kitchen, Jethro dug up worms and got the poles ready for a walk to the creek. For the first time he could remember, he wished for a dry creek. But they'd had plenty of rain lately. The sun had warmed the cool morning air to a most agreeable temperature of not too hot or too cold.

He hoped the missus was truly concerned about Heidi's happiness and hadn't hornswoggled him into spending the afternoon with her sister. Fishing with Heidi might well prove to be the imperfect ending to what could have been a perfect afternoon. Especially if he could have gone alone. After being with so many people yesterday, he could use some solitude.

Sooner than he wished, he set the bucket of worms on the porch then propped the poles against the porch railing. He forced his hand to knock on the door.

"Come on in. I think Heidi's about ready." Mr. Grimes ushered Jethro inside.

Heidi stepped into the parlor, empty-handed, a few moments later.

"Aren't you taking your pencils or paper?" Mr. Grimes stared, obviously expecting to see her carrying her satchel, maybe more.

"No. I haven't fished in so long. I'm going to enjoy that the way Lily suggested. If I find some spots for good paintings, I can go back later."

Jethro swallowed a groan. These days, later meant he *and* Heidi would go back since the rumors he'd heard after church yesterday about rustlers meant the lady wouldn't be going for walks alone. Which was probably why the boss had kept quiet while his wife schemed to get Heidi to go fishing. So here he was and would be. Escorting her. Again.

She paused as they walked by the chicken coop. "Thank you for allowing me to intrude on what might have been a quiet afternoon for you to think your own thoughts uninterrupted."

"You're welcome. May I ask who Otto was?"

"The brother Papa had expected to take over the wagon works."

"I see."

Her eyes twinkled. "I hope Lily was as genuinely concerned about how much I miss Otto and not just trying to convince us to go fishing. Regardless, we'll hope for enough fish for dinner and enjoy this time as friends, no matter that too many people seem to think we're more than that."

"Or should be." Her lack of enthusiasm for his company made him feel better. Somewhat. Part of him wished she didn't mind being alone with him.

She barely said a half dozen words by the time they walked past the barn, leaving him to wonder why she was so uncharacteristically quiet. But he had enough to think about he wouldn't ask for an explanation and ruin the unexpected silence.

The way Mr. and Mrs. Grimes had been acting lately must mean they didn't mind Jethro spending time with Heidi. Was he wrong thinking they would be unhappy if he and Heidi became more than friends? But that created a new problem. Heidi was not the kind of woman for him if he were looking. He'd hate to lose this job because he aggravated the Grimes for not liking Heidi enough.

When they got to the creek, Heidi stopped to take in the whole scene the way she usually did when observing a new place. "It's very pretty here with the cypress trees all along the creek bank. Listening to the water running is peaceful."

"It is nice. I can bait your hook if you'd like."

"Thank you. Otto always did that for me." Her sparkling smile shone into her eyes. "Why are you wearing your gun belt and with extra bullets too? It's too cold for snakes."

"Rustlers. Some men mentioned them after church."

"Rustlers are cattle thieves, aren't they?"

He nodded. "I told the boss this morning. He'll tell your sister to keep the children close just in case."

"Good." She threw her line into the water.

Only a one-word answer. What had come over the lady? But if he asked, she'd probably give him a long enough explanation to scare away every fish up and downstream. By the time they'd each caught a couple of fish, she'd barely said two sentences. Maybe she was concentrating on making a good memory the way her sister had suggested. Whatever the reason, he appreciated the quiet.

"Do you feel all right?" His curiosity got the best of him. Strange that he was the one asking questions this time.

"I feel fine. I've got a lot on my mind. Lily and I had a serious discussion this morning."

"It must have been very sobering."

"Yes, it was." She stared in the direction of the hook she'd thrown in the water. "We were talking about praying for God's will and knowing His will."

"That's a lot to think about."

She sighed. The kind of exaggerated one he'd come to expect. "Especially when I think or thought I knew for sure what God wants."

"And now you don't?"

"Yes. I mean no. But I can't tell Lily or Toby that with the way they're working to push us together." She turned her attention from her fishing line to look him straight in the eyes. "From what little you've said, I suspect you have no intention of taking a wife. Which is why you accept my plan to live alone."

Pretending to check on his fishing line, he peered away. She'd come to a somewhat wrong conclusion. He might settle down with a woman one day. But not her. He couldn't be that blunt, that cruel to a lady who'd been hurt enough already. "I do understand wanting to be alone."

"Exactly."

A quick, sidelong glance told him she was still staring. So intently he could almost feel her eyes on him.

"How did you determine God wants you single?"

He almost dropped his pole into the water. "How?"

Something tugged on the line, bowing his pole. "I've got a fish." Fish or turtle, he didn't care. What an answered prayer. He didn't have the slightest idea how to answer Heidi's question.

"What a nice catfish. We've got enough for supper now." He

put the fish into the bucket of water with the others they'd caught.

A horse neighed in the distance. Strange men's voices sounded from too close by.

Jethro froze, motioning to Heidi not to say anything. Grabbing the fish bucket and poles, he led her into the middle of a nearby small stand of trees and brush. They crouched, hiding as best as they could. With Heidi behind him and his hand on the handle of his gun, he listened for any other sounds.

Two men talked about the cattle they'd spotted a short distance away. No mention of hearing other people talking or seeing anyone. Maybe they'd just ridden up to the creek. Thank God they hadn't heard what he and Heidi had said.

A man's voice drifted from downstream. "As soon as the horses are watered, we'll round up a few longhorns and head out quick. A little night herding, and we'll be long gone in no time."

He wasn't sure how long they waited for the voices to fade away. His cramped, protesting muscles were more than ready to move again.

"Can we leave now?" Heidi whispered.

"Wait a little longer."

Both had to stretch their stiff limbs by the time they got to their feet. Jethro picked up the bucket. Heidi grabbed the poles then followed him. Neither said a word until the barn was in sight.

"Thank you." Heidi placed her hand on his arm.

"For what?" He choked out the words as he resisted the urge to cover her hand with his free one.

"For watching over me. You put yourself in front of me, closest to the opening of the thicket."

And he had. Without thinking about it. "I did what any good man should do for a lady."

"Perhaps. But not everyone would put themselves in danger for someone they hardly know."

"I'm nobody special."

"I disagree, but I'd rather get back to the house than argue with you." She dropped her arm to her side.

"You go on. I'll clean the fish first."

"What? Don't you have more important things to do such as tell Toby about the men after his cattle?"

"Send him to me. That way, the children won't overhear anything."

"Oh." Her eyes still full of questions, she turned to go.

Good. He had no intention of telling her he had more than rustlers to think about. How special did Heidi think he was? Especially since she might now doubt her decision to remain single. Just so she didn't decide he was the man for her. As he'd said, he'd protected her the way any man would. But without thinking about it? With no doubt, he'd have faced both rustlers to keep her safe.

**12**

As soon as she was out of Jethro's sight, Heidi pulled up her skirt and ran. Toby sat alone on the porch, still cleaning his gun. The children weren't in sight. Good. They didn't need to hear her news. Toby could tell Lily later.

"What's wrong?" Toby called to her before she reached the steps.

Heidi paused to catch her breath after trotting onto the porch. "Rustlers. Downstream from us." She gulped in more air.

"Rustlers?" Toby jumped to his feet. "Where's Jethro?"

"By the barn cleaning the fish we caught."

Toby's jaw dropped. "He's doing what?"

She sucked in another deep breath. "He wanted you to come talk to him to keep from scaring the children."

"Good idea. I'll go talk to him." Toby laid the rifle he'd dumped to the porch floor on his chair.

Heidi grabbed his arm as he reached the first step. Since she doubted Jethro would brag on himself for watching out for her, she'd tell Toby for him. "Jethro placed himself in front of me at the entrance to the thicket where we hid. I'm absolutely sure he would have confronted two men by himself to protect me."

"I'm sure too. I need to talk to him about those rustlers." He turned to fully face her. "You go inside. Get a drink of water and sit a while."

She nodded. "I won't tell Lily if Ella's close enough to hear."

"I'd appreciate that." He took the steps two at a time.

"Lily?" Heidi called to her sister as she stepped into the parlor.

"I'm in the kitchen."

Lily stood at the ironing board when Heidi walked in. Harvey sat in a corner with his toys. "Where's Ella?"

"She's dusting the bedrooms."

"Good." In hushed tones, Heidi told Lily about the rustlers and Jethro's willingness to protect her. "Toby told me to get a glass of water and sit. Then he went to talk to Jethro."

Lily grinned as she went back to the dress she was ironing. "A glass of water is Toby's way to fix almost anything, especially if it's cool, straight from the well. But do get a drink and take a chair. Your fishing trip wasn't supposed to have such a harrowing ending."

"I'm fine now. I can finish the ironing and let you rest." Heidi reached for the iron. Lily tightened her grip on it.

"Ella's dress is all I have left. Take Toby's advice." Lily pointed to the nearest chair.

Since she had little choice, Heidi poured herself a glass of water from the pitcher and took the end chair. "I understand now why you and Toby don't want me going off alone."

"And that Jethro is a much finer escort than you realized." The sparkle in Lily's eyes couldn't be missed.

"Yes, but not as fine as you look to be thinking. I'm praying about God's will as you suggested. But I'm still not planning to marry Jethro or anyone else." Heidi sipped her water.

"Just remember our hearts may plan our way, but the Lord directs our steps. I'll show you the verse in Proverbs later."

"Which means the Lord directed me here to help you whether you think you need help or not." Heidi was happy to try to direct Lily's conversation and thoughts away from Jethro.

"Maybe so. But I've washed and ironed clothes today with no problem."

"I'll be happy if you don't need my help before the baby comes."

Lily opened her mouth to reply but was interrupted by Toby and Jethro walking in through the back door.

Toby set the bucket on the worktable. "We'll let you ladies clean the fish. Fry them up whenever you want. Since we've got about an hour of daylight left, Jethro and I are going after the rustlers. He never heard more than two men talking downstream."

"Men like that can be dangerous. I'd rather lose a few cattle than either one of you." Lily set her iron on the board.

Heidi wasn't any happier than Lily. Her sister's tight lips and somber eyes signaled more distress than she voiced.

Toby walked over to Lily and caressed her cheek. "We'll fire in the air from a safe distance and scare them. That's enough to stampede whatever cattle they may be herding."

She held his hand against her face, her wide eyes pleading with him to stay home.

"Darlin', we won't do anything foolish. Keep supper warm for us. We'll be back." He tilted her chin up and kissed her.

She wrapped her arms around his waist, pressing her head against his chest. His arms went around her.

Watching their tender exchange caused Heidi's throat to tighten. What would it be like to have someone love her the way Toby loved Lily? But at what cost to the freedom she so needed and craved?

Lily stepped back. "You're going no matter what I say. God be with you and keep both of you safe."

"We'll be back. Maybe before supper's good and cold if those varmints haven't gotten too far."

A nod was Lily's only reply.

Toby strode toward the door. Jethro followed.

"Jethro, you be careful too." Heidi's words slipped out on their own.

"I will."

Neither Heidi nor Lily moved for a few moments after the door closed behind the men.

"This iron's too cold to finish. But since it's one of Ella's everyday dresses, she can do with a few wrinkles." Lily carried the iron over to the worktable. "I will let you put the ironing board away and hang Ella's dresses in her wardrobe.

Ella was dusting their room when Heidi came in to hang up Ella's clothes. "Did y'all catch some fish?"

"Yes. Plenty for dinner tonight."

"Yum. I like fish as much as Pa does."

"Your mother will probably start frying them as soon as we finish cleaning them." Heidi closed the wardrobe door.

Ella followed her back to the kitchen. "I finished dusting all the bedrooms, Ma."

"That's good." Lily hadn't budged from where she'd been when Heidi left the room.

"Heidi said you're gonna start the fish soon."

"Yes, soon."

Heidi couldn't miss her sister's absent-minded tone. Heidi's mind wasn't focused on dinner, either. Knowing Lily, she'd been praying the entire time Heidi had been putting things away.

Since the children were hungry, Heidi and Lily started cooking dinner a short time later. Heidi had no appetite and doubted Lily would unless Toby and Jethro returned sooner than they planned.

"Pa and Jethro will be late. They had to check on some cows that weren't where they're supposed to be.'"

Even Heidi knew Lily's explanation didn't make sense, but Ella's placid expression appeared to mean she took her mother at her word. Oh, to be six and so trusting again.

―――――――

Mr. Grimes dismounted to check for tracks along the creek bank. "Looks like you're right. Only two men and two horses unless they're meeting up with someone later."

"I didn't hear them mention anyone else. We were upwind, so maybe our voices were carried away. They spoke freely and in normal tones."

"Thank God they didn't realize y'all were close enough to hear them." The boss stood.

"Heidi was a lot quieter than usual, so there wasn't much to hear."

Mr. Grimes swung up in his saddle. "After we scare off some rustlers, I'd like to hear about that."

Jethro shrugged. "Maybe she likes fishing enough she didn't want to scare off the fish." Better to mislead the boss than betray what Heidi had told him. He doubted she intended for anyone else to know what she'd said.

Scanning the countryside for signs of the intruders, they rode in silence. Rustlers would be hard to miss seeing if they were rounding up cows to steal. And hopefully too busy to be watching for anyone else. A man cursed loudly enough for his voice to carry to them.

Mr. Grimes motioned for them to dismount. They ground tied their horses near a clump of mesquite trees. "Since there are only two of them and we only want to scare them off, we'll leave our rifles with our horses." He spoke close to Jethro's ear.

Jethro nodded, glad the boss didn't want to get into any kind of shooting match.

They crawled to the top of the ridge then ducked behind a big oak tree. One man was trying to rope a stubborn longhorn all but hidden in a mesquite thicket. His partner was holding a couple of others.

"I'll circle around to the other side of them. If we shoot from two different directions, they might think there are more than two of us. Fire when I signal you, but save a couple of bullets in case you need to actually shoot someone for your protection." Mr. Grimes whispered his plans.

Jethro gave another nod. The boss had war experience, so he'd do whatever the man thought best. Gun in hand, Jethro watched Mr. Grimes make his way to another thicket. At his boss's signal, he fired one shot after another, barely missing one man's horse. He saved his last two shots.

The startled cows took off at full speed. The men spurred their horses, riding toward the tree Jethro knelt behind. One of them fired in his direction. They'd found him.

Jethro got off a shot as a bullet whizzed past his head. He ducked but not in time to keep a second bullet from tearing into the sleeve of his left shoulder, burning his arm.

Before either man could shoot again, the boss fired a shot, barely missing one man's head. The next round hit the other man in his gun arm, sending his weapon to the ground.

Mr. Grimes stepped from behind the trees hiding him, standing in full view of the rustlers, pointing his gun straight at the unarmed man. "I killed my share of Yankees. I suggest you gents don't stay around long enough for my next shot."

The other man aimed at the boss the instant he'd stepped into the man's sight. Jethro fired his last shot. The two spurred their horses into a full gallop away from Jethro.

Mr. Grimes ran to Jethro. "How bad you hurt?" He checked the bloody tear on Jethro's sleeve.

"I don't know." Jethro winced as Mr. Grimes gently probed around the hole in his shirt. "It burns, but I don't think it's too bad."

"I can't tell without sunlight. It looks like they grazed you. I don't see any signs of a bullet in your arm." Mr. Grimes released Jethro's arm.

"If not for you, they might have killed me." Jethro noticed how fast his heart was racing for the first time since the whole incident had started.

Mr. Grimes lightly clapped him on the back. "Thank God they didn't count shots. That was my last bullet."

"Yeah, thank God. I was out too."

"I know. I appreciate that last one so I'm still in one piece." Mr. Grimes stood and extended his hand to Jethro. "Let's go home. I have a feeling a couple of women have been praying the whole time we've been out here."

"I'm sure you're right." Thinking about Heidi praying for him to be comforted rather than bothering him. The ride home was bearable despite his stinging arm. Why, he'd think about later.

As soon as they led their horses inside the barn, Mr. Grimes shut the door. He lit the lantern hanging nearby and then stared straight into Jethro's eyes. "Don't say a word to Lily or Heidi about what really happened out there."

"If that's what you want, but why?"

The boss sucked in a deep breath and then released it slowly. "My sweet Lily doesn't need to know how close her worries for our safety came to being true. She's been through enough."

"Right." Jethro didn't know the entire story, but he did know Mrs. Grimes had lost her first husband to a tragic accident with a bronco.

"So, here's what we will tell the ladies." Mr. Grimes uncinched his horse's saddle. "We'll have to sound good. Lily is sharp and hard to fool. So don't use the exact same words I use, but be sure to tell the same story."

By the time they'd taken care of the horses, Jethro knew exactly what to say and not to say. And how far Mr. Grimes was willing to go to protect the woman he must love with all his heart.

Mr. Grimes hung the lantern back by the door. "Let's go to your place first, clean up that arm, and get you in a clean shirt."

"I'm out of clean shirts. I'd planned to wash my clothes tomorrow."

The shadows from the lantern couldn't hide the boss's wide

grin. "That's even better. The ladies would wonder why you were wearing a clean shirt."

"I guess so." Amazing the way the boss wanted every detail taken care of to keep his wife from ever guessing the truth.

"After you've washed the blood out, you can bring your shirt over for Lily to mend."

"Yes, sir."

They walked in silence as they took a roundabout way to Jethro's place to keep the women from seeing them. Mr. Grimes helped wash the blood off his arm. "Doesn't look like those men are any better with their guns than stealing cattle. Your arm should heal up nicely."

"That's good."

The boss nodded. "Yeah. We have a lot to be thankful for."

A light shown through the parlor window when they walked up to the main house. Jethro followed Mr. Grimes inside, sure who the first man was the missus wanted to see coming through the door.

"Toby!" Mrs. Grimes jumped from her rocking chair and ran to her husband.

He kissed her full on the lips before wrapping her in his arms. She laid her head on his chest, pressing as close to him as possible.

Ella glanced up from playing with her doll in the corner. "Pa, did you and Mr. Bannister put the cows back where they're s'posed to be?"

"We sure did." He kissed his wife's hair.

From his spot by the door, Jethro peered past the Grimes toward Heidi still seated on the couch. Her glowing smile left no doubt she was happy to see him and her brother-in-law return. The way she had yet to take her eyes off him made him wonder what else she might be thinking.

Mrs. Grimes stepped back. "Your supper is in the oven. It should still be warm."

"Sounds good. Chasing ornery longhorns can give a man quite an appetite."

The slight shake of Mrs. Grimes's head indicated she'd probably want to hear more when Ella wasn't around. The lady had no idea how much of the truth she'd never hear. Heidi studied Jethro almost as carefully as Mrs. Grimes checked her husband.

A few minutes later, Jethro and the boss sat in their usual chairs enjoying their late supper. No matter everything wasn't freshly cooked, Jethro doubted he'd ever tasted better. Dodging bullets had a way of making every bite special since only God knew how close he and Mr. Grimes might have been to not coming home.

After his last bite of cornbread, Mr. Grimes scooted his chair back as if the day been perfectly normal. "Delicious as usual, ladies. Jethro, let's go to the parlor while Lily and Heidi wash dishes."

Since he didn't appear to have another choice, Jethro followed Mr. Grimes out of the kitchen. Why the boss wanted him to stay after dinner tonight, he wasn't sure. But after their story rehearsal in the barn, he'd best not ask. Good thing he knew exactly what he was supposed to say.

Mrs. Grimes insisted Ella and Harvey go to bed after she and Heidi cleaned up. Heidi took her sister's rocking chair by the fireplace while Mr. and Mrs. Grimes tucked the children in.

"I'm glad the cows are all right just as Toby told Ella."

"We didn't lose a one." He hadn't rehearsed that comment with the boss, but assumed he could safely say it.

Heidi nodded. The intense way she kept watching him made him doubt she thought he'd told the whole truth. If fooling Heidi was going to be hard, Mr. Grimes might have one more time convincing his wife of his version of scaring off the rustlers. Too bad he couldn't go to his place the way he so often did after supper.

"You've got a bad scratch on your cheek. Are you sure you're all right?" Her serious expression said her question was sincere, not just spoken to make polite conversation.

If that was all she was concerned about, maybe he and the boss would get away with their charade. But he couldn't tell her they'd gone to his place first. "I haven't had a chance to look at it yet." He lightly touched his cheek. The moisture around the scratch meant it must still be bleeding a little. Maybe that was good, since it wouldn't look like he'd already cleaned up some. "It stings some. Guess I got a little too close to the tree I hid behind."

"I'm so glad you came home with only a scratch."

"So am I." At least those words were truly spoken. Somewhat. He couldn't tell her about the nasty spot on his arm where a bullet grazed him. He'd stretched the truth to keep from getting in trouble as a kid, but he'd never told as big a lie as the one he was telling now. He forced himself not to squirm in his chair.

Mr. and Mrs. Grimes walked into the room hand in hand. Good. If the boss had said anything to his wife yet, she must believe him so far. They settled next to each other on the couch, their knees touching.

"Thank God, you're both all right." Mrs. Grimes placed her hand on her husband's arm.

"We did exactly what I told you we would. We snuck up on them then split up so we could hide behind trees and fire from more than one direction. That way, they thought there were more than two of us. Those two rustlers galloped off faster than the cows ran." He patted her hand as he smiled into her eyes.

"We prayed for both of you." Heidi clasped and unclasped her hands in her lap as if she were still concerned for them.

"We always appreciate your prayers." More words Jethro could truthfully say.

"Your prayers worked so well I got a new rope out of it all. I fired a single shot, and one man dropped his lariat. I brought it home."

Mrs. Grimes shifted to look her husband in the eyes. "That's good, but just because this time turned out so well doesn't mean I want you two to ever try scaring rustlers off again."

"I understand, darlin'." Mr. Grimes took her hands in his.

Jethro rose. "If y'all don't mind, I'll head to my place. From what Heidi says, the scratch on my face needs a little tending to."

"We'll see you tomorrow. I plan to stay close to the house so don't plan on much."

"Sounds good." He forced himself not to trot outside.

The women's lack of comments hopefully meant they believed the story Mr. Grimes had made up. But the less Jethro said and the sooner he left, the better. He had more than enough details to remember so he could repeat them again if necessary.

Telling the whole truth would have been easier. But like Mr. Grimes, he'd rather not scare the women with what had really happened. Heidi's broad grin had signaled she was as relieved to see Jethro as Mrs. Grimes had when she'd seen the boss walk in. Which made him feel better than it should.

## 13

The next couple of days, Jethro and Mr. Grimes stayed close to the house. The rustlers they'd chased off had probably gone looking for other cattle to steal. But the boss wanted to stay near his precious family just to be safe. Being careful and staying safe was fine with Jethro. He hadn't slept well since getting shot at.

Mr. Grimes leaned against the corral and checked his pocket watch. "Lily will be sending Ella out to tell us supper's ready soon. Since we've fixed every loose board on this fence, let's go wash up."

"Sure." Jethro covered a yawn.

"Have you slept since Monday night?" Mr. Grimes slipped his watch back into his pocket. "You've yawned all day."

"Not much."

"Sleeping after the first time you've been shot at isn't easy. I'll pray for you." Judging from the sober look in the boss's eyes, he knew exactly what he was talking about.

"Thanks." He wanted to ask how a man got to where he could sleep again, but he assumed Mr. Grimes was thinking back to his time during the war. As little as the boss mentioned those days, he must not like talking about them. His brother hadn't said much about it after coming home.

After finishing a small feast for dinner, Jethro hoped eating so much would help make him sleepy enough not to wake up from nightmares of someone shooting at him or Mr. Grimes.

"Since you made two apple pies this afternoon, why don't we take one over to Charlotte and David tomorrow?" Mr. Grimes grinned at his wife. "We'd better take advantage of days when you only need a shawl, and I can stay warm in my flannel shirt."

"You're right. We haven't seen them since roundup, so we should go." Mrs. Grimes took Harvey out of his highchair and set him on the floor.

"I always like to see Aunt Charlotte and Uncle David. Both *abuelos* will be there too." Ella bounced in her chair.

"They will be." Mr. Grimes turned his attention to Jethro. "You should come too."

"I'll think about it." A day alone to think and pray sounded much better than one with a house crammed full of two families. "Thanks for dinner. Every bite was good." He rose. "I need to go to my house and take care of the clothes I washed this morning."

"Smelling those pies while we washed up made me forget to put the bucket back in the well after we finished." Mr. Grimes followed Jethro out the back door.

Another lie Jethro would have to remember being told. The boss always lowered the bucket back into the well.

"I'd appreciate it if you'd ride with us tomorrow. The rustlers should be in the next county or farther if they're smart. But if I'm wrong, I'd like you on horseback with your gun loaded." The stars weren't out enough for Jethro to see the boss's face, but his somber-sounding words left no doubt how concerned he still was.

"I'll go."

"Thanks. I want to tell David about Monday night. He can decide what he wants to tell Charlotte and Francisca after we come home. He knows what happened to Lily and why I don't want her worrying something could happen to me like it did to Harvey."

"All right. I'll see y'all in the morning." Jethro turned to leave.

Mr. Grimes placed his hand on Jethro's arm. "I need one more favor."

"You do?"

"Yeah, and it's a big one."

Jethro braced himself for whatever must be coming next. He'd had enough surprises since Monday evening.

"I'd like Heidi to learn to shoot. But I think she'd be less worried about why if you showed her."

"Me?" He sounded almost like a kid whose voice hadn't changed yet.

Mr. Grimes chuckled. Nothing he'd said had been the least bit amusing, especially his request for Jethro to teach Heidi how to shoot. Worse, it sounded more like a done deal than a wish.

"Tell her she should know how to use a gun since she's bound and determined to live alone in town one day. Not spending time with Lily and the kids the way I usually do might make her wonder if something's wrong. She'd take the idea better from you."

Jethro doubted it mattered who taught Heidi to shoot. She'd sounded sensible not alarmed when she'd wondered about buying a derringer a while back. He sincerely hoped the boss wasn't hoping Jethro might come to think of the woman as more than a friend.

The ladies hurried to clean the kitchen after breakfast the next morning. Everyone rushed to leave but Jethro. He'd rather lose his favorite hat than spend the day with so many people. Plus, he hadn't slept well last night. Again.

Thoughts of Heidi interrupted him between dreams about gun shots. He hadn't been thinking of her as a sister while they hid from the rustlers. Hadn't thought of her the same way he did Louisa for a while. But her problems with her parents brought back his bad family memories so vividly he hurt. Not the kind of woman he wanted or needed after what he'd been through. Even if she could be quiet occasionally.

The drive to the *Double S* wasn't quiet. Ella, Heidi, and Mrs. Grimes carried on a lively conversation most of the way. Jethro grinned in their direction occasionally while scouting out the countryside as he rode. Mr. Grimes kept a careful watch of their surroundings too. Seeing only rabbits, lizards, and turkeys never made him so happy.

CHARLOTTE AND FRANCISCA stepped onto the porch to greet everyone before Lily or Heidi had a chance to get out of the buggy. No one could surprise the Shepherds with the two barking hounds announcing every arrival. Ella ran to them the way she'd done the last time.

"Jethro and I will tend to the horses first." Toby remained by the buggy.

"David and Eduardo are probably still cleaning stalls in the barn, so you won't have any trouble finding them." Charlotte reached to hug Lily.

"Thanks." Toby and Jethro turned to lead their horses out of the yard.

After hugs from Charlotte and Francisca, Heidi followed the other women inside. Lily and Charlotte settled Harvey and his two cousins in a corner to play then took what must be their usual spot on the couch. Francisca carried Lily's apple pie to the kitchen. Ella went with her, telling her *abuela* all about the new baby chicks at her house.

"What a nice surprise to see y'all." Charlotte's warm smile included Heidi.

"Toby wanted to tell David and Eduardo about some rustlers." Lily glanced at the kitchen as if watching for Ella and Francisca to return to the parlor.

Charlotte's brown eyes widened. "Rustlers?"

"Only two. Toby and Jethro scared them off by firing a few shots over their heads."

"That's good."

"Yes. Thank God. Jethro has a bad scratch on his face from a tree trunk, but that's all the harm they received."

Lily added a few more details before Ella and Francisca walked in. "I'm glad October's almost done. Father found out Heidi was staying with us and surprised us a few days after the men came home from roundup."

"Oh, no." Charlotte turned her attention to Heidi. "That must have been awful."

"It would have been if not for Toby and Lily." Heidi told Charlotte how Papa stayed one night then Toby escorted him back to San Antonio.

"So Heidi is staying to help me, and we're all happy to have her with us." Lily smiled in Heidi's direction.

The conversation soon turned to how fast the children were growing and other more pleasant topics. Heidi couldn't help wondering what the men were discussing. Lily might believe what her husband said about the rustlers, but Heidi didn't. Jethro had fidgeted like a child Monday night while Toby told how easily they'd scared the thieves away. She'd seen real fear in the foreman's eyes when Toby mentioned them firing on the men.

Add in Jethro telling her yesterday he'd like to teach her to shoot. Every time she'd glanced at him on the trip here, he was paying much closer attention to their surroundings than he'd done the Sunday they went to church in town.

By the time the men came into the parlor, Heidi was getting ready to help Francisca with lunch. She'd listened to as much talk about when a child started walking, talking, or losing teeth as she cared to hear.

Since the Shepherd's kitchen didn't have room for everyone, they ate on the porch. Just as she'd done in San Antonio, Heidi ended up sitting by Jethro. Lily, Charlotte, and Francisca had chairs close to the steps so they could watch the children seated there. The other men grouped themselves close to their wives, leaving her and Jethro a little off to the side. She couldn't help wondering if like her, Jethro felt as if he didn't quite fit here.

"We had a good visit with the Hawkins and Bridges a couple of weeks ago." Lily smiled the way she always did when mentioning her friends.

A sidelong glance at Jethro's serious expression told Heidi he probably didn't want to hear talk about that afternoon any more than she did. He was quiet even for him through the remainder of their visit. She didn't blame him. Despite how everyone welcomed her, she was quite happy when Jethro helped her into the buggy for the ride back to Lily and Toby's house.

Shortly before four, the buggy rolled into the yard at the *Tumbling G.*

"Jethro, I'll take care of chores if you'd like to start teaching Heidi to shoot." Toby helped Lily from the buggy.

"That's a good idea." Lily's smile was too bright to only be thinking about Heidi learning to fire a gun. "I can still start supper alone."

"Only if you're sure." Heidi wouldn't mind some time with Jethro to ask him the truth about Monday night. But she didn't want to sound too eager and have Lily and Toby think she was more interested in Jethro than she was.

About half an hour later, she stood with Jethro not far from the corral.

"I stacked a few bottles on the top rail for targets."

"May I ask you some questions about how you scared off the rustlers?"

His face blanched. "Mr. Grimes pretty much told y'all what happened."

"What didn't he say if he only told us pretty *much* what happened?" She clasped her hands in front of her as she waited for his reply.

His whole body stiffened. "That's not what I meant."

"Oh?"

"Mr. Grimes is no liar, and you know it. Every word he said was true." He looked toward the corral. "Do you want to learn to shoot or not?"

*Or not.* She clamped her mouth shut to keep from saying the words out loud. He obviously had no intention of telling her more. "Learning to use a gun would be good for my safety."

If she hadn't been so worried for his safety she might not care what he was leaving unsaid. But she did care. She'd also leave such words unsaid. Jethro wasn't the only one not speaking the entire truth.

He took his gun from his holster, aimed it at a bottle, and sent pieces of glass flying. "Don't expect to hit anything except maybe the fence on your first try."

"All right. Show me how to do it."

He showed her how to aim, how to cock the gun, and how to pull the trigger then placed the revolver in her hand. "Hold the handle with both hands until you get good at shooting." He took her hands in his, helping her to wrap her fingers around the handle.

Her heart sped up. She swallowed hard, concentrating on the weapon she held instead of how nice it felt to have his hands covering hers.

"Hold it steady and straight." Maintaining his grip, he lifted her hands until her arms were almost straight out. "Aim and cock it. Pull the trigger."

Having him so near unnerved her to the point she had to silently repeat his instructions in her mind. Had to remind herself to breathe. She jumped as the gun went off. The bullet missed the bottle and the fence.

"Like I said, it takes practice to hit a target." He released her hands.

"I suppose it does."

"Want to try again? This time without my help."

"All right."

Taking a step or two away from her, he talked her through the next shot. After the fourth try, the bullet nicked a bottle. The sixth shot broke the glass.

"I did it!" She couldn't hold her grin inside.

Jethro didn't smile back. "Yeah, you did."

She lowered the gun. Why wasn't he happy for her? "Did I do something wrong?"

"No. You'll probably be a good shot one day. Just remember a gun is only for protection."

"Of course. For snakes or wild animals. I pray I never need to aim at a person, much less actually shoot someone." She handed him his weapon.

His expression resembled someone who had just left the funeral of a loved one as he holstered his gun.

"Did you shoot someone Monday night?" She clapped her hand over her mouth. How could she have blurted out such a fearful idea without thinking first?

"Shot at the rustlers. Only to scare them off. I hope I never have to do it again." The agonizing look in his eyes tore at her heart.

She laid her hand on his arm. "I'm so sorry I asked. I shouldn't have."

"It's all right. I'm glad you don't want to shoot anyone." He placed his free hand over hers.

"I'm glad you don't." His intense gaze held hers. She couldn't look away.

How long he caressed her fingers as he stared into her eyes, she couldn't have said. He stepped away.

"We should go to the house."

"Yes, we should." She resisted the urge to take his hand as they walked side by side.

"If the boss doesn't have too much for me to do, we could practice again tomorrow."

"Or you could go with me so I can draw or paint. Not too far from the house yet, but far enough." She curled and uncurled her fingers. She mustn't reach for his hand.

He smiled for the first time since he'd handed her his gun. "I'd like that."

So would she. Perhaps more than she should.

## 14

The next Monday morning, Heidi was still thinking of what had happened the week before while she and Lily washed clothes. Especially since what Jethro had and hadn't told her confirmed he and Toby were hiding something from her and Lily. Something she doubted was good. Toby and Jethro had taken a short ride Saturday afternoon and hadn't seen any signs of rustlers. For that, she was grateful.

"I'm glad that norther blew in Saturday and not today." Lily picked up one of Toby's shirts from the pile of dirty clothes.

Heidi bent over the rub board scrubbing an apron. "We wouldn't be doing laundry if the sun hadn't come out to warm us up this morning."

"Tobias Lee Grimes." Lily held her husband's shirt in front of her, focusing on one of the sleeves.

"What's wrong?" Hearing Lily use Toby's full formal name she'd never heard and didn't even know meant something was far from right.

"I'm going to the barn to catch Toby before he and Jethro leave on their long ride. Keep an eye on Ella and Harvey for me." Clutching the shirt, Lily marched off.

By the time Heidi pinned the apron to the clothesline, Lily

returned with Toby and Jethro. Neither of the men appeared happy to be following her.

"I want the real story of what happened last Monday. Here in front of Heidi and me. Not whatever you and Jethro concocted for us." Lily's eyes flamed with anger in a way Heidi had never seen. She shoved Toby's shirt at him. "Why is there blood by this cuff?"

Toby's shoulders drooped. He stared into Lily's eyes as if they were the only ones standing in the backyard. Heidi wished they were. The way Jethro shifted his weight from one foot to the other and gazed off in the distance suggested his thoughts matched Heidi's.

"Darlin', I'm sorry. You were already so worried. I didn't want you to worry more." Toby kept his eyes focused solely on his wife.

Lily's arms went limp at her side. "Please. Tell me the truth, dear. Heidi too."

"We did fire at the men to scare them off. But the scoundrels galloped toward the thicket of brush where Jethro was hiding, firing at him. One bullet tore his shirt grazing his arm. I shot at them and hit a man in the shoulder. They rode off after that." He held out open arms. Lily walked into them.

After Toby said Jethro had been shot, Heidi heard little else of what her brother-in-law said. No wonder that night still bothered Jethro. She'd noticed it at her first shooting lesson.

Toby caressed Lily's hair as her head pressed against his chest. "Be mad at me, but don't get upset with Jethro. I told him what to say so our stories would match up." He went on to tell her he'd checked to be sure Jethro was all right, then insisted he change shirts before they went to the house.

Heidi looked past them to Jethro, standing with his hands in his pockets. As much as the man hated family problems, he had to be miserable being forced to be a silent witness to a family confrontation. Even one that had ended with Lily in her husband's arms after he apologized.

Toby's half-truths reinforced her longing for her own life. Well-intentioned or not, she never wanted to be close enough to anyone for them to lie to her. The way Papa and Mama lied about how a marriage with Johann would be for her own good.

Lily stepped back from Toby. "You and Jethro can finish saddling your horses." She patted his cheek.

"We'll be back in time for supper. I want to be sure we don't have rustlers roaming anywhere." He took her hand in his and kissed her fingers.

"If you find any, I want to know."

"All right, darlin'." Toby turned to Jethro. "Let's ride."

Jethro tipped his hat to Lily and Heidi before striding off with Toby.

"Now that we've got all of that settled, I'll get the blood out of this sleeve before it sets worse than it already has." Lily put Toby's shirt in the tub with the cold rinse water.

Heidi started scrubbing another apron.

"Toby knows how much I hurt losing Harvey. My dear husband would protect me to his last breath." Lily stared straight at Heidi. "Sometimes he protects me so much he forgets God gives me strength. Otherwise, I couldn't get through most regular days, much less the bad ones."

"I hope to have strength like yours one day." Heidi concentrated on the apron in her hands. With God's help, she'd be strong enough to live the life she wanted. Since Lily still didn't completely understand, Heidi kept her thoughts to herself.

---

JETHRO SWUNG up in his saddle, glad they'd be gone most of the day, wishing he could ride alone. If Mrs. Grimes hadn't insisted he be there too, he'd have been more than happy to let the boss explain everything by himself.

"Sorry for putting you in the middle of all that." Mr. Grimes glanced over at Jethro as they rode away from the barn.

"It all turned out all right." Especially since Mr. Grimes had been the one his wife had aimed her angry words at.

"Because my Lily is such a loving and forgiving woman who's a lot stronger than most people give her credit for." He grinned. "Sometimes including me. I'll tell her later we both ran out of bullets. Probably a lot later since she worries more than she lets on."

"My father always said God made women that way because someone besides the Lord himself had to watch over us foolhardy men." Recalling his late father's wise words was one thing from his past that didn't bother him the way it once had.

Mr. Grimes chuckled. "That sounds about right. But I will tell her sometime, so you don't have to shade the truth anymore to save my hide."

"Since you saved mine, I don't mind helping you." Jethro scanned the horizon, hoping the boss wouldn't say more about their encounter with the rustlers.

They said little more as they rode, still looking to be sure the thieves hadn't returned. Around noon, they halted by a creek to water the horses and let them graze.

"I never get tired of looking over the amazing country the Lord made. It'll still be pretty when the leaves fall and the frost turns the grass brown soon." Mr. Grimes took a dish towel bundle from his saddle bag. "Lily sent more than enough bacon and buttered biscuits for both of us. She worries I might go hungry without her around to cook for me." He sat on a fallen log.

Jethro grabbed his canteen before sitting on the other end of the log. A woodpecker tapped on a nearby oak tree. The water babbled over the rocks at the bottom of the creek. Peace and quiet like this was the very reason he'd left Georgia.

Unexpected thoughts of Heidi interrupted his tranquility. Or did they? Thinking of her sitting on her stool, paint brush in hand made for a pretty picture to go along with the nice scenery in front of him.

"Heidi would like to paint out here." The words he shouldn't have said slipped out of their own accord.

"Yeah, she would." The boss took another bite of his biscuit.

Jethro gulped water from his canteen. If he didn't get better at not talking about Heidi, Mr. and Mrs. Grimes would get worse at trying to put him and her together. Sweet Mrs. Grimes rarely lost her temper. But her short outburst had served as a reminder for why he'd vowed to never become entangled in family problems again. He'd best keep his mind on watching for signs of cattle thieves instead of wool gathering about a pretty blonde in a blue dress.

"Just so you know, you don't have to go with Heidi for her to paint. She can do that sitting on the porch or out in the yard just fine."

"Yes, sir. I know." Jethro popped a piece of bacon in his mouth to keep from saying more.

Mr. Grimes twisted to face him, propping his elbows on his knees. "Not that it's my concern, but she's growing on you like you told me a while back. Isn't she?"

Best to think how to answer such a question before saying something else he shouldn't. He washed the bacon down with a swig from his canteen. "In some ways. But maybe not like people are starting to think."

He paused, stretching his legs out in front of him while mulling over how truthful he should be. Without telling anything, she'd confided in him and him alone. "She's honest to a fault saying point-blank what she's thinking."

The boss nodded. "Sometimes when she shouldn't."

"She's probably got more spunk than she needs. Not many women want to make their own way without any help." He said no more, since he didn't want to explain the reasons he admired her for that. The boss knew only the barest facts about why Jethro had left Georgia.

"Lily's strong too but with different ideas." Mr. Grimes got to his feet. "Let's ride out a little ways more to be sure there are only cows out here then head home."

After they mounted their horses, Mr. Grimes turned toward Jethro. "If Heidi were to grow on you more, Lily and I would be all right with that. If she doesn't, we're fine too. The main thing is be sure you know what God wants."

"I understand. I appreciate you being so honest with me."

"A straight-shooting man like you deserves that. I don't intend to ask you to lie for me again." Mr. Grimes turned his horse away from the creek.

Jethro urged his bay alongside the boss. As much as he hid about his past in Georgia, he wasn't as honest as Mr. Grimes thought. Heidi was the only one who had the slightest idea how painful leaving Georgia had been.

They rode up to the barn around three o'clock. "Since the missus won't be starting supper for about an hour, I'll see if Heidi wants to try shooting again." No matter how much he shouldn't, Jethro was beginning to enjoy time with Heidi. Too bad he hadn't swallowed his words.

"Only if you want to." Mr. Grimes dismounted. "Don't offer just to please me. I was wrong about you being the only one to show her how to shoot."

"I want to. She needs to know how to use a gun."

"Thanks."

After tending to the horses, they walked together to the house. Nice to have a boss he could enjoy working with and talk with too. Maybe he could keep this job without woman problems making him leave.

They walked in the back door to find the ladies in the kitchen.

"You had a peaceful ride this time?" Mrs. Grimes smiled from her chair. "Jethro, I'm almost through mending the tear on this sleeve."

"Thank you, ma'am."

Mr. Grimes bent to kiss his wife's cheek.

Heidi glanced up from her ironing. "I'm almost finished too."

"Good. If you've got time, I'll help you practice shooting again." Jethro sounded more enthusiastic than he intended. "That is, if you don't have to start supper right away."

"There's time." Mrs. Grimes snipped the thread she'd used on his shirt. "You can take this with you on your way to set up bottles on the fence." She held out his shirt.

"Yes, ma'am."

Jethro used the time it took to walk to his house and gather up bottles to think. Mrs. Grimes's sunny smile signaled she might be more than fine with pairing Heidi off with him. For so many reasons, he wasn't. He had to be more careful with what he said and how he said it.

A short time later, Heidi joined him by the corral. "Do you truly want to help me do this?"

"Yes. I want—I mean a lady intending to live alone should know how to keep herself safe." He took his gun from the holster.

She cocked her head as if trying to decipher his jumbled sentence. He'd barely stopped himself from telling her he wanted to keep her safe by showing her how to use a gun.

"Again, I'm so glad you understand what I want." She held the gun with both hands.

While she took aim, he wished he could steady her hands in his the way he'd done a few days ago. No. He had to quit thinking like that. Two or three shots later, she squarely hit a bottle well enough she knocked it off the fence. He'd been so busy not thinking about holding her hands, he lost track of how many shots she fired.

"That's much better than the first time." She laughed.

"It is." He couldn't laugh with her while thinking why she needed to become a good shot.

She shot off a few more rounds and then lowered the gun. "Is something bothering you?"

"No."

"Yes. I doubt you've said a half dozen words since we started." She studied him much too intently. "I suspect something's bothering you about Lily's outburst this morning?"

He shook his head.

"Jethro, we're friends. Don't make me guess. Tell me the truth."

He'd heard too many mentions about telling the truth today when he hadn't done so with too many people over the years. "The truth is I don't like talking about one of the most harrowing nights in my life."

Her expression sobered. "You were in more danger than you or Toby will say. Weren't you?"

"Yes." He ducked his head.

"Put this back in your holster." She hand him his revolver. "The next time we have a chance to do something together, you may go with me to paint. There will be no mention of guns."

"Thank you." He holstered the weapon.

Next he needed to put away his growing admiration for the perceptive woman standing next to him.

## 15

Jethro walked into the kitchen on Saturday morning, thankful the rest of the week had been uneventful. Mr. Grimes had decided they'd made enough rides checking for rustlers and could stay home and tend to chores. Get things ready to go deer hunting soon.

"Mornin'." Mr. Grimes greeted Jethro from the corner where he had squatted down to help Harvey stack blocks.

"Good morning." Jethro stood near the table, waiting for the ladies to finish filling platters with bacon, eggs, and biscuits. No matter that he'd been in Texas for seven years, he still couldn't bring himself to sit before the ladies seated themselves.

His manners were some of the few things he hadn't left behind when he'd said goodbye to everyone in Georgia. His late father would be proud. Mother ... He shoved thoughts of her deep down inside. Her opinion of him no longer mattered after the way she'd sided with his brother over him.

Mrs. Grimes and Heidi set the food on the table. With her apron on, he couldn't tell for sure, but pieces of brown fabric peaked out. Was Heidi wearing the nice brown dress she'd worn the day he brought her here? Whichever dress she did or didn't put on didn't matter. That he remembered what she'd worn the first time he'd seen her did matter. He was doing a terrible job of not letting her grow on him lately.

Mr. Grimes said the blessing. Mrs. Grimes then passed the platter of biscuits after taking enough for her and Harvey. She smiled at Jethro. "After you left last night, we decided to go to town today in case another norther blows in soon. The easel and other supplies we ordered for Heidi should be in by now. You're welcome to come with us if you'd like."

"I could use a few things." Nothing he couldn't do without, but thinking of all the men in San Antonio who would be happy to see Heidi made the thought of the new rifle or knife he'd like a necessity. She might need a friend along to help corral admirers.

Reminding himself repeatedly he should stay home didn't work. While Mr. Grimes hitched Red to his wagon, Jethro saddled his bay then saddled Mrs. Grimes's mare for Heidi. She'd rather ride than sit in the back of the wagon with Ella.

Since the ladies hurried with the dirty dishes, everyone was ready to go to town not long after he and Mr. Grimes had the horses ready. Jethro couldn't help watching Heidi when she stepped out onto the front porch. He didn't mind at all she'd again chosen her brown dress for traveling. She'd be a little less noticeable today than she'd been in her green Sunday dress a while back.

"I still wish you'd sit with me in the wagon." Ella walked with Heidi down the steps.

"I do love being with you, but I want to leave plenty of room in the bed for my easel and paints."

The little girl looked satisfied with her aunt's explanation. For someone who never planned to be a mother, Heidi had a way with children. Anyone with good eyes could see Ella adored her aunt, and for good reason.

"Thank you for saddling Calico for me. I'll have a marvelous view of the countryside to look for things to paint or draw." She started talking before they'd ridden much over a hundred yards.

"You're welcome." He hoped she didn't talk the entire trip to town the way she'd done the day he'd driven her here. The day he'd decided she wasn't the kind of woman he'd ever want if he started looking to settle down.

But this time, he was interested in what she had to say. He liked the way she saw places and turned them into pretty paintings or drawings. How she'd never pressed him to tell her why he understood her struggles with her family problems so well. The woman who could talk enough to worry the horns off a longhorn but didn't mind how quiet he liked to be amazed him now in ways he'd never dreamed.

"I wish I could get close enough to a jack rabbit to draw one, but they don't stand still any longer than the one to the left of us now."

"You'll gradually see enough of them you can draw them from memory." He could if he could draw. Only Heidi would be fascinated by an ordinary jack rabbit with hundreds of others like him running around.

By the time they rode into town, Jethro feared his ears would soon be sore. He'd intended to ride close enough to the Grimes family's wagon she could talk with them instead of only him, but Heidi had wandered off a time or two to look at something to paint and never caught up to them until now.

As they rode toward the Hawkins's store, more than one man stared in Heidi's direction longer than he should. Not staying home was a good idea for the exact reason he'd figured. He dismounted and then helped her down. With her family present, he had no problem not holding onto her waist longer than he should.

Holding Harvey by the hand, Mrs. Grimes went straight to the back counter where Owen was working. Heidi walked with her.

"Morning, Lily, Heidi."

"Good morning to you. Did the easel and art supplies we ordered for Heidi come in?"

"They did. Only a few days ago." Owen's smile was dim compared to the one that lit up Heidi's face and sparkled into her eyes. "I'll have Sam get the crate while I fill your order." He called to his nephew to go to the back of the store as Mrs. Grimes handed him her list.

"I can help him with that." Mr. Grimes stepped around the counter and headed to the back.

Doris came over to greet them and handed Ella a piece of penny candy.

"Thank you so much." The little girl popped the piece of hoar hound into her mouth before wandering off to look at dolls.

Doris and Mrs. Grimes soon walked away for a visit the way they usually did. Heidi handed Owen a folded sheet. "I'd like to send this to a good friend in New Braunfels." She kept her voice so low Jethro struggled to make out her request. No matter. Who she wrote to was none of his concern. She remained by the counter, probably waiting for Sam to bring the crate with her easel and paints.

Jethro wandered to the other side of the store to look at guns and knives. He could use a new rifle for hunting. But a knife he could hide in his boot might come in handy if he ever faced down someone again after he'd run out of bullets. The coldness that gripped his heart caused him to shiver.

No. Living in that kind of fear wasn't healthy or right. Especially since he had no doubt God had and still did watch over him. He'd finally banished the nightmares about rustlers and started sleeping again. He ran his hands over the stock of a nice rifle he *did* need.

The bell jingled over the door. With a newspaper tucked under his arm, Andrew Bridges sauntered in. He pretended to be interested in watches as he checked the store over. Jethro had no doubt the man was hunting for Heidi. If the pastor's son had been standing somewhere on the sidewalk as they rode by, Jethro hadn't seen him. But Andrew Bridges must have seen Heidi.

"Miss Schultz, what a pleasant surprise to find you here." The man walked over to her the instant he spied her, halting too close by her side.

"I didn't expect to see you today, either." Her dimmed smile seemed more of a polite response than delight.

A derringer next to the rifles caught Jethro's eye. He snatched it up and pointed his boots in Heidi's direction. "Heidi, this would be a good weapon for you now that you're learning to shoot." He hoped Bridges noticed his use of Heidi's first name.

Wide-eyed, she took the gun he handed her. She examined it a moment. "I don't need this for now. Thank you for showing it to me." She pressed the gun back in his hand. Her brusque tone sounded as if she weren't happy with what he'd done. If so, he was sure he'd hear about it later. She had yet to fail to speak her mind with him.

"That's a nice weapon for a gentleman, but I don't know why a lady such as you would need one." Bridges's tone sounded condescending.

Heidi grabbed the derringer from Jethro's hand. "Since I intend to buy one soon, I should look at it more closely." She turned the gun over in her hand as if examining every inch of it.

"Not that it's any of my concern, Miss Schultz, but why would you need a gun?"

Her head jerked up at his question. "To protect myself if necessary. Jethro says I'm already a good shot." Good. She used his first name the way she'd done at the Hawkins's house.

"Oh, I see. Since I work at the newspaper, I always bring my parents the latest edition at noon. I'd best be on my way." Gripping the paper in one hand, he tipped his hat to her with the other one. "Have a good day."

"The same to you, Mr. Bridges." Heidi's stiff posture relaxed. Was she as relieved to see the man leave as Jethro was? She handed the gun back to him again. "You may put this back. I do want one when I can pay for it myself."

"I'm glad you do." Jethro hated to think she might need any

kind of weapon. But whenever she moved to town, he wanted her to be safe.

While Jethro inspected guns some more, Mr. Grimes and Sam carried the crate over to Heidi then set it at her feet. Mr. Grimes helped her open it.

"Ohhh." Heidi clasped her hands together as she stared into the crate. "I ... I can't thank you and Lily enough for this." She knelt to run her fingers over her treasure. "As much as I'd like to look at it better, I'll wait to take the easel out after we're home. It's best to leave it in the crate while it's in the wagon."

"That's a good idea." Mr. Grimes grinned ear to ear as he watched her.

The missus and Doris soon joined Heidi by the counter. "I'm so glad we could get this for you. We should have thought to bring your satchel and show Doris and Owen the nice pictures you do."

"Thank you." Heidi rose and then enveloped her sister in a hug.

From his spot by the rifles, Jethro's crazy heart wondered what it would be like for Heidi to hug him like that. *Stop it, man.* If he were alone, he should be shouting the words to himself. No matter how much Heidi had grown on him lately, she would never think of him as more than a friend. As long a list as he could make of the problems she was saddled with, he had no reason to be thinking about her embrace or embracing her if she did like him. He returned his attention to the guns.

Mrs. Grimes next insisted Heidi pick out material for more serviceable dresses, which kept the ladies occupied for a while. Since no other single men wandered into the store, Jethro picked out a new rifle in peace. Then helped Owen and Mr. Grimes load the supplies into the wagon.

Heidi rose to stack dirty plates after lunch on Sunday. "I'm going to set up my easel on the porch this afternoon."

"Would you like to go to one of the places you wanted to paint instead? You saw several on our ride to town." Jethro handed her his silverware and plate.

"That would be wonderful." Judging from Lily and Toby's bright smiles, they agreed. Sounding so eager to be with Jethro was not the way to convince her family she wouldn't be bound to any man. She carried the plates to the dish pan, glad she could turn her back on everyone without them wondering why.

"I'll hitch the horse to the buggy and meet you outside after a while."

"Thank you." She kept her back to Jethro as she poured hot water from the tea kettle into the dish pan.

Lily set the meat platter on the worktable. "Ella and I will do the dishes. Go gather up your paints. Since we never know what November weather will be, enjoy this pleasant afternoon while you can."

"I don't mind helping you."

"I know." Lily nudged Heidi away from the dish pan.

By the time Heidi gathered everything she needed, Jethro had the buggy in the front yard waiting for her. "I filled my canteen already in case we get thirsty." He grinned as she stepped out the door, carrying a stool in each hand.

"Thank you."

"We can leave sooner if I help you." He reached for the stools.

"That makes sense."

He followed her back inside to get her satchel and the small basket holding her brushes and paints. She carefully carried her precious folded easel outside as Toby held the front door for her.

Jethro set her satchel on the porch by the rail. "Let me help you down the steps. I don't want you to fall." He took her elbow and guided her off the porch.

"Thank you." She focused on the easel in her hands instead

of his fingers touching her arm. The only reason she'd accepted his gentlemanly assistance was to give her more time to paint.

After they loaded all her supplies, Jethro helped her into the buggy. If she could be sure no one was watching, she wouldn't allow him to assist her. He then climbed up next to her, holding the newspaper he'd bought in town. "On our ride to town, I saw an interesting group of mesquite trees that almost twine together. I tried to pay special enough attention to find it again. I should drive since I'm the only one who knows where I want to go."

He chuckled. "That sounds about right most of the time."

"I hope you mean that as a compliment." She glanced over at him.

"I do."

She turned her attention back to looking for the spot she wanted, hoping he'd elaborate on his short answer. He didn't as usual. Yet she appreciated his quiet ways more all the time. He hadn't once tried to convince her she shouldn't forge a life of her own.

"I found it." She halted the horse about a mile later. "See how the branches look as if they're twisted together from one tree to the other?"

He studied the trees a moment. "I've probably ridden by here a hundred times and never noticed that. Maybe I should pay closer attention to what's around me. I might see other things I never realized were right in front of me." He stared straight ahead as if to avoid looking at her.

What he might mean by his last remark, she wouldn't ask. Especially if he were hinting about paying closer attention to her. He'd done enough of that in town yesterday. She climbed out of the buggy as quickly as possible. He ground tied the horse then picked up his paper off the front seat. Folding the paper under his arm, he stood and watched her set up her easel and paints.

"I'll stand at my easel today, so you don't need to remain on your feet until I sit, the way you usually do." One of his gentlemanly habits she didn't mind.

"I can't remember ever sitting before a lady did. But if I can let one unload a buggy without helping, I guess I can manage to find myself a comfortable spot on the ground." He settled onto a clump of grass.

She laughed. Talking with a man who didn't mind her ways was refreshing. Unlike Andrew Bridges's patronizing remarks about a lady not needing a derringer. She doubted the man would like her future plans any more than he thought she should have a gun.

As she moved her easel around to give her the best view of the entwined trees, Jethro unfolded his paper. "I'll also keep my promise to you of no guns this afternoon. I'd much rather hold a paint brush."

He nodded. "I'd rather do this today too."

"Even though you showed me a derringer you thought I should buy some day?"

"Yes. I want you safe."

"Thank you." While being sure to get the right amount of paint on her brush, she reminded herself to study the mesquites in front of her instead of the man sitting a few feet off to her side. The man who didn't seem to like guns wore his gun belt now. To protect her if necessary. Which he'd proved he'd do.

Such comforting yet disquieting thoughts. A woman with plans like hers shouldn't welcome Jethro's watch care or consideration. But she did. No, she didn't. She couldn't. The life she wanted would allow her time to paint where and when she wanted without worrying about anyone else's dictates. Thinking too highly of Jethro would risk not only her heart but the freedom she so badly craved.

Once the trees had taken shape, she changed colors. "I'm adding a jack rabbit to the picture. As you said, I've seen enough of them to memorize what they look like."

"There are plenty of them around." He went back to whatever he was reading.

"I think I'll put a longhorn or two on one side."

"It's your painting. Put as many cows in it as you like." He answered without glancing up from his paper.

"Thank you."

He shifted to look up at her. "For what?"

"For not thinking you know what's best for me better than I do. The way Mr. Bridges did in the store yesterday." She added more strokes to the rabbit now sitting in front of the trees. "As quickly as he left, I think he was quite perturbed with me."

Jethro laughed. "If he has a list of prospects for a wife, you won't be included."

"That's good. I don't want to be on any man's list."

His broad grin morphed to a barely perceptible frown that clouded his eyes. He ducked his head, turning the page of his paper so quickly the top corner almost tore. "So you keep saying."

Exactly what he meant, Heidi feared to ask. His voice sounded thick with emotion. But what kind? Yes, he wanted her safe. But he hadn't been interested in showing her a gun until Andrew Bridges had walked up to her. Mr. Bridges wasn't the sort of man to put her or any woman in danger. What else other than her safety did Jethro have in mind?

She gripped her brush to keep from dropping it in the dirt. Surely, Jethro wasn't jealous of Mr. Bridges. He'd said he'd helped her keep the man at bay at the Hawkins' house the way he'd have done with any other friend. She could have handled Mr. Bridges quite well yesterday without Jethro's help. But Jethro was at her side before she had exchanged a dozen words with the pastor's son.

*Oh, dear.* She hadn't anticipated Jethro changing his mind about her and wanting more than her friendship. Or that such an idea didn't bother her as much as it had or should. Entertaining thoughts of being more than friends with Jethro would mean the end to the completely independent life she wanted.

Which brought to mind the letter she'd mailed to Frieda for her parents, falsely stating she and Jethro were engaged. She told such a lie only to be sure her parents disowned her the way they had Lily after she eloped with Harvey. Surely, since they despised cowboys, they'd never bother Heidi again.

With broad strokes, she painted the sky in darker, more ominous shades than she'd planned. Perhaps she should add in storm clouds on the horizon to go with the emotions now causing such a storm in her heart.

## 16

After Sunday afternoon, Heidi determined to stay as busy as possible. To avoid Jethro as much as she could. If she found time, she'd sketch or paint close enough to the house that she wouldn't need an escort. So far on this Friday, Jethro had accidently cooperated with her. As soon as they'd finished chores, he and Toby had taken the wagon out to gather wood. They wouldn't be back until supper time.

"Toby mentioned this morning he's hungry for chicken, I'd like to take care of the chicken and fry it all myself." She grinned at Lily as she dried the last plate from the noon meal. "If I'm to truly be of help to you, I need to learn to do things by myself in case you can't later."

"As I keep telling you and Toby, I feel fine."

"I'm glad you do." Heidi picked up the dish pan to go empty it outside.

Since talking with Toby Monday night, she'd been doing her best to do the heavier work and leave the easier tasks for Lily. She'd do all she could to see this next baby didn't come early the way Harvey had two years ago. Toby said the August heat had helped keep such a tiny baby warm. But if this baby came early in January, they wouldn't have such an advantage.

Lily was wiping off the worktable when Heidi walked back into the kitchen. "We'll go out to the henhouse after I put Harvey down for a nap."

"Good." Heidi hugged Lily, being careful of her sister's protruding abdomen.

By the time Heidi cut off the chicken's head, scalded it, and plucked the feathers, she was ready to move to San Antonio tomorrow. Tonight, in the dark, if possible. No matter how good the chicken smelled frying in the skillet, she'd never take town living for granted again.

Lily put the cornbread in the oven. "For someone who'd never gathered an egg in her life until September, you've done wonders."

"Thank you."

"Now you can even milk a cow and tend a garden. You're much better at sewing too. Maybe the Lord is preparing you to be a rancher or farmer's wife?"

Heidi turned a piece of chicken in the skillet. "I don't think so."

"You are still praying about whatever God might have for you, aren't you?"

"Yes, I'm praying."

Lily patted Heidi's shoulder. "Good. I can tell you from my own life, sometimes God answers our prayers by giving us what we should have instead of what we think we want."

"I'll remember that." Her sister's prayers weren't the same as the ones Heidi had been praying, but she'd keep that to herself. The more she talked to the Lord about her future, the more God helped her learn to do things for herself. Surely, that meant He approved of her wish to one day live alone in San Antonio or some other place.

Ella skipped in the back door. Heidi wanted to hug her sweet niece for interrupting a conversation her aunt didn't want to continue. "Pa and Mr. Bannister are cleaning up at the well. I told them Aunt Heidi said the chicken's almost done."

"Set the table before the men come in." Lily emptied the butter mold onto a saucer.

"Yes, ma'am."

Toby and Jethro came in as Heidi put the last piece of chicken on a platter. She carried it to the table while Lily got the cornbread, potatoes, and corn. As usual, Jethro waited until she and Lily were seated before he took his chair. Lately, Toby had been doing the same.

After Toby said grace, he passed the platter of chicken while Lily put pieces of cornbread on Harvey's highchair tray. "Heidi fixed the chicken." Lily went on in detail telling how Heidi had killed and then plucked the chicken by herself. "As I told her, she's doing so well here she should think about one day being a rancher or farmer's wife."

Not at all the kind of praise Heidi wanted. If only a giant prairie dog would dig a hole under her big enough to swallow up her and her chair this exact moment. She couldn't miss Jethro's barely disguised smile before he ducked his head. Nothing about Lily's remarks should make him happy. She'd remind him the next time they were alone she still didn't intend to ever find a husband. No. Since she planned to be with him as little as possible, she wouldn't be telling him anything.

Toby grinned at Heidi. "You fried the chicken just right."

"Thank you. Lily helped me." Both men needed to realize she wasn't as good at doing everything herself as Lily bragged. She didn't want Toby joining in with Lily's matrimonial encouragements. Especially if they had their hearts set on Jethro.

The conversation soon turned to when Toby and Jethro intended to go deer hunting and how much longer they had until the first frost. Heidi hoped no one noticed her silence. She wasn't in the mood to talk after Lily's pronouncement in front of everyone that Heidi should wed a farmer or rancher. Having her mention it to Heidi alone would have been enough.

Thunder rumbled as Toby scooted his chair away from the

table. "Jethro and I saw clouds off to the north when we were coming home."

Lily set Harvey down from his highchair. "We could use some rain."

Jethro rose. "I'll go to my place now in case the rain's coming this way. Heidi, the chicken was delicious. Maybe you should look for a job in a restaurant when you leave here."

Heidi wanted to jump up and hug the man. "Thank you. I'll think about it." She worked to keep her voice calm and not betray her elation. This friend might be the only one here who understood her longings.

—

JETHRO SLIPPED OFF his jacket as he walked into the kitchen for breakfast. "I'm a little early to eat, but I came in between showers."

"We don't mind. Good morning." Lily nodded toward him as she fried the bacon.

"Good morning to y'all."

Heidi gave him a sidelong glance while flipping a pancake. After his comment about a restaurant, she wanted to be with him more instead of ignoring him. Someone who accepted her goals was getting rare, especially as bold as Lily's suggestions had been last night. Heidi suspected Lily already had one certain rancher in mind.

"Doesn't look like we'll be chopping wood or splitting logs this morning." Toby squatted down by Harvey, chuckling at the little boy's efforts to stack too many blocks on top of each other.

Memories of Papa smiling at her as she played made Heidi's throat tighten. She hoped someday that remembering pleasant times wouldn't make it hard to take a breath. Lily spoke of her life in New Braunfels only when prodded. Was that the best way to deal with what Papa and Mama had done?

"That's why Heidi decided we had time for pancakes this

morning since they take longer." Lily set the syrup pitcher and butter on the table, bringing Heidi's thoughts back to pancakes.

"I've got cleaning I can do inside my place this morning." Jethro inhaled as Heidi set the last pancake on the platter. "I appreciate eating with y'all and how well you ladies feed me."

"You're welcome." Heidi set the platter on the table. Perhaps she'd tell him later how welcome his comments had been last night.

The off-and-on rain continued until it was almost time to start supper. Just as Heidi's thoughts went from yes to no back to yes about talking to Jethro. Telling a sympathetic friend about her frustrations with Lily was tempting. Until she recalled what he had and hadn't said while watching her too closely as she painted Sunday afternoon. The more she thought about it, Jethro was jealous of Mr. Bridges. His actions had been too much like a possible suitor than a friend.

She carried the butter churn out to the front porch when the sun started coming out. After so much time inside, time to think alone outside would be good. She gasped as she looked toward the barn. A brilliant yellow, green, and pink arch stretched across the bright blue sky making the most glorious rainbow she'd ever seen. She jumped from her chair so quickly she almost knocked the churn over.

"Lily, you and Ella must come see the most beautiful rainbow." Heidi rushed into the parlor, almost colliding with Ella who was dusting the furniture. "Lily, could you finish the churning? I have to get my pencils and paper."

"Go enjoy it before it's gone," Lily's voice drifted to Heidi from the other part of the house. "Harvey and I'll come see it too."

"It's sooo beautiful." Ella clapped her hands together as Heidi joined her family on the porch.

"I have to sketch it now."

The four of them were still on the porch when the men trotted toward them. "We wanted to be sure y'all noticed the rainbow, but looks like everyone has." Toby paused to stare at the sky before joining them on the porch.

From his spot in the yard, Jethro grinned at Heidi when she glanced up from her paper. "We hurried over here to be sure you could draw a picture before the rainbow faded."

"I want to drive out from the house tomorrow afternoon. I started a painting with the barn in it. Adding the rainbow over it would be the perfect way to finish it. I'll settle for sketching it now so I can remember how it looks."

"I'd like to see you do that." Jethro's quiet, wistful-sounding words spoke much too loudly to her heart.

She concentrated on her drawing. The man who understood and accepted her future plans couldn't be thinking about enjoying her company as more than her friend. The possibility he might shouldn't thrill her. Such contradictory thoughts were scarier than the worst thunderstorm she'd ever seen.

As Heidi drove the buggy to where she wanted to set up her paints, Jethro chided himself for letting his thoughts and his words overrun his common sense again. The more he volunteered to go with the woman sitting close to him, the more muddled his mind got. She hadn't surprised him by assuming yesterday he'd come with her today. But how comfortable was she becoming with him? And he with her.

No matter. She still was not his kind of woman, although he'd found too many things to admire about her lately. He must remind himself they'd never be more than friends. She must think highly of him, trust him the way she often shared her thoughts and problems with him. If she changed her mind about a husband, he'd want her to consider anyone other than him. Or would he?

Heidi reined in the horse on a ridge overlooking the barn.

"This is perfect. I want to paint the rainbow before I forget such amazing colors."

"Good idea."

Again, he pressed his hands against his trouser legs while watching her unload her things. Making this woman happy was so different than what any other woman he'd known would like.

"Use the extra stool so you aren't sitting in the mud." Heidi handed a closed stool to him.

"I appreciate that." He didn't seat himself until Heidi had her easel and paints set up. His late father would be furious Jethro dared sit while a lady was standing. But Father had never met anyone like Heidi. Neither had Jethro.

"Rainbows have always fascinated me." She studied the painting a few moments as if deciding where she wanted to start on it today.

"As much as ranching and cowboys?" He couldn't resist teasing her a little since she sounded as enthusiastic as she did when talking about anything concerning a cow.

She flashed a quick smile his way. "Yes. Just as much." A yellow arch took shape as she worked. "God picked such a beautiful way to promise He wouldn't send another flood. And a wonderful way to mark Noah and his family's new beginning." Her hand stilled. "I do hope God is as pleased with the way I'm starting over."

"I'd say He is. He helped you get here. All the things you've learned lately will help you take care of yourself better." His gut knotted at the thought of her leaving in a few short months.

"I'm so glad God sent you to me for a friend. I can't tell you how much I appreciate the way you understand me." She kept her gaze focused on her art.

He hadn't thought of her friendship as a godsend. But the more he got to know her, the more he might agree. As long as he was careful to think of her only as a friend. He stared off toward the horizon. Better to get his mind on something else. Say something else to keep this conversation from getting any more serious than it was.

"I enjoyed the chicken you fixed the other day. You'll soon be as good a cook as Mrs. Grimes."

Her eyes shone as she glanced over at him. "Thank you. Learning so many new things hasn't been easy." She painted a bright green into the rainbow, leaving him to his own thoughts.

As she worked, she studied the canvas in front of her so intently he couldn't help wondering what she might be thinking. Amazing how quiet she could be whenever she stood in front of an easel.

She paused as she dipped her brush into the paint. "I do miss sausage and sauerkraut." She licked her lips. "And Mama's *apfelkuchen*."

"What is that?"

"It's like an apple cake. It's delicious." Brush still in her hand, she stared at her painting. "Lily has somehow set aside her memories." She added a pink arch next to the yellow. Laying her brush down, she turned to face him. "I don't know what kind of hurtful things you've endured, but do you have some pleasant memories too? And does thinking of them haunt you instead of making you happy at times?"

He gripped the edges of the stool to keep from losing his balance. Her words were like a large rock hurled into his chest, robbing him of his breath. He'd long preferred Mrs. Grimes's method of setting aside—shoving aside—old memories. The good and bad as well as he could.

"I'm sorry." Her voice quivered as she studied him. "I shouldn't have asked you such a thing." She turned back to her paints.

One by one, his fingers released the stool frame. He closed his eyes, breathing in and out.

She nibbled on her lip as she painted a blue sky around the rainbow. "I have a terrible habit of blurting things out before thinking first." Again she peered directly in his eyes. "Please forgive me."

"Of course." His dry throat made it hard to speak.

She bent to retrieve his canteen propped beside her easel. Then handed it to him. "Would you like a drink?"

"Thanks." The water moistened his throat but did nothing to calm his soul.

She turned back to her canvas. He stood. Maybe walking around a little would clear his head. He had happy memories of his childhood before the war. Before one of Sherman's Yankee soldiers killed his father. But like Heidi, remembering the good times could still haunt him some days. Could still remind him of unhappy days.

After yesterday's unsettling afternoon with Heidi, Jethro welcomed the hard day's work Mr. Grimes had planned. Cutting a wagon full of wood and splitting logs should make him tired enough to sleep tonight. The boss took one end of a large branch while Jethro grabbed hold of the other as they heaved it out of the wagon bed.

"Like Lily said, we needed the rain, but I'm glad we can finally get to the wood we hauled in Friday."

"So am I." How glad Jethro wouldn't say.

Memories, good and bad, had kept him awake through much of last night, praying more than he'd slept. He hadn't dreamed about the day he left home for a good two years. Until last night. He'd been wrestling with his heart fighting not to get too close to Heidi. Her probing questions had won that battle and more than confirmed she wasn't the woman for him. She was much too good at helping him remember what he'd worked too hard to forget.

"With Thanksgiving coming next week, the ladies need plenty of wood for the stove. Especially since Lily invited the Shepherds."

"Hope the weather's good since you'll have a houseful." Of

course, the weather would be nice or the Shepherds would stay home. He wasn't very good at making conversation on a good day. Being so tired made it worse.

"We'll pray it is." Mr. Grimes grabbed the end of another branch.

Before they finished unloading the full wagon, they stopped to take their jackets off and get a drink of water. The light breeze made working in flannel shirts comfortable. Mr. Grimes screwed the top back on his canteen. "Good way to work up a sweat."

"Yes, sir, it is." Jethro wiped the back of his neck with his bandana.

"Do you feel all right? You've been too quiet even for you this morning." The boss studied Jethro as if searching for the answer to his question.

"I feel fine."

Mr. Grimes cocked his head. "No. No, you don't. I've noticed a difference in you since that night we ran off the rustlers."

"I never want to shoot at a man again." Jethro slumped against the side of the wagon. He'd tell the boss only part of what was bothering him.

"Or get shot at." The boss sucked in a deep breath. "Lily told me losing a few longhorns to rustlers wasn't worth putting you and me in danger." He clapped his hand on Jethro's shoulder "If I'd listened to her, you'd be sleeping a lot better than you have lately. Today's not the only time I've noticed circles under your eyes."

Jethro shrugged. "You didn't drag me along. I've survived other things. I'm doing a lot better than I was."

The slight shake of Mr. Grimes's head indicated he doubted Jethro's words. "You're too honest to be a good liar. Something tells me you've got more on your mind than guns. If you want to talk about it sometime, I'll listen."

"Thanks."

Mr. Grimes kept his hand on Jethro as he stared into his eyes. "I can tell you from my own experience holding everything inside yourself is hard on more than your digestion." He turned and grabbed another piece of wood.

Jethro spent the remainder of the morning thinking over the boss's words. Heidi should be the picture of health since she rarely kept any thought to herself for long. Maybe he should quit going off alone with her. The boss didn't expect him to do that if he didn't want to. But as much as Mrs. Grimes had come to hope Heidi might one day change her mind about a man, he hoped the lady didn't think Heidi should change her mind for him.

"We'll rest up some tomorrow then go deer hunting Wednesday. It won't hurt to have some venison laid by in case we get a few days of cold weather." Mr. Grimes grinned as they threw the last limb from the wagon.

"Good idea." *Not really*. Jethro would rather go hunting tomorrow. An easy day meant extra time for Heidi to want his company while she painted if Mrs. Grimes could spare her help. Which the missus would probably be all too happy to do.

They sawed and stacked a few logs before quitting to clean up for the noon meal. After his restless night, Jethro felt as if he'd already worked until sundown. But despite his fatigue, Heidi was prettier than she should be, sitting across the table from him. Even with an apron over it, her new dress with small purple flowers all over brought out her blue eyes. He was more than grateful Mrs. Grimes had insisted Heidi should buy fabric when they'd gone to town.

Thoughts of helping Heidi aggravate Andrew Bridges made him smile. He ducked his head lest she think he was grinning at her. Better to concentrate on buttering a slice of bread. The bad memories her words had triggered last night were the reason he was already bone tired at noon.

By supper time, Jethro felt as if he'd spent a straight twenty-four hours in the saddle during a cattle drive. He had to find a way to sleep tonight. Plus figure out how to avoid time alone with Heidi. No use causing himself more problems and pain by getting too close to the woman who planned to leave here and start her own life in a few short months.

Except carrying out what he should do would be hard. Thinking about not going with her while she painted didn't sit well with his heart no matter what his head told him. Regardless of how he felt about her, Mr. and Mrs. Grimes now assumed he'd accompany Heidi and watch over her. Since he wanted to keep his job, he'd probably still go with Heidi even if he came to hate her. Which he doubted would happen since he found more to admire about her almost every day.

Mr. Grimes scooted his chair back from the table the way he did most nights. "Jethro, if you weren't so tired from our busy day, I'd say we should play some checkers while the ladies wash dishes. But that can wait for another night."

"I'll take you up on that some other time." Jethro stifled a yawn, glad for a good excuse for being exhausted. The less he said about being tired, the less someone other than Mr. Grimes might wonder why the boss wasn't too tired to play checkers and Jethro was.

"Heidi might want to play after we clean up." Mrs. Grimes nodded toward her sister. "You'd played enough games with Otto by the time I left you were becoming good at checkers. Do you still play?"

"Not since Otto died."

"Then you and Toby can play."

"Can I play too?" Ella looked from Mr. Grimes to Heidi. "I want to learn how."

"You're not quite old enough." Mrs. Grimes smiled at Ella. "Heidi was about ten when Otto started showing her how to play."

"Oh." Ella's downcast expression said much more than her simple reply.

Heidi patted her niece's arm. "You and Annie can watch your pa and me play."

The little girl's eyes sparkled. "I'd like that."

Once again, Jethro couldn't help noticing Heidi's way with children. Maybe she should reconsider her vow of spinsterhood and have a family of her own. Only if she chose a man other than himself. As soon as the ladies started clearing the table, Jethro rose. "Thanks for another delicious supper, ladies. I'll see everyone in the morning."

Mr. Grimes nodded. "I'll set the checkerboard up in the parlor."

Jethro headed out the back door. Being tired could be better than he'd thought. If Heidi liked to play checkers, he might have ended up playing her instead of the boss. He wouldn't put it past Mr. or Mrs. Grimes to see he and Heidi did most anything together.

---

LILY GRINNED at Heidi as they finished fixing lunch. "Since Toby plans to finish a little early this afternoon, you should have time to work on your new painting."

"I'd like that."

"I believe Jethro would too. He doesn't seem to mind going with you." Lily's eyes twinkled as she watched Harvey playing with his toys in the corner.

Heidi turned her back to her sister while reaching for a platter on the shelf. "He does. From what little he says, he likes thinking and praying outside. I paint or draw while he talks to God or ponders whatever is on his mind."

"I hope he's not the only one doing that while you stand in front of your easel."

"He's not." Heidi grabbed a knife to slice the bread. "I often think how Papa and Mama tolerated my art, but never truly encouraged me the way everyone here does. I'm still praying about how much that pains me."

"I understand." Lily handed plates to Ella for her to set the table. "God gave you such a wonderful talent for a reason. Not very many people can do what you can."

"Aunt Heidi, can you paint a picture of Ruckus some day?" Ella walked over to get the silverware to set by the plates.

"Yes, I should do that." Her niece would be thrilled if she knew Heidi had already started a small painting of Ruckus for Ella's Christmas present.

"Thank you, thank you." Ella hugged Heidi with all her might.

Lily turned from stirring the gravy. "If I can take butter and eggs to town to trade for groceries and help us make ends meet, you should be able to sell paintings. There are people in San Antonio with the money to buy them."

"Maybe I could." Heidi wouldn't mention she'd already thought about, dreamed about selling her art but not to someday help her husband with family finances. She was still honestly praying for God to show her His will for her life. Lily's confident words could easily be another sign God wanted Heidi to live on her own, relying totally on Him to care for her. Not a man, who unlike the Lord, might betray her in the future.

The men walked in a short time later. "We've got wood stacked by the smokehouse, wood for Jethro and plenty for us for a while."

"That's good." Lily set the gravy on the table.

Heidi picked Harvey up to set him in his highchair. The little boy probably wasn't too heavy for Lily to lift yet, but Toby had recently asked her to do more for Lily whenever she could manage. Some days the way Toby so carefully cared for Lily made Heidi wish for a husband who would cherish her.

While they ate, Ella happily told Toby and Jethro Aunt Heidi was going to paint Ruckus someday. "He'll be the happiest dog in the county when I show it to him."

Toby chuckled. "He'll for sure be the only hound around here with his own picture."

"Aunt Heidi knows he's an extra special dog, same as I do."

Toby grinned. "Yeah, he is."

She was still amazed how Toby treated Ella and Harvey as if they were his. Another thing he did that sometimes made Heidi long for someone to love her. But Papa had turned on his own flesh and blood. Twice. With Lily and her.

"Heidi wants to paint this afternoon, but probably not a portrait of Ruckus." Lily smiled at Ella as she put more carrots on Harvey's tray. "Jethro, I can't thank you enough for going with Heidi."

"You're welcome." Jethro grabbed his glass.

Heidi hoped she wasn't imagining his voice didn't sound as welcome as the words he'd said. Maybe he was still tired from yesterday. "I don't want to go so far off I can't be back in time to help Lily fix dinner."

Lily set her fork on her plate and stared straight at Heidi. "You deserve some time to yourself. If y'all walk into the kitchen the minute I'm setting the food on the table, it won't hurt one thing."

"As I keep saying, I'm here to help you."

"Ella is good help too, aren't you?"

The little girl beamed at her mother. "Yes, ma'am."

"All right. Jethro, do you mind hitching up the buggy after we finish eating?" For once, she didn't mind not being able to go out alone. Jethro had become more pleasant company than she'd thought he'd be.

"Not at all."

After Heidi helped clean the kitchen, she gathered up her paints and brushes. Jethro picked up the painting she wanted to finish and laid it on the backseat of the buggy as carefully as she would. When she carried her easel onto the porch, he reached to help her down the steps as he'd done before.

"Will you let me carry that for you? I worry about you tripping over your skirt coming down the steps."

"Thank you, but you understand why I need to do this myself." She said no more. Thinking about loading everything into Papa and Mama's buggy alone hurt too much to talk about.

After they finished loading the buggy, Jethro helped her up. "I wouldn't do this if I weren't concerned about someone in the house watching us."

"I know. I wouldn't want to cause problems between you and Toby, since he's your boss."

"I appreciate you seeing things my way." He grinned. "For a change."

She laughed. "I suppose I can be a little stubborn at times."

"Only a little?" He climbed up beside her.

How nice to be so at ease with him. The fact he wanted nothing more than friendship from her made her more comfortable with him all the time. Which caused her discomfort lately if she thought about Jethro too much. Praying had forced her to consider the possibility God might have different plans than she envisioned.

But if He wanted her to reconsider, why did she keep finding ways to support herself such as selling her art? Or make friends with a man who didn't mind she wanted to maintain her independence?

She snapped the reins. The buggy rolled out of the yard. Better to concentrate on going where she wanted to go to paint. Jethro didn't say a word as she drove to the creek not far from where they'd heard the rustlers. "I hope you don't mind coming here after what happened the last time. I should have asked you first."

"I figured out where you were heading a while back. I'd have told you if I didn't want to be here."

"Yes, you would. I appreciate your honesty."

"As I do yours. I won't live my life in fear because of something bad, especially since neither of us could help it."

"I'm glad we agree." Another thing to like about him. She set the brake then scrambled out of the buggy before Jethro could assist her.

"You know I don't mind helping you." He rubbed his hands along his trouser legs as if he had to constrain himself from picking up something for her.

"I know." He understood why she didn't want help, but she didn't want to have that discussion again today. She grabbed her satchel off the seat.

He took his usual spot on the ground without offering again to help get any of her equipment. Good. Whether he was beginning to accept her wishes or giving in to her to avoid a conversation he didn't want to have, she didn't care.

"I have something for you." She slipped the sketch of him she'd finished yesterday and handed it to him.

"This is like looking at me from the shoulders up in a mirror, except for the mustache." His voice held an unmistakable tone of awe. "Thank you."

"Do you like it?"

"Yes, I do." He grinned. "Wonder if someone will think I'm conceited if I make a frame for it and put this on a wall in my house?"

"People display family portraits all the time. Plus, a simple pencil sketch could never be considered ostentatious."

"I wouldn't call this simple. I could never do what you do with pencils."

His praise warmed her entire soul. "Thank you."

"So why'd you give me a mustache?" His twinkling eyes signaled he must not be displeased with her embellishment.

"Because ... because I think you'd look good with one." She hoped he didn't notice her hesitant answer. She'd barely stopped herself from blurting out how handsome he'd look with a mustache. Some other woman could utter such words one day, but not her. "This is a small thank you for helping me so many times."

"You're welcome." The way he stared into her eyes hinted his gratitude might go deeper than he'd said.

Making the needed trips to pull her stools, easel, and canvas from the buggy, gave her a much-needed excuse to turn her back and not continue looking up at him. "You could also give it to a relative if you have one nearby."

"I don't think I'd do that even if I had anyone around here."

"You wouldn't?" She turned to face him after she set her basket on the ground. He must truly like her gift. "You have no family in the area?" She was prying, but she had to think of something other than how pleased she was he wanted to keep the portrait for himself.

He shook his head. "I left everyone behind in Georgia somewhat similar to the way you left New Braunfels for good." His somber expression signaled his departure might not have been a happy one.

"I'm sorry. With everything I've been through with my parents, I should know better than to ask about your family."

"You're blessed to have someone left who cares." His tone sounded wistful as he stared off toward the horizon.

"Yes, I am." She unfolded her stools. "But I'm looking forward to living on my own and not depending on Lily and Toby."

"Nothing wrong with wanting to take care of yourself."

"No there isn't. I wouldn't impose on your time like this if Toby and Lily didn't insist."

"I appreciate your consideration. And this fine drawing."

"Thank you." Much more than she cared to say.

She finished getting out her paints. Concentrating on the rolling landscape was safer than thinking about her growing admiration for the man sitting near her. Not many men would be so accepting of her wishes for independence. Perhaps his similar break from his own family made him more understanding of her situation.

Heidi helped Lily rush through cleaning breakfast dishes while Ella did last minute dusting in the parlor. "We're wasting our time cleaning anything in here." Heidi grinned at her sister as she set the last washed plate on the shelf.

"We are, but all the extra work will be worth it when everyone gets here." Lily's bright smile emphasized her anticipation for the special Thanksgiving Day she'd planned.

Extra work was an understatement with Charlotte and her family coming plus Eduardo and Francisca. Getting the large turkey Toby had shot ready to go in the oven had taken considerable effort.

"Wait until you taste Charlotte's mincemeat pie and Francisca's bread pudding." Lily licked her lips.

"I'm sure they're delicious." Heidi slipped her apron over her head. "You need to sit in the parlor before we have to start the vegetables for lunch."

"You can be worse than Toby some days."

Heidi gave Lily a nudge toward the door. "I'll consider that a compliment." Which she did. Toby was like another older brother now. Unlike Otto, Toby admired her paintings and drawings. No matter how much he believed she should start a family, he never belittled her when she continued to talk about what she'd do when she moved to San Antonio.

By the time their company arrived, the turkey in the oven was almost done. Corn, carrots, and potatoes with onions simmered in pots on the stove. The house filled with laughter, love, and conversation. A lot of conversation with so many people in one place.

Toby halted inside the kitchen as he carried in Francisca's bread pudding. He took a long, deep breath. "I could get too fat for Smoky to carry me just smelling all this."

"If you don't move and let David in the door with my pies, you won't be fat." Charlotte put Matthew, her youngest, on the floor by Harvey. Jeremiah joined his brother and cousin.

"I'll be in the parlor out of the way until you ladies say everything's ready." Toby set the pan on the worktable.

Charlotte, Lily, and Francisca set about finishing the feast they'd planned. Ella did her best to help. The last time Heidi remembered being in such a crowded kitchen was the Christmas before Lily, then still Suzanne, eloped with Harvey. Greta hadn't married yet, so all three girls were helping Mama. At almost twelve, she hadn't understood why Mama and Lily weren't getting along. The first week of March, days after Heidi's twelfth birthday, Lily disappeared. Their parents never allowed the other children to mention their wayward sister's name again.

Heidi took a deep breath as she opened the oven door to check the turkey. Like Jethro, she wouldn't allow bad memories to ruin today. Coming here was an answer to prayers she hadn't known to ask in August.

With two extra chairs squeezed in, the table had just enough room for the adults. Someone—probably Lily—had seated Heidi next to Jethro. Ella and Jeremiah sat at the worktable. Harvey had his highchair. Matthew perched boosted on a couple of pieces of wood and tied into his chair with a dish towel.

Eduardo rose after everyone was seated. "I want to thank God for so many blessings. For giving me my beautiful Francisca after I gave up on having a loving wife again. For my family." He beamed, opening his arms wide as if to include everyone in the room. His beautiful prayer of gratitude was part Spanish, part English.

No matter that Heidi couldn't understand every word, her heart filled with her own thanks as Eduardo continued to pray. She had family. Some by blood. Some by love. She stole a sidelong glance at Jethro. His thin smile hadn't traveled up to his eyes as Eduardo talked. Everyone here accepted him. Thought highly of him.

But Jethro had no family. Not even in love. Being a well-respected foreman wasn't the same. Her heart ached for him. Could she become his family? Give him someone to love? She squeezed her eyes shut. Had such thoughts come from God or from emotions overwhelming her because of the moment?

The longing to choose her own path shoved out her thoughts of marriage. Living alone meant never risking betrayal again. Even if she had her own house one day, she'd still have family. Something she realized she now wanted. Being independent but not completely.

Like Jethro. Or with Jethro?

Everyone said a hearty amen when Eduardo finished praying. She quickly chimed in, lest anyone realize she'd probably heard less than half of what Eduardo said to the Lord. Toby carved the turkey, and the feasting began.

Charlotte and Toby traded stories of each other's antics as children. Eduardo added details since he'd started working for their father when Charlotte was about ten. God had cobbled together an amazing group of people who now claimed her. Thoughts that someone should claim Jethro intruded into her mind again.

After the ladies cleaned the kitchen, the three little boys were settled into Harvey's room for naps. The adults gathered on the porch to visit more while Ella and Ruckus romped in the yard. The men grouped their chairs on one end. The ladies sat on the other. Heidi and Jethro ended up on the edge of each group almost in the middle of the porch and very near each other.

But this time, she couldn't blame Lily. She'd chosen her chair, because she wasn't completely comfortable talking with three married women about the things they liked to discuss. Had Jethro done the same? He could easily talk about cows or hunting but not family matters.

As the men and women turned their conversations to things that didn't pertain to Heidi or Jethro, she glanced over at him. His stiff posture seemed to indicate he was as uncomfortable as she was. The desire to ease his discomfort welled up in her heart. "We talked about playing checkers last week, but I haven't had the chance to beat you yet." Her words slipped out before she thought. Jethro might not want to walk off alone with her in front of so many people.

"Is that so?" The mischievous look in his eyes said he'd accept her challenge.

She nodded. "We could play in the kitchen if we carry our chairs back inside."

"I'll carry yours in too." Jethro rose then picked up his chair by the back.

After following him into the house, Heidi went to get the checker game. Jethro had their chairs at the table when she walked into the kitchen. She took the chair at the end, leaving the one he'd placed next to her for him. "I should have thought more before asking you about checkers. Everyone on the porch was much too happy to see us walk off alone."

---

JETHRO SHRUGGED, hoping to appear more nonchalant than he felt. "I was already trying to figure out a way to make a graceful exit without being rude."

The smiling woman setting up the checkers had an uncanny

ability to figure out what he was thinking. She'd somehow done that since the first time they'd gone off alone. Not very many people were as perceptive as Heidi.

The better he got to know her, the more things he discovered that made her different from any other woman he'd known. Yet because of her own family problems, she reminded him as no one else had about his past troubles. Incidents he'd worked years to bury deep inside himself had haunted his dreams too often lately.

He really needed to leave her alone. But his heart kept interfering with what his mind told him was best. He liked this fiercely independent, too-talkative woman more than he should. Especially if she decided to go through with her plans to go in February or March and leave him behind.

"Are you ready?" Heidi interrupted Jethro's wool gathering.

"Yes. Prepare to lose. My father taught me well."

"We'll see." She made the first move with a red checker. "You took too long thinking."

As usual, she didn't ask him for details. Another trait of hers he liked.

Their game turned into a duel.

"Otto taught me well. So well, few people in New Braunfels would play either one of us." She jumped two of his kings with one of hers.

He soon maneuvered his checkers to where he could jump two of hers, only to open himself up for her to jump him back. Twice.

"See. I told you." She jumped his last checker.

"I demand a rematch."

She laughed. The urge to make her happy and hear her laugh often overwhelmed him. He set his checkers back on the board.

"Do I see the beginning of a mustache?" She pointed toward his upper lip.

"Yeah. You flattered me too much in your sketch. I thought

I'd see if looking more like the handsome version of the man you drew would make me look better."

"I'm not surprised someone like you doesn't spend much time looking in a mirror. I draw only what I see. And what I see ... Would you like to know?"

Judging from her sparkling eyes and saucy tone, he'd swear she was flirting with him. He'd pretty much done the same with her when she asked if he wanted to play checkers. "Why wouldn't I if you see me the way you drew me?'

Another lilting laugh he could listen to all day. She was flirting. He was flirting. Not something he'd planned to do today or any other day. But he was enjoying it immensely.

"Mind you as quiet as you are, learning anything about you is difficult. But I see a hard-working, honest man. And a handsome man even if you don't."

"I appreciate your kindness." Which he did. She'd asked to play checkers about the time being with so many people was beginning to get the best of him. Especially being with so many people who had family when he didn't. Again, she'd somehow figured out his thoughts.

"You're very welcome." Her grin stretched across her face.

Was she changing her mind about her future? If so, could he? He was getting used to listening to her talk. Some days enjoying listening to her. But what did he do about so many vivid memories about Georgia coming back to haunt him again? Keeping his promise to himself not to become entangled with anyone with family problems was getting harder by the day.

"I made my first move. Again." She leaned closer. "Is something bothering you? You look deep in thought."

"I've had a lot on my mind lately." He moved a checker.

She took her eyes off him long enough to slide another checker forward. "I'm willing to listen if you'd like. You've spent hours and hours listening to me."

"Maybe not that long." He studied the board to figure out his next move. He'd rather flirt than have a serious discussion with her or anyone else.

"Whatever your past troubles are, you've learned to handle them and forgive the people who caused them. I hope to make peace with my past hurts as well as you have."

"Some days are more peaceful than others." He jumped one of her checkers.

"Days like this with a crowd of people where you can't have your solitude aren't pleasant for you." She flashed him an impish grin. "Especially if you think you can beat me." She maneuvered a checker in front of his, forcing him to take a jump. She took three of his checkers, including his only king, with her next move.

He appreciated her diversion and the way she changed the subject. Maybe if he ever told anyone the entire story about leaving Georgia, Heidi would be the person he'd feel most comfortable talking to. She knew firsthand what it was like for family to turn on you.

They played and talked until Charlotte and Francisca, followed by Lily, came into the kitchen to gather up their dishes and go home.

Lily paused beside them. "Who's winning?"

"We've won one apiece. This game will break the tie." Heidi moved a king closer to one of Jethro's kings.

They set the game aside to return to the porch and tell everyone goodbye. Charlotte and Francisca hugged Mrs. Grimes and Heidi then Ella and Harvey. Charlotte hugged her brother. David, Eduardo, and the boss shook with each other. Looking each other in the eyes while exchanging heartfelt expressions of "take care of yourself" as Jethro watched the whole proceeding. David and Eduardo shook with Jethro after that.

The Grimes family and Heidi stood in the yard and waved their company off until the Shepherd's buggy and the men riding horseback were well on their way. Jethro stood slightly behind

Heidi. Not close enough to be a part of the family farewell but near enough to not appear standoffish and uncaring.

As Heidi had observed, a day like this wasn't peaceful for him. But not because he couldn't have his usual time to himself. For the first time in years, he wished he wasn't alone. That he had someone to miss when they drove away. Someone who would miss him.

## 19

Heidi stacked the last clean plate on the shelf. "With the men not here, it doesn't take as long to do dishes."

"Yes, but they'll be back from their ride in time for supper tomorrow and expecting a big meal, so we'd best enjoy cooking a little less while we can." Lily rubbed her back as she spoke.

"I'll bring the clothes in since it started clouding up while we ate. You put Harvey down for his nap and rest some too." Heidi didn't like how tired Lily sounded and acted even after their usual easy Sunday yesterday. Maybe Thanksgiving had been too much for her.

"An aching back is normal for this time."

"Maybe so, but I'll do the ironing too."

"We'll see about that." Lily slipped her apron over her head. "I'll be out to help you after I settle Harvey in his room."

Heidi grabbed both laundry baskets off the back porch while Lily tended to Harvey. The clouds were getting darker to the north. This time of year, northers could come in quickly. She didn't want a downpour soaking all their dry clothes and sheets. Ella came with her. She was too small to carry much, but Heidi could hand her shirts and towels to put in the baskets and unpin the clothes faster.

189

"Ruckus must know the weather's fixin' to change. He wanted in the barn before lunch." Ella glanced at the sky as Heidi handed her a dish towel.

"God made animals so they know before we do sometimes." The wind picked up enough to whip Heidi's skirt around her legs. "I'll finish this. You go on in the house."

"Yes, ma'am." Ella scampered off, looking glad to do as she was told.

Hoping Lily would stay inside, Heidi returned her attention to the sheets now billowing in the wind. Lily stepped outside as Ella reached the porch.

"Aunt Heidi told me to go in."

"Good idea. I'll go help Heidi."

"I can take care of this myself." Heidi gripped a sheet with both hands as she unpinned it.

"As I keep telling Toby, I'm not a delicate china doll." Lily hurried off the porch.

Halfway to the clothesline, Lily cried out as she fell to the ground. Heidi tossed the sheet in the basket then ran to her sister.

"Are you all right?" Heidi knelt next to Lily.

"I tripped." With her skirt wound around her ankles, Lily struggled to sit.

Heidi took hold of her arm. "So I saw. Let me look at you before you try to stand. Can you move your arms?" She'd seen Lily try to catch herself as she fell.

Lily flexed her fingers then bent and unbent her arms. "My arms are all right."

"I think so. I didn't see you hit your head." Heidi studied her sister, carefully checking for signs of damage.

"No. I'm rattled but fine. Help me unwind my skirt so we can get the clothes in case a storm is coming in." Lily tugged at her skirt.

"I'll help you to your feet and into the house. Nothing else."

Lily groaned as soon as she put her weight on her right foot.

Heidi grabbed her arm to keep her from collapsing. "Lean on me. We have to get you inside. If it rains, it rains. I can wash the clothes again later."

Heidi managed to settle Lily onto the couch in the parlor as a concerned Ella trailed behind. "Your ma fell and needs to rest. If she wants a glass of water, you can bring it to her."

"Ma, are you going to be all right?" Ella hovered inches from the couch by her mother.

"Yes, dear. I need to rest a while."

"I'll bring the clothes in. You be a good helper for your ma and me." Heidi smiled at her niece as she patted her shoulder. "Your ma will be fine after she rests."

Ella nodded.

Heidi rushed back outside. The temperature was dropping. She could see shafts of rain in the distance and smell it coming. She carried the laundry baskets in minutes before the rain started. Dumping the baskets in the kitchen, she went to check on Lily. "How are you?"

"I'm all right."

"I should check your foot and ankle."

Lily shook her head. "That's not necessary."

"I think it is." Heidi knelt then started unbuttoning Lily's right shoe. She gently massaged her right ankle. "It doesn't feel swollen or broken."

Lily gingerly flexed her foot. "No. I probably twisted it a little."

"I think you're right. But you need to stay off your feet for a while. Thank God you didn't break your arm or worse." Heidi stood and then studied Lily once more to be sure she was truly all right.

"Yes, thank God."

"Do you need anything before I go to the kitchen to heat the irons?"

"Bring me my mending basket, please. I might as well do something useful."

"I'll get it." Ella was halfway out of the parlor by the time Heidi stepped back from the couch.

The gentle autumn rain beat a soothing rhythm the rest of the afternoon. Heidi did the ironing while Ella helped her mother and watched Harvey after he woke from his nap. After putting away the clean clothes, Heidi went to the parlor to check on Lily. "How are you feeling?"

"A little sore, but I can walk carefully and help you start supper soon. The men might come back later today since the rain hasn't let up. We should fix a stew that's easy to keep warm for them."

"Stew would be good. I can do that."

"I've darned every hole in Toby's socks, replaced every missing button on his shirts, and let out the hems of two of Ella's dresses. I've done enough sitting this afternoon." She pushed to her feet and winced.

"I disagree." Heidi took hold of Lily's left arm. "I'll help you walk around a little so you don't get stiff, but that's all you need to do for now."

Lily shook her head.

"You don't need to fall again." Heidi grinned at her sister. "As you keep saying, I'm worse than Toby."

"Yes, you are."

By the time the stew was done, Heidi was quite proud of everything she'd accomplished. She walked beside Lily to see her sister seated at the table safely. Then set Harvey in his highchair. "I'll fill the bowls, and we'll be ready to eat."

Lily offered the blessing for the food and thanked God for Heidi. "I'm so glad God sent you here."

"So am I." She hated to think what might have happened if she hadn't been able to come here. Frieda would have still helped her escape. But starting a new life totally alone in a strange town would have been so much harder than having Lily and Toby's help and loving support.

If Papa threatened her again, she might have to move

somewhere unknown. Such complete isolation no longer appealed to her. Heidi hoped and prayed the letter she'd sent to Frieda would keep her father from ever seeking her out. What if they burned her letters too? Then they'd never learn the tiny lie she'd told about being engaged to Jethro.

Toby threw open the back door, letting in the colder air. He shut the door behind him and then removed his hat. "Sure feels good in here. Smells good too."

"Pa!" Ella sprang from her chair and ran to hug him then stepped back. "You're all wet."

Toby patted her head. "Yeah, I am."

"Ma hurt her foot. Aunt Heidi and I've been taking good care of her."

"What happened?" Toby closed the distance between him and Lily in an instant.

"I twisted my ankle. I can still walk if Heidi would let me."

"Sounds like Heidi's been doing exactly what I'd have done if I'd been home." He caressed her cheek as he gazed into her eyes.

"She tripped and fell in the back yard." Heidi wanted Toby to know what had happened.

Toby knelt beside Lily, taking her hands in his. "Are you really all right, darlin'?"

"Yes, I am. My ankle is only a little sore."

A look of sheer relief played across Toby's face. He kissed her hands and then rested his head on her lap. "Thank God."

Heidi tried to concentrate on the bowl of stew in front of her instead of staring at the intimate exchange between Lily and Toby. What would it be like to have someone care for her the way Toby adored Lily?

"Where's Jethro?" Blurting out her question wasn't a good way to interrupt Lily's and Toby's moment, but Heidi needed to know why Jethro hadn't walked in yet. Not needed, wanted. Just as she'd be concerned about any friend.

Toby stood then grinned in her direction. "He's at his place changing into dry clothes. I'll get out of my wet clothes and be back real quick to eat what smells like a delicious stew." He kissed Lily's cheek before leaving the room.

As Heidi stood by the stove ladling stew into a bowl for Toby, Jethro walked inside. He must have scrubbed any dirt from his face and taken extra care with his still damp hair. Which would explain why Toby had already changed clothes and returned to the kitchen. "Smells like I picked the right time to come."

"You sure did. Have a seat." Toby motioned toward Jethro's usual chair.

While Heidi filled a bowl for Jethro, Ella told him what had happened to her mother. "I helped Ma watch Harvey while Aunt Heidi did everything else."

"I'm glad you and your aunt were here to help." Jethro smiled at Heidi as she set the stew in front of him. His fingers brushed hers for just a moment.

Heidi could feel Jethro's touch the rest of the meal. No matter how quickly it had happened, he'd deliberately lifted his hand from the table to hers. More than the stew warmed her from head to toe as she ate. Then chilled her as she pondered what her next step would be after she left this house.

---

JETHRO SPENT the next morning helping Mr. Grimes check the roofs on the house and outbuildings after yesterday's high wind had blown a few shingles off the bunkhouse roof. He tossed the hammer to the ground after nailing down the last loose shingle. Ella and Ruckus approached Mr. Grimes as Jethro climbed down the ladder.

She grinned up at her pa. "Ma says lunch is ready."

"Jethro and I'll be ready to eat as soon as we clean up." The boss matched the little girl's steps the way he usually did as they walked toward the well.

Ella told him what she'd helped her mother and Heidi do the way she did whenever she walked with Mr. Grimes. After he cleaned up, she'd take his hand and not let go until they stepped inside the kitchen. His sister had trailed along with Father like that when she was Ella's age. Another memory he could think about that didn't make his heart ache. Wouldn't haunt him at night and rob him of sleep.

The simple lunch of dried beef, buttered bread, and onions tasted wonderful after climbing up and down a ladder all morning. He hoped the next front that blew in didn't damage roofs again. Riding for miles checking on cattle was a lot less work.

After everyone finished eating, Heidi rose and started stacking dirty plates. Mrs. Grimes placed her hand on Heidi's arm. "Ella can help me with the dishes. You've earned an afternoon of painting or drawing. Especially since the wind died down and the sun's out."

"Thank you, but not today. I promised Toby an apple pie for dessert. Remember?"

"It can wait. So can what little I planned to do this afternoon. Jethro, if you want to, go relax while Heidi paints. After riding home in the rain yesterday, you deserve an easy afternoon."

Heidi looked across the table at Jethro. "If you don't want to go with me, I can stay close to the house."

Her intriguing blue eyes no longer reminded him of Louisa. Instead they were like an invitation to get to know her better. Which meant he should tell her no. "I wouldn't mind soaking up a little sun while you draw or paint." He had to get better at keeping his heart from overrunning his mind and his mouth. He hadn't had any nightmares about Georgia lately. He'd like to keep it that way.

"Thank you."

He hitched the horse to the buggy and then drove into the yard so Heidi could load her paints up more easily. As had become her routine, she stepped onto the front porch carrying her satchel when she saw the buggy. "I'll help you carry whatever else you want to take."

"I only need my stools today. I'm not going to paint."

He followed her in the house to get the stools. With Mr. and Mrs. Grimes watching them, she let him carry both stools outside.

After he helped her into the buggy, she took the reins. "The way that norther blew in yesterday, I was afraid it might be cold instead of pleasantly brisk today. I'm glad for good weather in December."

"So am I. This is much better than our ride home yesterday."

"I'm sure it is." She halted the buggy not far from the barn. "I only need to be out of sight from Lily today. I'm doing special drawings for her for Christmas."

"That's nice." As she climbed out of the buggy, he ground tied the horse. He doubted he'd ever see the day it didn't bother him to not help her down. Why she didn't want his assistance bothered him much more now than worrying about losing his manners. He didn't like thinking about her leaving in a couple months.

She soon settled onto a stool with her sketch pad and pencils. "I brought the other stool so you don't have to sit on the wet cool ground."

"I appreciate that." He sat close enough to be able to see her drawings but not so close she'd wonder if he had other motives. He thought more highly of her every day. But unless she decided to change her future plans, he needed to rein in his wayward ideas. As badly as Mr. and Mrs. Grimes seemed to want him and Heidi together, he hoped his job wouldn't be in jeopardy if Heidi continued to shun marriage with anyone.

As usual, she was soon concentrating on her sketches to the point he might as well have been in the next county. She was meticulously copying a drawing of a man about his age.

"You're not doing a landscape today?" He hoped his innocent-sounding comment didn't give away why he was so curious about who she was sketching. Since she had no intention of being romantically involved with any man, he assumed her subject was a relative. But the desire to know for sure overwhelmed him.

"No. I'm copying a sketch I made from the last photograph of Otto. It was taken not long before he died. Hopefully Lily will like this for Christmas."

"I'm sure she will."

Heidi sighed. "I drew the first picture not long before Johann came along. I intended to give my parents sketches from old photographs of me, Greta, Otto, and my other brother, Heinrich, for Christmas this year."

"But not one of your sister?"

"No." She sucked in a shaky breath. "They destroyed every likeness of Lily."

Heidi's admission made Jethro wonder what his family had done with the few photographs they had of him as a boy. Probably torn them to pieces or burned them as angry as they'd been with him.

Maybe they'd keep the likeness of the whole family they'd had made before his brothers left for the war? Depended on how much they might still hate him. Thank God bitterness toward them no longer boiled up enough inside him to almost choke him.

"The way they acted is so sad. I will not become bitter like my parents. I tucked sketches I made of them in my trunk." Her pencil started moving again and then paused. She glanced over at him. "But the small canvases I brought with me I intended to use for miniatures of those sketches will be used for other paintings. One of them of Ruckus to give to Ella."

"Better to turn them into something good than stare at them and let them remind you of bad times." He'd learned to do that the hard way too. But had never come as close to sharing his thoughts with anyone as he was doing with Heidi.

She smiled for the first time since she'd started drawing. "Ella will be delighted with a painting of her dog. A very happy use for one of my small canvases." She stared off toward the barn. "I'll have to think of something happy for the other one."

"Good idea." Maybe if he could do what he'd suggested she do, he could better cope with the memories that had come back to disturb him again.

"But what do you do when you can't think of anything happy about the way your family betrayed you? I don't ever want to see my parents again unless they tell me they were wrong and apologize." Her exaggerated sigh didn't bother him the way it used to.

"What do you do?" He shifted on the stool, almost tipping it over. "They may never say they're sorry. Forgiving people anyway takes God's help. Not forgiving can eat *you* up."

"Says the man who has experienced such a thing, or he couldn't be so helpful to me." Her tender expression offered sympathy as no one had ever done before.

He nodded. He couldn't choke out a single word if he had to.

"I've done more than enough meddling in your life again. I'll work on my sketches and leave you to your thoughts." She turned back to the pad of paper in her lap.

"Pray for me, and I'll pray for you." Something else he'd never asked for or offered to anyone since he'd left Georgia. Her bright smile gave him her reply.

## 20

Heidi took care of Lily and the household for the next week as much as possible. As much as her stubbornly independent sister would allow. Yet this same self-reliant woman persisted with hints Heidi should carefully pray about God's will for her life, especially concerning marriage. Preferably to Jethro the way Lily and Toby worked to see Heidi and Jethro had plenty of time together. Lily, of all people, should understand Heidi's wishes.

She truly was praying for God's will. But the more she learned to do while staying with Lily and Toby, the better she'd be able to take care of herself. Or her and Jethro? Thoughts of the man who listened to her as no one else ever had popped unbidden into her mind much more than they should. Especially if she wanted to never answer to anyone again.

While Lily put Harvey down for a nap on Wednesday afternoon, Heidi carried the butter churn to the porch, intending to start churning before her sister could come out to do it herself.

"Look how fast I can run, Aunt Heidi." Ella rushed past the steps, followed by her faithful dog.

"I see."

Lily stepped out the door. "We'd better take advantage of such an unusually warm day while we can." She pulled a chair over to the churn before Heidi could grab one. "Thank you for carrying this outside for me. I can still sit and churn butter. I'd appreciate it if you'd get a ham from the smokehouse."

"I'll start supper in a little while too."

Lily shook her head.

"I'm not arguing with you about the butter. Don't argue with me about cooking now that you don't have to worry about me ruining everything." She grinned at Lily.

"You're worse than Toby telling—"

A ferocious bark from Ruckus interrupted the rest of Lily's words.

"Ma, I see a buggy coming." Ella pointed east. "There's a man and a lady this time. Nobody's riding next to them."

Heidi trotted down the steps. Lily made her way off the porch as quickly as she could, shading her eyes with her hand to get a better look at the approaching buggy.

"*Gutentag*." Papa waved as he called to them.

"Father? Mother?" Lily's hands covered her heart as she stared in the direction of the buggy, a couple of hundred yards away.

Heidi groaned. "I have to talk to Jethro. Now"

"What?" Lily turned her full attention to Heidi.

"Remember the letter I mailed to Mama and Papa the last time we went to town?" Heidi kept her voice low, wishing Lily would do the same.

"The one you said you wrote to say goodbye?" Lily switched to a whisper.

"Yes. I added a little more than I told you. I wrote that Jethro and I are engaged."

Lily's jaw dropped. "You didn't. "

"I did. The letter I put in with yours to Frieda was the truth. I told her what I'd written to Mama and Papa and why. I asked her to tell them I was engaged if they didn't read my letter."

"Why? What were you thinking?" Lily's knitted eyebrows and curt tone said she was not sympathetic.

"Since they hate cowboys so much I thought ... well, hoped, they'd leave me alone the way they did with you after you and Harvey married. Please pretend what I said is true until I can explain everything to Jethro."

Heidi grabbed her skirt, hiked it up, then ran toward the barn, hoping Jethro and Toby hadn't finished fixing the barn door and gone to do something else. She'd worry later about what everyone thought of her for exposing her stockings and petticoats.

She halted by the door, gasping for breath as she caught sight of the men.

"Something wrong?" Toby tossed his hammer to the ground as his gaze darted past her toward the house.

"Very." She sucked in air. "Not Lily. *Mutter* and *Vater*—my parents." Heidi took another frantic breath before she could manage more words and get her rattled thoughts together enough to keep from speaking German again. "Their buggy should be—in the yard by now."

Toby scowled as he marched past her. Heidi grabbed his sleeve and stared into his eyes. "They think Jethro proposed."

"How?" Toby and Jethro asked in unison.

She turned her gaze toward Jethro. He clenched his jaw. She hoped his Christianity would win out. Before he spoke, she answered Toby. "I told them in a letter." Words flooded out so fast she hoped the men would understand. "Please pretend I didn't lie. Jethro ... I ... I'm sorry."

Toby jerked his arm from Heidi's grasp and trotted toward the house. "Sorry to leave you to this mess alone, Jethro, but I'm going to see about Lily."

"I'll be fine, boss." Jethro called to Toby's retreating back. His stern looks aimed in her direction signaled Heidi might soon be anything but fine.

She gulped in more air. "I'm sorry I lied about you—about us to my parents."

His stony expression didn't change as he continued to glare down at her. She'd never seen this calm man look so upset. Yes, she'd lied. But judging from the way he'd been acting lately, hadn't he been thinking about being more than friends with her? Just a little?

"I'm not trying to excuse what I did, but could I explain why?" She wrung her hands. "Please."

"This should be interesting."

"I've told you some of how Papa and Mama disowned Lily when she married Harvey. She hadn't seen or heard from them in seven years until Papa surprised us in October. I wrote them saying you had proposed, thinking they'd never want to see me again."

"Really?" His countenance softened slightly.

"Yes, really." She licked her dry lips. "I didn't think they'd read my letter."

"They must have if they're here now." His sarcastic tone combined with his severe scowl might not bode well for her.

"Or Frieda told them what I wrote and asked her to say. I didn't lie to Frieda."

He shook his head. "Either way, you lied to them."

She swallowed hard. "Yes. I didn't intend to cause you problems or drag you into mine. If I'd known they'd come here, I wouldn't have done such a thing." She took in another deep breath. "I'm so sorry. As awful as it sounds, I wanted to find a way to be sure they'd never want to see me again. It hurts too much to see them ..." She couldn't finish the rest of her explanation. "As strange as it may seem to you, I can't put my feelings into words right now."

HER ADMISSION of pain ended every bit of Jethro's resolve to stay furious with her. Being even a little aggravated with her wasn't possible now. Not after all he'd been through with his family. He knew too well how it felt to not want to hurt anymore. Plus, he still understood her desire for independence despite sometimes wishing she might change her mind. Crazy as her idea was, she'd meant well.

"So what exactly did you tell them?"

She closed her eyes as she took another deep breath. Maybe this was her way of mustering the courage to answer his question. Or think of an excuse she'd said she wouldn't give him. When she opened her eyes, she stared straight into his.

"I told them you proposed about a week before I wrote the letter. You were watching me paint a sunset. You complimented the beautiful colors and as you gazed into my eyes and said what you were really looking at was more beautiful than any painting in the world. Then you told me you wanted to share moments like this with me forever and asked me to be your wife. And I said yes, of course."

"Of course. I doubt I've ever met a lady who'd say no to such an eloquent proposal."

"I suppose so." She sighed. "Except you're a man of few words and would never make a speech like that. I hope Toby doesn't laugh out loud if my parents mention the details."

She'd come to know him better than he'd planned while she painted. But the way she assumed he'd never say any such thing to any woman bothered him. He might. Maybe even to the talkative one standing in front of him. She'd grown on him much more than he'd like to admit, especially to her. "I'm assuming your parents won't stay here long since your papa only spent one night here in October?"

"Probably. I can't imagine Papa leaving his wagon works for too long."

"Then I think I can pretend to be your fiancé for a couple of days or so. Sometime after Christmas, you can write them and tell them we decided we weren't suitable for each other." What she'd do after that to keep her papa from bothering her, he wasn't sure. But such a resourceful woman was bound to think of something.

"You'd really do that for me?"

He nodded. "Friends help each other out."

"Thank you. I can't tell you how much this means to me."

Except without an easel in front of her, he was sure she could and would tell him if they lingered here too long. "So should we head toward the house?"

"Yes ... I suppose we should."

She didn't sound the least bit enthusiastic. At least lying seemed to bother her. He extended his hand toward her. Her eyes widened. "I've never seriously courted a lady, but I think we should hold hands if we want to properly convince your parents we're in love."

"Oh, uh, yes." She took his hand.

"And smile when you look at me." He grinned down at her. "You have to have some experience with male callers. Just treat me like one you're glad to see."

"The only caller I was happy with married another woman. The other one was probably more interested in Papa's wagon works than me the way Johann behaved."

"Oh." No wonder she wanted to be on her own so badly. If so, why did she flirt with him one day and then talk of friendship the next? She might be as unsure about what to do with him as he was with her.

"One more thing." She halted. "I told Lily a quick version of what I wrote too. So I'm hoping she and Toby will pretend and not be too shocked when they see us holding hands."

"Right."

During their walk to the house, he tried not to think how perfectly her hand fit in his. How natural it felt to be beside her, to match his steps to hers. Maybe because she was upset or fearful of her parents, she said little. He wasn't in the mood for talking, either, as he battled the crazy thoughts being so near her caused.

Everyone stood talking on the front porch when they walked up. The conversation ceased when he and Heidi reached the steps. Mrs. Grimes's grin stretched across her face. Mr. Grimes appeared to be almost as happy as his wife. He doubted they had to pretend to look so thrilled.

"Papa, you met Jethro in October. Mama, my fiancé, Jethro Bannister." She gripped Jethro's hand tighter with every word she spoke.

With his free hand, he tipped his hat to Mrs. Schultz. He'd have to jerk the hand Heidi held away from her so hard he'd make a scene. "Pleased to meet you, ma'am."

Which had to be one of the biggest lies he'd ever told. Knowing how this woman and her husband had tried to force Heidi into a loveless marriage, didn't please him in the least. Mr. Grimes had little regard for his in-laws. Jethro felt the same despite the charade he and Heidi were conducting.

"We'd both like to join in the conversation now, but I need to get a ham from the smokehouse as I told Lily I'd do. I'm sure Jethro wants to clean up and make himself more presentable before visiting with you. So please excuse us." Heidi released his hand and all but bolted in the direction of the smokehouse.

Hoping his forced smile looked natural, Jethro tipped his hat to everyone. "As Heidi said, we'll be with y'all later." He pointed his boots toward his house, wishing he could run instead of walk as if he had all day to get there. Never had he been so grateful for how much or how well Heidi could talk.

He took his dear, sweet time cleaning up. He couldn't remember the last time he'd shaved twice in one day. The mustache he'd started growing a while back was starting to look nice. He'd leave it be. What had come over him that he'd agreed to help Heidi out the way he had? Her pleading blue eyes and quivering lips had bothered him more than they should, especially since he hadn't thought of her in a younger sister way in quite a while.

Which he shouldn't be doing. Breaking his promise to himself about never becoming entangled in family problems again could cause him more heartache than he ever wanted to experience again. And that was only one reason he should avoid the woman he'd spent too much time with lately.

By the time he sauntered over to the main house, everyone had settled into the parlor. Everyone except Heidi. Mrs. Grimes sat in her rocking chair near the fireplace, keeping an eye on Harvey as he stacked his wooden horses and cows. Mr. Grimes had his usual favorite chair by his wife. Leaving the only empty chairs in the room by the couch where Mr. and Mrs. Schultz sat. Two days or so wasn't very long, but the rest of this evening might be one of the longest he'd ever endured.

"Where's Heidi?" He worked to keep his irritation from showing in his voice. She had no right to disappear anywhere and leave him in this kind of situation after what he'd volunteered to do for her.

"She insisted on fixing supper so Lily wouldn't do too much and could have more time with her parents. Ella's helping her." Mr. Grimes's stiff posture hinted he wasn't any happier to be in the room than Jethro was.

Mrs. Grimes smiled included him and her parents. "Heidi has been a godsend coming at just the right time to help me. I don't know what I'd do without her now."

"I'm not at all unhappy she came." Amazing such a whopper didn't choke him. The woman had upset his normal routine since the first time she'd wanted to wander off alone to sketch the house. Upset the promises he'd made to himself in so many ways. Lately trying to decide what to do about her bothered him more than all the changes she'd made in his life.

"*Ja,* I'm sure you aren't." Mrs. Schultz's words didn't sound warm or welcoming.

Mr. Schultz shifted to look straight at Jethro. "You don't

sound like a Texan. Heidi's letter had very few details about the man she wants to wed."

Wants. The man's meaning couldn't be clearer. Which meant he had about two days to help Heidi convince her parents she'd never go back to New Braunfels or anywhere else with them. "*Will* marry, sir."

"Tell me about yourself since my daughter hasn't."

Jethro sat as straight as possible. "I left Georgia about a year after the war was over. One of my cousins had already moved to Texas. He spoke so highly of life here I came to see for myself. I've been here since then."

"He's a very good foreman. He can hire men, completely handle a roundup or a drive into Kansas, or anything else I need him to do." Mr. Grimes's compliment and effort to help the conversation were greatly appreciated.

"How will a ranch foreman take care of my daughter?"

Bristling on the inside, Jethro hoped he wasn't glaring on the outside as he stared back at the man who sounded too determined to challenge him. So determined that he was asking questions he should have saved for a man-to-man talk between him and his future son-in-law instead of in front of others. "Mr., uh, Mr. Schultz, I can provide nicely for Heidi. I'm paid fairly. I also have a house here."

He hoped no one paid too much attention to his obvious verbal stumbling. But beginning his explanation the way he'd almost done by saying Mr. Grimes had built a nice house for his foreman might not be the right thing to say. If he and his boss were supposed to be family soon, they should probably be on a first name basis. The same with Mrs. Grimes. He'd have to ask the boss about that later.

"And you would be content to never give Heidi more than what a foreman can offer?"

No wonder Heidi never wanted to be under this man's roof again. He wondered if he could give Heidi the biggest ranch in Texas if it would be good enough for her father. "I'm saving money every month. But what else I might do someday is up to the Lord. He brought me here and hasn't told me to move on." Finally, a truthful statement.

"How old are you? Heidi's letter didn't mention that either." Mrs. Schultz's thin smile didn't look genuine, but he welcomed the change in the direction of the conversation. Liked the possibility they'd read Heidi's letter.

"Twenty-four, ma'am."

She studied him, maybe thinking about his simple answer. "You were quite young when you left Georgia."

"Yes, ma'am."

"Why did you leave?"

*None of your concern.* Only God knew how he kept from saying aloud the words he wanted to spit out. "Reconstruction and the Yankees ruined a lot of people's way of life in Georgia. I came to Texas for better opportunities."

Mr. Schultz's jaw tightened. His wife's eyes widened. Jethro wasn't sure why. Maybe they had no idea what had happened in a place as far away as Georgia. Reconstruction in Texas wasn't pleasant, but it hadn't upended this state the way it had in his old home.

What he did know, they could pry all they wanted. He'd say no more about why he'd parted ways with his family. If Mr. or Mrs. Grimes were the type to interfere in his business, he wouldn't have worked here two days, much less a little over two years.

"Toby and I are thrilled to welcome Jethro into our family. He's a good, godly man." Mrs. Grimes smiled straight at Jethro.

Her parents said little after that. Mr. and Mrs. Grimes talked about weather, their family, and other routine topics. He hoped no one minded he didn't add much to the conversation.

What felt like an eternity later, Heidi and Ella finally stepped into the parlor.

"Supper is ready." Heidi's unsmiling eyes signaled her pleasant expression was as painted on as one on her canvas. She led the way to the kitchen. "Mama, Papa, please sit here." She pointed at the intended chairs as Mr. and Mrs. Grimes took their usual spots at each end of the table.

"I get to sit by Aunt Heidi and Ma." Ella seated herself in one of the three chairs across from her grandparents.

Jethro appreciated the girl's unwitting hint the chair next to Mr. Grimes would be his. After he and Heidi seated themselves, she smiled into his eyes while giving his hand a quick squeeze. He smiled back. Mr. Grimes blessed the food and somehow managed to thank the Lord for their guests. Jethro got through the tense meal without choking on anything. Something he was truly grateful for.

"I will help with the dishes." Mrs. Schultz picked up the empty ham platter as Heidi rose to start clearing the table.

"We'll go back to the parlor and wait for you ladies to join us." Mr. Grimes led the way.

Jethro followed behind him and Mr. Schultz. How he wished he was walking with Heidi to her favorite spot to paint instead. He'd be happy to listen to her talk for the next day or two rather than spend more time with her papa. She could even ask him questions about his past.

***

Heidi watched Lily, leaning over Harvey to wash his hands and mouth with a rag. Lily probably didn't want time alone with their mother any more than Heidi did. "Mama, we don't expect company to help in the kitchen. Lily, Ella, and I will clean up."

"Heidi's right, Mother." Lily set her son down from his highchair. "Go visit in the parlor."

"*Nein.*" Mama finished her sentence in German, insisting she'd stay and help.

"I'm sorry if Father didn't tell you we don't speak German in our house." Lily's tone was kind but firm as she slipped her apron on.

Mama shook her head as she carried the last of the dirty dishes to the sink. Heidi braced for whatever her mother might say, surprised she hadn't responded to Lily about language choices. She'd overheard a few bits of conversation from the parlor. None of it had sounded relaxed or friendly, judging by everyone's tone of voice.

"When are you to be married?" Mama's somber expression gave Heidi the impression the date was an upcoming funeral rather than celebration.

"We haven't talked about it yet. Sometime after Lily and Toby's baby comes." She hoped Jethro hadn't already been asked that question and said something different. They had to find a way to go off alone and decide on answers for whatever else her parents might ask.

"I got the table all washed off." Ella set her rag on the counter.

"That's good." Heidi grinned at her niece. "You can help your grandmother dry dishes while I wash and your mother sits back in her chair where she should be."

Instead of her usual protests, Lily did as Heidi said. Why, Heidi couldn't begin to guess. She'd ask Lily later.

"Grandmother, I'll introduce you to Ruckus tomorrow. My dog is the best in the county."

"He's a noisy creature." Mama didn't look too happy about Ella's plans.

"Yes, ma'am. He's real good at stirring up a ruckus. That's how come he got his name."

Ella spent the next several minutes telling her grandmother more about Ruckus than Heidi guessed Mama wanted to know. But what a wonderful way for Mama to learn more about the granddaughter she *should* know. As little as Lily said, Heidi couldn't help wondering if her sister were thinking the same thing.

Heidi used the time to try to think of ways to keep from being alone with her parents tomorrow in case they were planning to try to corner her. Too soon, the dishes and kitchen were clean.

Lily scooped up her son. "Let's go see what the men are doing. Ella, you should take your doll and her table and chairs to play with."

Since she had no other choice, Heidi followed Lily, Mama, and Ella to the parlor. Mama seated herself on the couch next to Papa. The only spot left for Heidi was on the other side of Mama. Next to the chair Jethro occupied. She smiled in his direction as he'd suggested. His eyes sparkled in a way she'd never seen while he held her gaze. He must be as relieved to have a friend sitting beside him as she was.

Did their exchanged glance look adoring? "I assume you and Toby have been telling Papa all about the ranch the way you were so good to do the day you drove me here."

"We've talked some ranching." Jethro's tone didn't sound as if whatever they'd talked about had made for a pleasant conversation.

"Good." She turned her attention to the others "If the weather is still nice tomorrow, I think we should have a family picnic on Toby and Lily's favorite ridge. Ours too."

"That's a wonderful idea." Lily replied before Mama finished opening her mouth. "Don't you think so, dear?"

"As long as you feel up to it." Toby grinned back at her.

Toby and Lily supplied more details about why their ridge was one of the best picnic spots on the ranch, leaving Mama and Papa little chance to say much. Heidi resisted the urge to jump up and hug her sister and brother-in-law.

Harvey left his horses and cows to toddle over and grabbed for one of Ella's treasured doll chairs.

"No!" Ella jerked the toy out of her brother's reach.

The boy whined.

Lily got to her feet. "Time for bed, little one."

"I'll help you make him a pallet in our room." Toby picked up the still-crying boy. "Sorry to end our night like this, everyone."

"Ella, you may stay up a little longer. Heidi, will you show Mother and Father to Harvey's room when they're ready?" Lily asked before following Toby out of the room.

"Of course." How Heidi hoped her parents were tired from their stage ride and would want to retire soon. "Ella, did you show Grandmother your doll or her furniture? Grandfather made a table for my dolls when I was little."

"He did?" Ella picked up her toys and carried them over to the couch. "See how pretty they are?" She went into great detail about how her ma had made Annie's dress and her pa had made Annie's furniture. "They made them for me when I was little, because I was only four then."

Mama's entire countenance softened as she gazed into her granddaughter's serious brown eyes. "Oh, so you're not little?"

"No, ma'am. I'm big enough to help now just the way I helped Aunt Heidi fix supper and helped you dry dishes."

"I'd say you're right." Mama's indulgent smile warmed Heidi's heart.

"I think so too." Papa reached for one of the chairs. "Let me have a better look at this fine chair."

Whatever her parents' motive for coming had been, this special moment had to be one of the real reasons for their visit. She prayed they'd realize that. Perhaps this evening could be one small step toward their family's reconciliation. Except she doubted they were willing to accept she'd take care of herself from now on and never live under their roof again.

Lily soon returned to the parlor. "Time for bed now, Ella."

"Yes, ma'am." Ella leaned toward her grandparents. "I have to hug Grandmother and Grandfather goodnight first."

Heidi's eyes misted as she glanced toward Lily, whose eyes were also glistening with tears.

"Goodnight, everyone." Lily led Ella out of the room.

"Would you please show us where Harvey's room is?" Mama rose. "I'd like to retire a little early. And I assume you and Jethro would like some time alone."

Heidi remembered to smile in Jethro's direction as she stood. "I could get my shawl so we can sit on the porch a while?"

"That sounds good."

She guided her parents to their room for the night, breathing a silent prayer of thanks for how well this unexpected day was progressing so far. Hopefully, time alone with Jethro wouldn't upend things again.

Her heart sped up when she walked into the parlor and spied her supposed fiancé standing by the door, waiting for her. He was a nice-looking man. Handsome really with his wavy light brown hair, kind green eyes, and mustache he'd grown because of her. A little thin. Not as tall or broad-shouldered as Toby, but still quite nice to look at. Add in his pleasant personality, and he might make a wonderful husband—for another woman. A woman who didn't mind having a husband who could tell her what to do.

"Thank you for waiting for me."

"You're welcome." He opened the door for her then took the chair next to her after she seated herself. The lamp still burning in the parlor shone through the window behind them, affording a little light on the porch. He stared off toward the moonlit sky casting dark shadows across the yard.

Maybe he liked to look at the stars, but she wasn't here with him to discover his likes. "Mama wants to know wedding details. Did Papa ask you about it?"

"No."

"Good." She told him what she'd said to her mother. "So we're saying the same thing."

"Right. When she asked me how old I am, I thought we should know each other's birthdays just in case." He scooted his chair to where he could look at her.

The night shadows meant he couldn't see her well. Which she didn't mind since this was only a meeting between friends. "Yes. Um, how old are you? I should know that."

"I'll be twenty-five in April. You're nineteen. When's your birthday?"

"I don't remember telling you my age."

"You mentioned it at supper the first night you were here. Maybe you were so upset you don't remember?"

No, she didn't. But he did? How much attention had he been paying to her? Too much if he could recall anything from the day she'd come here. "My birthday is the twenty-fifth of February."

He sat as if studying her for a moment. "Then maybe you shouldn't write you parents about our disagreement until March so they don't think we ruined Christmas or your upcoming birthday."

"That's a good idea. Plus, by March, I could be living and working in San Antonio without them knowing about it."

"Possibly."

She shifted in her chair. Why was he still watching her so closely? "We should probably know some about each other's families."

"You know family isn't one of my favorite subjects. I left Georgia to never return the way you've left New Braunfels." He stared straight ahead, as if she were no longer sitting next to him.

"I do understand. Only bare details should suffice. I'm the youngest of five. My other older sister, Greta, lives in Minnesota with her husband. They have no children yet. My youngest brother, Otto, died of pneumonia in February last year. That's why Papa wants to find me a husband who can run his wagon works and keep it in the family."

He sucked in a deep breath. "Sometimes businesses should be sold."

"Yes, they should." His terse, bitter-sounding words made her wonder if family businesses were another subject he didn't like mentioning. "Heinrich, the oldest, died fighting in the war. He left home when I was seven. I barely remember him." Since Jethro was from Georgia, she wouldn't tell him Heinrich had slipped out of Texas and fought with the North. No use possibly upsetting Jethro more than he already appeared to be.

"I'm the youngest of five sons. My oldest brother died fighting in the war. Two others died as children, as did my younger sister."

"So you have one brother left?"

He nodded.

"And you'd rather not speak of him?"

"Yeah."

"All right. I doubt I need to know more since Papa and Mama said they're leaving Friday morning."

He turned toward her once more. "I'll head back to my place unless you can think of anything else we should talk about."

"Not right now. Hopefully, Mama or Papa won't ask too many more questions of us."

"I'll see you tomorrow." He rose.

"Yes. Tomorrow."

The slight night breeze chilled her. But she watched him walk away, staring at his back until he disappeared into the night shadows. What painful secrets lay in Jethro's heart? And why did she hurt for him whenever her questions caused him distress?

## 21

Breakfast the next morning was almost pleasant. Heidi's parents didn't ask Jethro any more personal questions. Whatever the reason, he didn't care. He scooted his chair back after everyone had finished eating.

"I'll tend to chores so we can all enjoy the picnic later." He hoped no one noticed he didn't call it *our* picnic. An engaged man would probably think about our more, but he'd never been good at pretending.

"I'll help you." Mr. Grimes stood. He kissed his wife's cheek. "Let us know when to hitch up the wagon, darlin'. I'll tend to your horse and buggy, too, Mr. Schultz."

"*Danke.* Thank you."

"I'll send Ella out when we're ready." Mrs. Grimes patted her husband's arm before he turned to follow Jethro out the back door.

Mr. Grimes let out a long breath as they walked toward the barn. "Never thought I'd be so happy to do chores."

"Neither did I."

The boss grinned in his direction. "I hope they're not going to start surprising us with visits like this whether you might become really engaged to Heidi or not."

"Right. But while I'm pretending to become family soon, what do I call you and Mrs. Grimes? Mr. and Mrs. sounds strange."

"Yeah, it does. Probably better call us Toby and Lily until after they leave."

"I'll try to remember." Jethro opened the barn door, glad something was repaired and working as it should.

"You can practice on me while we work. I'll be sure to tell Lily what we decided before we leave for the picnic."

"Thanks, uh, Toby."

Neither of them rushed through chores. Jethro had thought seriously about volunteering to milk the cow for Heidi to give himself something else to keep him away from her parents. But Heidi would probably welcome milking this morning.

Ella, with Ruckus at her side, came to tell them to hitch the horse to the wagon just before he and Mr. Grimes—Toby—finished. "Ma says saddle her mare for Heidi. She'd rather ride with Mr. Bannister than in the back of the wagon."

Mr. Grimes raised both eyebrows. "That's so? Tell your ma, we'll have everything ready soon."

"Yes, sir."

"Is riding with Heidi all right with you?" Mr. Grimes's eyes twinkled as he waited for Jethro to answer.

"It's better than sitting as close to her in the wagon as a fiancé should."

"That's probably what Heidi's thinking too. Too bad she didn't think clearly before she wrote to her parents." Mr. Grimes led the horse over to the wagon. "But y'all will have to sit next to each other while we eat and visit."

"Yes, sir." He jerked a bridle from a peg.

"Better not call me sir either."

"Right." Something else he hadn't thought of. The Schultz's were leaving tomorrow. He only had to get through today. "At least she didn't tell them we're married."

"Yeah, with her imagination, she could have done a lot worse."

Jethro nodded as he finished saddling Calico for Heidi.

By the time everyone and everything was loaded up, the late morning sun had a good start on a warm day for December. Jethro hoped the temperature was the only thing that heated up. If some kind of family squabble were to start, he'd have no way to escape being in the middle of it. A pretend fiancé would stick up for the woman he loved if needed.

He and Heidi rode behind the Grimes's wagon and her parents' rented buggy.

"I can't thank you enough for being such a wonderful, considerate man." The smile she sent in his direction was the most genuine she'd given him since they'd begun their ruse. Real enough to reveal dimples he'd never noticed before.

"You know I'd do anything for you." If he got any better at lying, the Lord might send a lightning bolt to strike him down without a single cloud in the sky. But as well as every sound carried on such a still day, he'd best say what a man madly in love would say. Good thing his father had been such a fine example of expressing love to his mother so he had an idea what to tell her. What might he say if his heart could speak for itself?

"I'm sure you would do anything I wanted."

Her shining eyes emphasized her too confident-sounding tone of voice. Carrying on a charade to help her lies from being found out didn't make him the kind of self-sacrificing man his words implied. Her too-active imagination had better not be picturing more than he was willing to do. Unless he could come to terms with his painful past and the way she kept reminding him of it.

"I'm so glad we're going to the ridge today. I still want to do some drawings there. We should come again, just us."

"Maybe we should wait. It's a lot prettier in the spring when the grass is greening up and the wildflowers start blooming." He hoped her suggestion wasn't a serious one. Since she might be gone soon, he didn't want to remember one of his favorite spots as one he'd been to with her.

"I'm sure it is. But the contrast of the brown landscape stretching toward the bright sky is pretty in its own way."

She continued talking about sketches and paintings the rest of the way, leaving Jethro to listen and nod the way he usually did during their evenings together. Maybe today wouldn't be too bad.

Mr. Grimes soon halted the wagon at the top of the ridge. "This is why we wanted to bring y'all here. God's handiwork at His finest." He beamed as he gazed out over the rugged, rolling landscape below them. A hawk soared overhead while a half dozen mustangs ran past the grazing cattle.

"Oooh." Heidi sucked in her breath as she took in the scene. "I've never seen so many horses at once. I'd love to paint them too."

He braced for another hint she wanted him to come back with her later. Instead, she sat in silence still looking over the land. With her riding sidesaddle, he had a decent view of her face. A view that might rival the landscape. The blue dress he liked more than he should perfectly emphasized her eyes. The loose pieces of medium blonde hair made a pretty frame for her face. No. She'd be back to talking enough to worry the horns off the nearby cows before the day was over.

Mr. Schultz helped his wife down from the buggy while Mr. Grimes got his family out of the wagon. Jethro dismounted to help Heidi off her horse. He grinned, hoping she'd realize a real fiancé would do such a thing. Her mouth formed a too-pretty *O* as his hands spanned her waist. He couldn't keep himself from looking into her eyes as he set her on the ground while telling his uncooperative hands to let go of her.

She stared back as if she'd never seen him before. A side-long glance told him her parents were carefully watching them. He bent to kiss her, intending to brush her lips with his. She kissed him back. His arms wrapped fully around her waist of their own accord as he deepened the kiss. Then released her and stepped back to gaze into her wide eyes.

She brushed her lips with her fingers. "I'd better help get the food unloaded."

He nodded.

Once the old quilts were spread on the ground and the meal set out, he took the spot next to Heidi. A good distance across from her parents. For a change, Heidi said little while they ate the simple meal of ham sandwiches. Too bad this picnic had come about so quickly Mrs. Grimes didn't have time to make one of her delicious molasses pies.

After everyone finished eating, Mrs. Schultz got a basket from the buggy. "When Lily said she had dried apples, I had to make *apfelkuchen*. My grandchildren must know what this is."

"I helped, didn't I?" Ella beamed at her grandmother.

"Yes, you did. Quite well."

Heidi had mentioned missing the dessert he couldn't pronounce. Whatever they'd made smelled delicious when Mrs. Schultz lifted the towel from the pan. Mrs. Grimes's wrinkled brow signaled she was far from pleased. From what Heidi had said about the way the family had disowned such a sweet lady, he couldn't blame the missus for not wanting anything German around.

Ella watched her grandmother cut the cake and then put pieces on plates for everyone. "Take a plate with a fork to your papa. He has to taste this too."

"It's apple cake, Pa." Ella handed a plate to Mr. Grimes.

"It looks good." Mr. Grimes took a bite. "Very good."

After Jethro tasted his piece of cake, he had to agree with his boss. But only Ella and her grandparents appeared happy about how good the desert tasted. Heidi's wistful expression reminded him of the day she'd talked about German foods she missed. Yet today, she only nibbled on her dessert. He'd probably hear later what she was thinking. Mrs. Grimes wore a much too serious expression for being at a family picnic. She had yet to take a bite of the cake. He understood the bad blood between them. But he hoped he wasn't fixin' to learn more.

After everyone finished eating, Mrs. Schultz nudged her husband's arm. His slight frown indicated he didn't appreciate his wife's gesture. He shifted as if he'd sat on a sharp rock beneath the quilt. Clearing his throat, he looked from Heidi to Mrs. Grimes. "We discovered Johann was not the kind of man he pretended to be."

"Really?" Mrs. Grimes turned her full attention to her father.

"*Ja.* I caught him taking money out of my office. He pushed me so hard he almost knocked me down. He ran away before I could turn him over to the marshal."

Mrs. Schultz rubbed her husband's arm. "Thank God he only ran and didn't try to hurt anyone. He pulled a gun on Kurt Mueller and stole his horse to get out of town."

Heidi's face blanched. Jethro resisted the urge to reach for her hand. Thank God her parents hadn't succeeded with their plans for her and that man.

"He didn't hurt anyone?" Mr. Grimes eyed his father-in-law.

"*Nein,* no."

"Good. Good too that kind of scoundrel is gone before he caused more harm to more people." Mr. Grimes continued staring down Mr. Schultz.

Jethro couldn't help wondering if the boss's statement was a not too-veiled hint about how much harm could have come to Heidi.

"*Ja.* Yes. I'm hoping to find a better man to replace him."

But not a better man to pair Heidi off with. Jethro swallowed his words rather than risk causing a confrontation. Heidi and Mrs. Grimes might still be wishing for or hoping for a reconciliation. Even if they weren't, he didn't want to end up in any kind of family squabble if he could prevent it.

"Right. Someone honest who can be trusted the way I trust Jethro." Mr. Grimes set his fork on his plate.

Jethro appreciated the compliment despite the

circumstances. Heidi's slight smile in his direction hinted she might agree with her brother-in-law.

Mr. Schultz stared past Jethro to Heidi as if he weren't next to her. "So, Heidi, you should come home after Suz—Lily no longer needs your help."

"No, sir." Jethro draped his arm around Heidi's narrow shoulders. She leaned against him close enough he could smell the soap she used to wash her hair. "She's staying here with me where she belongs." Words he did and didn't mean. He couldn't allow this man to bully Heidi, even if she never became more than a friend.

"No, Papa. I won't be coming with you." Unlike her body, her voice didn't tremble.

Mr. Schultz rose then reached his hand toward his wife. "Mathilda, we'll go back to the house and get our things now."

"*Ja.*" Whatever they said to each other was in German.

The boss stood before they got into the buggy. "Please think about what you're doing. Hurting two loving daughters all over again. Deserting grandchildren you've just met."

They halted by the buggy. Mrs. Schultz took a step toward her son-in-law.

Her husband snagged her arm, shaking his head. "We're going. Now." He helped his wife up onto the seat. They drove off in silence, Mr. Schultz's clenched jaw set in a stubborn frown. Mrs. Schultz's mournful expression was the only indication Mr. Grimes's plea might have hit any kind of mark in her heart.

"Where are they going?" Ella turned to her parents.

"Back to New Braunfels." Mrs. Grimes's toneless reply didn't indicate if she were angry, resigned, or what. She reached to pat Ella's back.

Heidi slipped from under his arm and got to her feet. "I'll help you put everything away." Heidi grabbed her and Jethro's plates off the ground then shoved them into the basket.

Mr. Grimes shook his head. "We'll take care of it." Since his wife had yet to move, he turned his attention to wiping Harvey's sticky hands and mouth. "We need some time. Why don't y'all go for a ride."

"Are you sure?" Heidi's gaze went from Mr. Grimes to her sister.

"Yeah. Don't rush back."

Ella still sat pressed into her mother's arms, a look of bewilderment on her face as Jethro helped Heidi up on Calico. Poor Mr. and Mrs. Grimes were going to have one more time explaining to a six year-old girl what had happened.

---

As Heidi and Jethro rode off, Toby started putting the food away while watching Harvey. Lily remained on the quilt. Ella hadn't moved away from her mother. Lily's soft tone sounded as if she were doing her best to comfort Ella. Heidi's heart ached for her niece. The child would never know her grandparents. Which might be for the best as stubborn as Papa and Mama were.

She sighed as she guided her horse south away from the house. She'd gladly give Lily and Toby all the time they needed to talk to Ella and get back home. Jethro rode beside her. For once, she was glad the man wasn't talkative. She wasn't in the mood for conversation.

"You wanted your parents to leave you alone. Sad to say, you got what you wished for." He broke the silence after they'd ridden far enough Lily and Toby couldn't hear them.

"Yes, it is sad. I thought I'd feel so happy, so relieved to never have to worry about them interfering in my life again. Shakespeare lied. There's nothing sweet about the sorrow of parting. Especially when it might be for the rest of your life."

"No, but sometimes it's necessary, even for the best, no matter how upsetting it is." He stared straight ahead.

"Your personal experience mirrors mine more closely than you'd like to say."

He tightened his grip on his reins. "It does."

"But you still don't want to talk about it."

"Right." He kept his gaze focused on whatever he was watching, probably to avoid looking at her.

"But you do agree I'm making the right decision not to go back to New Braunfels." Why she wanted his advice or approval was something she'd have to figure out later. Perhaps because he'd willingly rescued her from having to tell her parents she'd lied about being engaged.

"Yes. I'm guessing if you went back it wouldn't be long before your parents found another business man to saddle you with for life."

"That's why I refused to go with them."

"Yeah. It's rough right now, but God never promised doing what's best or right would be easy."

How she wished he'd give her even a quick glance. Making him so uncomfortable wasn't what she wanted. But she desperately needed reassurance from someone she trusted who had successfully dealt with a problem similar to hers. "Are you at peace with the hard thing you had to do?"

His stiff body relaxed. His lips turned up in a slight smile as he looked her straight in the eyes. "I hadn't thought of it like that. But yes, I do have peace. I have no doubt God wants me right here where I am."

"How long has it taken you to realize that?"

He shrugged. "About the last two years or so I've been here. Watching God work bad things for my good during the years before that. I worked my way to Texas to be with my cousin, but he died of a fever a few weeks before I got to San Antonio."

"Oh, my."

"I ran across a rancher in town looking for hands. I was hungry enough I offered to do any job he needed. He felt sorry for a young man with no roof over his head and hired me. He taught me everything I know about ranching. But that didn't end well, so I started working for Mr. Grimes."

"Then I should consider myself fortunate I could run to Lily and Toby." Perhaps staying here to help her sister and postponing her desire to be on her own had some kind of purpose in God's plan.

"Very fortunate. You couldn't be with better people."

"That includes you too."

"Me?" His eyes widened.

"Yes. You didn't have to volunteer to pretend to be my fiancé and save me from my own lies."

He grinned. "I wouldn't want you back in New Braunfels."

Why exactly, she wouldn't ask. She suspected his concern was more than that of a friend. "Thank you for standing up to Papa for me. You've incurred my parents' wrath from now on. They'll despise you even after I tell them we're no longer engaged."

"That won't matter since I'll never see them again. I'll be fine."

"Just the same, I do appreciate you doing so much more than you had to do."

"You're welcome." Jethro guided his horse closer, his gaze clearly going to her lips.

Was he thinking of stealing another kiss?

"I didn't appreciate you kissing me." As much as she hated to admit it, she hadn't minded. But such a thing could never happen again. She wouldn't be beholden to any man. Even a good man like Jethro. "That wasn't necessary to convince Mama and Papa we're in love."

His jaw dropped. "You kissed me back. Soundly."

"Yes, but I really didn't intend to."

His raised eyebrows hinted he didn't believe her. "I hadn't planned to kiss you, but your parents were watching our every move. The crazy idea came into my head, and I acted without thinking. I'm sorry if I offended you."

"No real harm was done. I accept your apology." Except she wouldn't be upset if he didn't apologize. His kiss upset her only because of the questions it stirred in her soul, causing her to wonder if she could relinquish her dreams of independence for him.

"Shouldn't I have an apology too? You did kiss me back. And soundly."

"I, uh, I ... Well, I suppose so. I shouldn't have kissed you either." As much as she needed to say the words *I'm sorry*, she couldn't force them past her lips.

"Thank you. Mr. and Mrs. Grimes should have had enough time to talk with Ella. Should we turn our horses toward home?"

"Yes, we should. I'm glad Ella is too young to realize everything that happened."

If only Heidi could still be an innocent, naïve little girl. But she wasn't. The afternoon had and hadn't ended well. As Jethro said, she now had her wished-for freedom from her parents even though her hopes for reconciliation had been dashed. Now if she could somehow understand why she'd welcomed Jethro's defense of her as well as having his arm around her shoulders. Not just accepted, but enjoyed his kiss.

She would sort through all those events later. A woman who wanted to live her own life couldn't allow such things to happen again. If God had different plans for her, He'd have to show her in a way she couldn't doubt or mistake His leading. Soon.

## 22

When Heidi and Jethro rode up to the barn, Toby was cinching his saddle. He halted as soon as he saw them. "Ella and I are going for a ride and a little talk while Harvey is napping. Lily's in the kitchen." He huffed out his breath as he glanced up at Heidi. "Lily says she needs time alone, but I'd appreciate it if you'd go see about her. Keep her company if she'll let you."

"I'll do that."

"Thanks." Toby led Smoky away.

Jethro helped Heidi dismount, holding on to her longer than necessary. Again, she didn't mind. "I hope you can help your sister."

"So do I. Especially since this whole fiasco is my fault."

"Not completely. Yes, you lied. But they might have showed up even if you hadn't sent that letter." His gentle voice comforted her.

"You really think so?"

"Yes. I'm glad you're rid of someone who'd trade you off to a man as he would a horse to secure his business. I'm happy I could help you."

"So am I." The tender look in his eyes made it impossible to look away.

But she must. With her parents no longer threatening her, she'd soon be free to make her own choices. What to do with the man in front of her? His kiss. His willingness to stand up to Papa even when defending her lies. He understood her dreams better than anyone else she knew. "I should see how Lily is doing." And walk away from the man she did and didn't want to be so near to.

"Yes, you should. I'll be praying for both of you." His fingers brushed her cheek as he reached for her horse's reins.

She mustered every ounce of strength she had not to lean her head into his hand. "Thank you. I can always use prayers."

He nodded. Again, his gaze lingered on her lips. She stepped away. If he took her in his arms, she'd stay right there. Instead, she turned toward the house.

"Go try to help your sister. I'll see to our horses."

*Our* horses. She walked away without mentioning the word he must have misspoken since he hadn't acted surprised at what he'd said or corrected himself. Even if Calico belonged to her instead of Lily, Heidi was not thinking of anything she owned in terms of ours. With Jethro or anyone else. If she moved to town, there would be no ours. Only hers.

When Heidi walked into the kitchen, Lily stood at the worktable stirring something in a mixing bowl. "What are you making?"

"Molasses pies. I have to get the smell of *apfelkuchen* out of my kitchen." Lily cracked an egg into the bowl so hard she almost crushed it. "I threw the rest of Mother's desert out before we loaded up the buggy. I'd rather leave it for the animals to eat."

"I can make the pie crust while you stir the filling." Heidi had no desire to eat *apfelkuchen* again either. She slipped her apron over her head.

"I'd like that. The sooner the pies are baking, the better."

Lily stirred the eggs in with a fury Heidi never dreamed she'd see from her sister.

With both of them working, they soon had two pies in the oven. "Sit. You need to rest." Heidi pulled out Lily's chair.

Lily slid into the chair. Heidi took the one beside her. "I'm so sorry."

"For what?"

"If I hadn't written that letter, none of this would have happened." Heidi closed her eyes, wishing she could undo what she'd done.

"Look at me." Lily placed her hand on Heidi's arm. "*You* are not to blame. Father probably started thinking how to get you to come back as soon as he found out the truth about Johann. He'd have come anyway."

"Jethro told me that too."

"Listen to him. He's a good man." Lily's smile lit up her tired-looking eyes.

"I'm praying about that." Which she was, but she didn't want to talk about Jethro right now. "I feel terrible about what happened." Heidi breathed in the welcome scent of molasses, and nutmeg beginning to waft through the kitchen. "After watching Mama and Papa with Ella, I hoped they might want to get to know their only grandchildren."

Lily sighed. "I see little hope for them if our sweet Ella can't soften their hard hearts."

"I'm working to forgive them. I think one day I have, then on days like this ..." Heidi let the rest of her words go unfinished, sure Lily would know what she meant. How Lily stayed so calm, was more than Heidi could fathom.

"I understand what you mean." Lily patted Heidi's arm. "Forgiving is one thing. Forgetting is another. Jesus said to pray for our daily bread. Sometimes we have to pray to forgive daily. At least I do."

"How do you keep from being bitter?"

"A lot of prayer. I never want to be like them. Even though

we were the ones to leave, they pushed us away. Forced us to choose between love or a business arrangement that benefitted Father instead of us."

Now wasn't the time for Heidi to mention she hadn't chosen to leave for love as Lily had. Yet or not at all? The stress of last night and this morning had muddled her mind and emotions. "They tried to force you too?"

Lily nodded. "Gunther Eichmann. Having a family blacksmith to make the tires for Papa's wagon wheels would have been very good for business."

"That's why Toby says Gunther's not welcome here." Heidi had wanted to know why since the day the man guided Papa here in October. Too bad the opportunity to satisfy her curiosity had come at such a trying time.

"Partly. Toby and I might tell you the rest some other time. But don't hold me to that."

Whatever else Lily was holding inside, Heidi wouldn't ask. For once, she'd keep quiet instead of blurting out what she shouldn't. Jethro would be happily shocked to know she could hold her tongue at times.

If she told him. She'd confided so much to him lately. When she moved to San Antonio, he wouldn't be close by to talk to. She didn't want to think about what missing him might mean for her future.

"You must to be doing some deep thinking since you look just shy of a frown." Lily interrupted Heidi's musings.

"I am. I might tell you about it someday."

"I'll wait until you're ready. When you asked why I'd given up our German roots, I didn't tell you the answer completely."

Heidi leaned toward her sister. "I'd like to know but only if you feel up to telling me."

"Maybe explaining can help you. I did it at first out of anger. But I gradually discovered speaking only English or not having things that reminded me of what had happened help me not to hurt as much. I fill my mind with pleasant memories or thoughts of blessings I have. What is here now instead of dwelling on the pain Father and Mother caused me."

"I think I understand." Jethro had done the same thing by not talking about or thinking about whatever had hurt him years ago. Something else she'd keep to herself, since Jethro had told her things he hadn't told anyone else. He'd be so proud of her for not saying what she shouldn't twice in such a short time.

"Enough talk about this morning." Heidi smiled at Lily. "Have you and Toby decided what to name your new little one?"

The sparkle returned to Lily's eyes. Not continuing to relive their painful past was good for both of them.

"Daniel Peter for a boy. After Toby's father and late younger brother. Rebekah Ann after his mother for a girl"

"I like both of those."

While the pies finished baking, they talked of Christmas coming soon and gifts each of them was making for other family members. Lily thought Heidi's idea for painting a miniature of Ruckus for Ella and one of Smoky for Toby was wonderful. Heidi was happy to have decided how to use her other small canvas to make a pleasant memory for her and someone else. Another thing Jethro would be happy to know.

---

Jethro walked toward the main house for breakfast, thankful for a Sunday to rest and focus his thoughts on the Lord. The last two days had been blessedly uneventful. After the short visit from Heidi's parents, he'd thank God for every mundane day he could have. He paused to watch the sun finish coming up over the nearest ridge where Heidi liked to go to and paint sunsets.

Maybe they'd start their days together someday, and he could watch her paint a sunrise instead. He shook his head to clear his mind of such a crazy idea. The short time her parents had stayed proved again why he didn't want to entangle himself with a woman who had her kind of problems. Mr. and Mrs. Schultz were probably gone for good. But if not, he wanted nothing to do with any future visits from people who reminded him of how his own family had turned on him.

Plus, Heidi still intended to leave after Mrs. Grimes's baby came. Or so she said often enough whenever they were alone. The more he thought about how she'd kissed him back, the more he wondered if she might change her mind.

If so, with God's help, he might be able to change his mind about loving her despite her problems with troublesome parents or how much she talked. Yet the better he got to know her, the less her wordiness bothered him. She wasn't the only one who'd been doing a lot of praying about what God might want. For them. If she weren't praying about possibly including him in her life, he was already setting himself up for the kind of heartache he'd promised himself he'd never endure.

"Mornin', Jethro." Mr. Grimes greeted Jethro from his spot on the floor next to Harvey.

"Good morning." He inhaled the smell of bacon and eggs as he closed the door.

"Aunt Heidi is fixing pancakes." Ella beamed at him as she set plates on the table.

"That's good." As was the sight of Heidi, even with her back to him as she stood by the stove. He wasn't the least bit unhappy to see her wearing the blue flowered dress she'd made a while back.

Breakfast was delicious as usual. With Mrs. Grimes's help, Heidi was becoming a fine cook. Cutting up his egg with the too soft yoke reminded him how he might tell Heidi one day the way he liked eggs.

After the unsettling visit from Heidi's parents, Jethro looked forward to the time of Bible reading, prayer, and singing they'd have once chores were done and the kitchen cleaned. He gladly followed Mr. Grimes to the parlor after they washed up from finishing chores. The ladies and children soon joined them.

Mr. Grimes picked up his Bible after everyone was seated.

"I'll read from the fourth chapter of Philippians, verses eight and nine. These are some of Lily's favorites, for good reason."

Jethro turned to the verses in his Bible. He could quote them from memory. He closed his eyes to think about the words that had helped him so often after leaving Georgia. Think about whatever is true, honest, just, pure, lovely, things of good report or virtue.

"If I had done what the Bible says, I would have had a lot less problems after I came home from the war. We've all had a rough time this week. Don't make the mistakes I made. Take care of your troubles God's way."

Mrs. Grimes reached over Ella sitting between her and her husband on the couch to pat his arm. "I'm so proud you do things with God now."

They talked about the verses for a while. No one mentioned Mr. or Mrs. Schultz by name. Jethro didn't know if it was because Ella was with them or because no one wanted to say their names any more than he did.

After praying with each other, Mrs. Grimes led them in singing *Amazing Grace*. As he did every Sunday, Jethro thanked God for giving him a good job with a Christian boss. He had so many blessings.

Yet he enjoyed his usual time to himself the rest of the morning. The barn, corral, and bunkhouse were closer to him than the boss's house. Another thing he liked about working on the *Tumbling G*. Looking out from his porch and doing nothing but soaking in the quiet was one of his favorite times to think and pray. After a little over two years of enjoying his own place, he was quite comfortable with his own company.

A few minutes before noon, he walked to the main house. The simple cold lunch would be fine too. If Heidi wanted to enjoy the pleasant sixty-five degree day, he'd go with her and watch her paint. She'd definitely grown on him. Like her, he was till praying about that.

By two o'clock, Heidi guided the buggy out not far from the

outbuildings. "I'm still working on family sketches for Lily. I could do these from the yard if I didn't want to surprise her. Thank you for coming with me so she doesn't suspect what I'm doing."

"You're welcome." He ground tied the horse while she took her stools out of the buggy. Something else he'd never thought he'd get used to doing while watching a lady carry things herself.

As he'd done the last time she'd sketched, he seated himself on the stool she wasn't using. This time he scooted it close enough to watch her draw while he soaked in the stark beauty of the fall countryside. "I thought of a possible problem for you since the last time we were out here."

"Yes?" She turned to look at him.

"Your sister has never said a word about family since I've worked here. Will she like these drawings you're spending so much time and effort to do?"

"I wondered the same thing, so I asked Toby before starting. He said she'd like pictures of her siblings."

"That's good."

"We do have some happy memories. Like the verses we read this morning said, I'm choosing to think about lovely and true things. Lily and I had a good talk about forgiving and not dwelling on the bad parts of our past." She lifted the satchel leaning against her stool onto her lap. "I'll draw Heinrich in his uniform today. He's the brother who died in the war who I barely remember."

"If he left at the start of war, you were only seven. Right?"

"Yes. I never saw him again. We didn't find out until after the war that he'd died in '64."

"Maybe that was for the best. You have only good memories even if they're vague. I was twelve when my oldest brother went to war in '61. The brother I was closest to." He took a deep breath. He'd never mentioned such things to anyone since he'd left Georgia. "Michael died in battle the next year. I remember my parents receiving the letter from a friend telling how my brother died and everything that happened after the letter came."

"But you can talk about such a horribly sad time now. I admire your strength."

"That's all from God, not me. It wasn't and sometimes still isn't easy." He didn't elaborate. Her problems had brought back too many bad memories lately he didn't want to talk about.

As if she sensed his reluctance to say more, she slipped the drawing she wanted to copy out of the satchel. How she managed so well to figure out his feelings was something he should ask her one day.

Looking over at her original sketch from her brother's photograph, he froze. The insignia couldn't be mistaken. "Was he a Yankee?"

Her face paled. "Yes."

"And you didn't mention that before when you know where I'm from?"

Her eyes widened, probably because of his sharp words and harsh tone of voice. "We've always been told not to talk about him. My brother wasn't the only man from a German town who went North."

Too stunned to speak, he stared at her in silence, trying to absorb the secret she'd purposefully kept from him.

She nibbled on her bottom lip. "I didn't tell you because of where you're from. He died fighting in Georgia."

"Really." Jethro's pulse thundered in his ears. "Where?" He choked out the word.

"Somewhere between Atlanta and Savannah with General Sherman. I don't remember exactly where." Her voice trembled.

Jethro shot to his feet, toppling the camp stool he was sitting on. "No!"

"No?"

Shaking in fury, he stared down at the woman who had no idea of the raging storm she'd unleashed inside him at the mere mention of that general's name. "One of that ... that Yankee's men murdered my father. Shot him when he was trying to protect our home. The rest of them laughed as they stole every bit of food they could carry off from us." Jethro stalked off as she rose then stuffed the picture and her pencils into her satchel.

"Jethro, please." She grabbed his elbow from behind.

He jerked away from her.

"I'm sorry. I ... I didn't intend to hurt you. I had no idea."

He whirled to face her. "Had no idea and still don't." He hurled his words at her.

She shrank from him as if he'd hit her with a real rock. "I was a child. I had nothing to do with the war."

"Your brother did, and you hid that from me."

"Was everything you said about forgiving nothing more than talk?"

Shaking his head, he closed his eyes. "I ... I can't."

"Can't what? Can't forgive my brother? Can't look at me or ... forgive *me*?" Her voice cracked.

He managed one quick glance into her tear-filled, mournful eyes before turning away. "I'm going for a walk. I need to be alone. To think."

"And pray. You'd better do that after all you've told me. I'll drive the buggy to the barn and unhitch it myself. Feel free to walk all you want before heading home."

23

Heidi's hands shook as she snapped the reins to drive the buggy back to the barn. She'd prayed for some definite sign from God to show her if she should move to San Antonio or not. But not anything like what had just happened.

She took her time unhitching the buggy and tending to the horse. The way she had when she'd done everything by herself in New Braunfels. Jethro had broken her heart, as she'd feared. If only she hadn't fallen in love with him. He was no different than Karl or her parents. Tears threatened. She brushed them away. She'd be living in San Antonio on her own by the end of February. No later than March.

With the handle to her satchel slipped over her arm, she grabbed one stool then the other from the back seat of the buggy. Squaring her shoulders as best she could, she left her barn sanctuary to go to the house. As she approached, Lily and Toby sat next to each other on the front porch. Ella, Harvey, and Ruckus played in the yard.

"You're back sooner than you usually are." Lily studied her as Heidi stepped up on the porch, probably already wondering about more than she'd asked.

"I am." Heidi propped the stools and her satchel against the porch rail, working to keep her shock and disappointment from coming across in her voice.

"Where's Jethro? Why isn't he with you, carrying your stools?" Toby's gaze shifted toward the barn as if expecting to see Jethro walking their way.

Heidi leaned against the rail, hoping her distress didn't show on her face. "He went for a walk."

"After he took care of the buggy and horse. Or he'd better have." Toby scowled as if he might be ready to tell Jethro what he thought.

"No. I'm perfectly capable of doing it all myself and told him so. Don't be upset with him."

"Tell me why I shouldn't be." Toby's gruff voice sounded as if he were already upset or worse.

"I decided to come back without him. He wasn't happy to hear I'm sure I'll be moving to town after the baby comes. Please don't fire him because we don't agree on what I want to do." As much as he'd hurt her, she didn't want Jethro to lose his job. He didn't deserve that.

"I won't fire him. It's not my place to decide if he loves you or not. That's between the two of you."

"Thank you." Heidi took the chair on the other side of Lily. Her sister was quiet. For now. She doubted that would last once the two of them were alone.

"We won't pry into your affairs, but we will pray." Lily's thin smile appeared forced. Her sad eyes telegraphed she wasn't happy about anything Heidi had said.

Heidi hoped her pretend smile looked natural enough to keep Lily and Toby from guessing how miserable she was. "Are you going to let the children play outside a while longer?"

"Probably. We'd better enjoy this pleasant day."

"I'll go to Ella's room and draw in there. I'd like to finish the sketch I started this afternoon." Heidi gathered up her stools and satchel. She wasn't in the mood to draw, but keeping to her normal habits might prevent anyone from seeing through her ruse of pretending to be all right.

By the time she heard everyone coming inside, she'd made some progress on a sketch of Greta. She'd finish the one of Heinrich another day or give Lily the one she'd drawn before coming here.

To Heidi's relief, Jethro didn't join them for supper. She wasn't up to looking at him from across the table after the way he'd turned on her. Lily told a curious Ella Mr. Bannister must have overslept from his nap and would be fine. Since Ella helped clean the kitchen, Lily didn't say anything to Heidi about her time with Jethro earlier.

The children played in the parlor until time for bed. Again, sparing Heidi from anything Toby or Lily might have wanted to say. Heidi gave Ella time to go to sleep before getting ready for bed herself. She crawled in next to her niece then lay on her back, staring at the ceiling.

Another man had disappointed her. She'd risked falling in love with Jethro, hoping he might care for her, love her. But he'd proved otherwise today. Exactly why he couldn't forgive her, she wasn't sure. She'd meant to protect him from his painful memories by not telling him Heinrich fought for the North. Protecting someone you love wasn't wrong.

What was it he really couldn't forgive her for? For having a brother who fought for the Union? Nothing that happened to Jethro during the war was her fault. She sighed. Better to find out now he wasn't as good at forgiving as he'd said. Before he could hurt her more than he already had. She heard the clock in the parlor strike three before she finally drifted off to sleep.

---

THE BACK DOOR opened the next morning as Heidi rolled out biscuits for breakfast. Jethro walked in. She focused on the dough.

"Mornin', Jethro." Toby offered his usual greeting as he helped Harvey stack blocks.

"Good morning."

Heidi took extra care with the biscuits then checked the coffee that didn't need checking. Jethro waited for her and Lily to sit before taking his chair across the table. Lily and Toby talked with Ella about the chickens and the new kittens born in the barn.

"Aunt Heidi, could you draw a picture of the kittens?" Ella paused between bites of biscuits to smile at Heidi.

"Not since we're washing clothes today." Heidi's words sounded normal enough to fool a little girl.

"All right. Some other day." Ella popped the last bite of her biscuit in her mouth.

"Yes, some other day."

"I'll be working in the barn most of the day." Toby made his announcement after finishing his last bite of eggs. "So you ladies will have to come get me whenever it's time to eat lunch."

"We'll do that." Lily set Harvey down from his highchair.

Toby had been working on a simple house for Ella's doll for a while plus a wagon for Harvey. He was such a good father. Such a good man. But the Lord hadn't seen fit to put someone like Toby in Heidi's life. She'd focus instead on the future she'd dreamed about.

"I'll chop the wood we need." Jethro watched his boss. He'd done an excellent job of ignoring Heidi.

Which was fine with Heidi. He'd freed her to concentrate on the new life she'd soon begin. If only knowing for sure what God wanted her to do would make her heart feel whole again instead of empty.

Heidi again did as much of the laundry as she could. She let Lily hang only the smaller pieces now, insisting she hang out the heavier sheets.

"I might forget how to wash my own clothes if you keep

spoiling me like this." Lily wrung out a dish towel before hanging it on the line.

"I doubt that." Heidi returned her attention to the shirt she was scrubbing on the rub board.

"I'll be happy to listen if you'd like to talk." Lily took another wet towel out of the rinse water. "Toby and I are praying. Your expression reminds me of someone who's come from a funeral. You didn't sound any better either when you walked up on the porch."

"I don't want to talk."

Lily pinned another dish towel on the line. "Jethro looks as miserable as you do."

"He should be." What a terrible time to speak before thinking. She must get better at not doing such a thing.

"I see. I'll say one more thing, and then I'll be quiet. Anyone watching the two of you, can see Jethro loves you. You love him. Toby and I are praying you both realize that and find a way to be happy together forever."

"He doesn't love me." She returned her attention to the shirt she'd soon ruin if she scrubbed it any more vigorously. "Pray I find the right job in San Antonio."

"You're sure?"

"Very sure." If Jethro loved her, he wouldn't have hesitated to assure her he didn't blame her for simply having a brother fighting on the side of his enemies.

"Toby and I are not sure." Lily pinned a petticoat on the line. "I'll say no more."

"Thank you."

Heidi spent the week mulling over her problems with Jethro. By Saturday, she'd decided she'd done nothing wrong and shouldn't have asked for his forgiveness. She hadn't hurt him on purpose. Not telling him her brother fought for the Union had been the right thing to do, considering how badly such news upset him. She'd been all of ten when Heinrich was in Georgia with Sherman. For a man who so often mentioned forgiving people, he held a lot of grudges.

She'd be better off without him.

JETHRO SETTLED onto the chair on his small porch with his Bible, glad for a Sunday to rest. Not happy to be sitting here alone. This past week had been the worst he'd had since his last fight with his brother. He doubted Heidi had said a dozen words to him. Something that made him miserable now.

Mr. Grimes had assured Jethro he wouldn't fire him because of his problems with Heidi. While not hesitating to tell him Heidi loved him. The boss and the missus were both praying he and Heidi settled their differences.

Every night this week, he'd read and reread the same verses on forgiveness he'd agonized over after leaving home. With God's help, he'd forgiven his brother and mother. But how did he forgive the Yankees who killed his father? He'd thought he had. He should do the right thing. He needed to for his peace of mind. As Heidi said, she had nothing to do with any of Sherman's atrocities. He'd hurt her as no other man had. She didn't deserve that.

He closed his eyes and tried to pray. "Dear God, help." He gripped the Bible in his lap. "Lord, show me what to do and how to do it."

How long he sat hoping for an answer, he wasn't sure. He opened his eyes in time to see Heidi walking in the distance carrying her satchel. Trudging would be a better description. She glanced in his direction then turned away the instant she saw him.

She knew not to go too far alone. With no snakes to bother her this time of year, she should be safe alone wherever she was heading. He watched her until she walked behind the barn, obscuring his view of her.

The urge to follow her almost overwhelmed him. No. Her brother had ridden with the men who murdered his father. She hadn't known he could have been with those soldiers. But she had deliberately not mentioned her brother had fought with the Yankees. If she'd hid that fact, what else had she not told him?

A shrill scream ripped through the silence.

The noise sounded as if it came from around the barn, it's echo pierced the air and his thoughts. Heidi! He bolted inside, grabbed his rifle from over the door, and ran. Praying as he'd never prayed before.

"Let me go!" Heidi yelled.

Jethro halted, trying to think of the best way to help her without Heidi getting hurt.

"*Ow!* You won't bite me again." The masculine voice continued, but Jethro couldn't understand. Was that German?

Heidi yelped in what sounded like pain.

The voices came from behind the barn, still blocking his view of what sounded like a fight Heidi might be losing. He crept along the side near him. He still couldn't see anything. They must be behind the middle part of the barn somewhere. Hopefully, he could continue to creep along the side and surprise the man as he got around to where they were.

The man spied Jethro the instant he stepped from around the side of the barn. He grabbed Heidi's arms, pinning them behind her back as he jerked her to him.

"You're hurting me, Johann."

Johann, the man her parents chose for her husband.

He growled something in German in Heidi's ear while watching Jethro's every move.

Heidi's face lost all color as her eyes widened.

The wild rage flaming in the big man's icy blue eyes made Jethro's heart race faster, almost taking his breath away. Whatever evil this madman intended, he wouldn't accomplish.

Jethro raised his gun. "Let her go." Thank God his hands and voice were steady.

As Jethro aimed his rifle, the man jerked Heidi in front of him. He wrapped one arm around her neck while aiming the pistol in his other hand at her head. "Throw your gun down. Easy, so it doesn't go off."

Jethro bent to lay the rifle at his feet while keeping a wary eye on the villain threatening Heidi, then stood straight with his hands out.

Johann took aim at Jethro instead of Heidi. "Heidi is my promised intended. She's coming with me."

"You'll have to kill me first." How the man could think Heidi was still his didn't make sense after what he'd done to her parents. He stared straight into the man's hard eyes, praying for what to say or do next to keep the maniac from hurting Heidi, or worse. "Mr. Schultz told us the last time he was here how you stole from him. How you stole a horse too."

The man's jaw dropped. He loosened his grip around Heidi's throat but not enough for her to get away.

A ferocious growl from behind Johann was the only warning Ruckus gave as he ran from around the other side of the barn and lunged at the man. Johann's gun went off as he fell to the ground, the shot barely missing Heidi. She scrambled away from Ruckus and his now prey.

Jethro grabbed his rifle the instant Johann hit the ground. "Kick his revolver away." He yelled to Heidi, who stood staring at the scene in front of her as if frozen to the ground. He'd never seen her so pale.

She did as he said.

Ruckus stood with all four paws squarely on Johann's back, growling as he clamped his teeth into the man's shoulder near the base of his neck.

"Get the dog off." Johann gasped as the hound's jaws tightened.

Jethro kept his gun aimed at Johann's head. "Heidi, get behind me."

She rushed toward him. Stepping in front of her, he couldn't miss the large welt on her cheek or the blood on her now swollen lip. Pure fury surged through him.

"This dog is going to kill me."

"Better him than me after what you did to Heidi." For the first time in his life, Jethro wanted to shoot someone. Wouldn't hesitate to do it.

"What happened?" Mr. Grimes ran up to them, revolver in hand. "We heard a gunshot." He looked from Jethro, with his rifle still aimed at Johann to Heidi and then to the whining man on the ground now cursing Ruckus in English and what sounded like more German.

"I won't have a shoulder left."

Heidi stepped to Jethro's side. He kept his gun aimed at Johann. "That is Johann Merkle. The man my parents ..." She took in a shaky breath. "He tried to force me to go with him."

"Looks like Jethro and Ruckus said no." Mr. Grimes holstered his pistol.

She nodded.

"Jethro, since he's not going anywhere, I'll get some rope from the barn. We can decide when we take him to the marshal in town while we tie him up."

"Now. We'd have to guard him all night to be sure he didn't get away. We've both done enough night trailing to get him to San Antonio." Jethro wasn't sure what he might do if he were left alone with the man.

"Yeah, you're right."

Mr. Grimes soon returned with the rope. With Ruckus standing guard, he straddled the man then jerked Johann's hands behind his back. "How tight you want me to make these knots?" He turned his attention to Jethro.

"Not as tight as I'd do it. Did you see Heidi's face?"

"Yeah." Mr. Grimes's eyes flashed in undisguised anger as he tightened the rope.

The man yelped.

After the boss tied Johann's hands and ankles, Jethro lowered his gun. Heidi still stood next to him, wide-eyed, silently taking everything in. "We need to get Heidi to the house and let Mrs. Grimes look at her."

"You take her. Ruckus and I will watch this varmint. When you can, hitch Red to the wagon. We'll toss this scoundrel in the bed and take him to town."

"Guard him with this." Jethro handed his rifle to the boss. "I don't want him getting away."

"Neither do we. Right Ruckus?" Mr. Grimes patted the dog's head. Ruckus had yet to take his eyes off Johann.

Jethro took Heidi's arm and led her away. While they walked past the barn away from where they could see Mr. Grimes, silent tears ran down her cheeks. He reached to brush them away. "I'm sorry."

She flung herself against him and sobbed. He wrapped his arms around her. "You're safe now." His lips nuzzled her hair as he spoke. "You're all right."

His shirt was wet by the time she stepped back. "Thank you."

"You're welcome. Let's get you to the house."

They walked hand in hand into the parlor.

Mrs. Grimes gasped as she ran to her sister "Oh, Heidi. What happened?"

"She can tell you the whole story later." Jethro held his hand over one side of his mouth to muffle his words as he glanced toward Ella playing with her doll and Harvey stacking blocks into a pan.

"All right. Let's go in the kitchen. I want to wash off your lip and look at it." Mrs. Grimes took Heidi by the arm. "Ella, watch Harvey for me. This time, Aunt Heidi has tripped over something."

"Yes, ma'am."

Jethro followed the women into the kitchen and led Heidi to a chair at the table. "Heidi can tell you everything. Mr. Grimes and I are taking Johann Merkle to the marshal tonight, so we'll be back late."

"What?" Mrs. Grimes's hands went over her heart as she stared at her silent little sister.

Jethro patted Heidi's uninjured cheek. She gazed up into his eyes. "I need to go."

"Yes, you do. I'm all right now as you said." She placed her hand over his.

Fighting the urge to bend and kiss her, he marched himself out the back door. He wasted no time hitching the horse to the wagon. By the light of the lantern he grabbed from the barn, he helped Mr. Grimes toss Johann into the wagon bed.

"I'll ride with him and guard him. You can drive." Mr. Grimes grabbed Jethro's rifle from where they'd propped it against the barn.

"I'll guard him. You drive."

"You sure?" The boss had to be remembering their talks about guns.

"Yes, sir. He tried to hurt the woman I love. I'll watch him."

The shadows from the lantern couldn't completely hide the boss's wide grin. "Does Heidi know how you feel?"

"She will."

"I'll keep quiet. Get situated in the wagon before I climb up on the seat and turn my back on you."

---

"Let me look at you." Lily dabbed a wet rag on Heidi's lip.

Heidi winced.

"No matter what you told Jethro, you don't look like you're all right. Your lip is swollen. I'm afraid you'll have a bad bruise on your cheek. The hem is torn on your dress. And your hair ..." Lily's whisper got louder with every sentence.

"After the children are in bed." Heidi kept her voice low.

They returned to the parlor after Lily finished cleaning the dirt off Heidi's face.

"You all right, Aunt Heidi?" Ella clutched her doll as she got to her feet.

"I'm fine now." Heidi forced what she hoped was a natural-looking smile as she took a spot on the couch beside Lily, praying for what to tell her niece. "I drew until it was almost dark and tripped coming back. Jethro found me and walked me back here."

"Where's your satchel?"

"My satchel?" Heidi had no idea what had happened to it.

"She must have dropped it when she fell." Lily patted Heidi's arm. "Pa or Jethro can get it tomorrow and bring it back."

"Where's Pa?"

"Um, he and Jethro decided to go for a ride and check the cows at night." Lily's thin smile didn't look genuine.

Ella tilted her head as if thinking about her mother's answer.

"They won't be back until after you're in bed, so Pa won't tuck you in tonight."

Lily let the children play a while longer before putting them to bed then returning to the parlor. "I laid out your nightgown so you can go to bed when you're ready. But if you feel up to it, I'd like to know what happened." She seated herself next to Heidi.

"I was going a little way behind the barn as I'd told you. Johann must have been hiding around there, watching for me from what he said. I think he's been doing that a day or so."

"Which is probably why Ruckus has been barking more than usual, but I'm interrupting. Go on." Lily shifted to where she was facing Heidi.

"He insisted I come with him. I'd been promised to him, and he wouldn't let me go back on that promise."

Lily shook her head. "The man sounds as if he's gone mad."

"Probably. He'd somehow decided if he dragged me back to New Braunfels, Papa would be so happy to see me he'd still force the marriage as well as forget Johann's a thief."

"Thank God he didn't hurt you any more than he did."

Tears stung Heidi's eyes. She blinked them away. "Thank God and thank Jethro. He heard me scream." She took in a shuddering breath before telling Lily how Johann had jerked her in front of him then aimed for Jethro. "Jethro was willing to die for me." Her voice cracked in spite of her efforts to stay calm.

"'Greater love hath no man than this, that a man lay down his life for his friends.'" Lily quoted the familiar verse in John.

Heidi nodded. Jethro had proved his love was deeper than friendship. But she'd talk to him about that later. She shivered when she got to the part of Ruckus knocking Johann to the ground. "When Johann's gun went off, the bullet missed Jethro, me, and the dog."

A slow smile played across Lily's face "I didn't want that noisy dog at first. I may tell you about it one day." She patted Heidi's arm.

"He deserves a big bone. He may have saved Jethro's life." Another clear realization to think about now she was calm enough to recall more details of what had happened. Heidi stifled a yawn. "I think I'll go to bed too."

"Rest would be good for you." Lily hugged her close. "Good night."

Resting wasn't easy once Heidi laid her head on her pillow. Not thinking about everything that had happened was impossible. As Lily said, thank God she and Jethro were safe. So many things to ponder. She'd fallen in love with Jethro, no matter how much she'd fought against it. He loved her enough to give his life for her.

Could she set aside her fears of being betrayed again?

## 24

Jethro awoke to a sunlit bedroom. He couldn't remember when he'd slept past daylight. The last time he'd gone to bed around two in the morning was after rounding up stampeding longhorns on this spring's cattle drive. This morning, he could sleep late instead of climbing back into his saddle.

He got up to check his pocket watch on the dresser. Eight o'clock. Past time to dress and shave and then help the boss with chores. If Mr. Grimes hadn't already done them alone. The boss had planned on sleeping late too but probably not this late.

Amazing, how he'd slept so well. The best in a week. Most people would think he'd gone crazy sleeping all night after what happened yesterday. But as terrifying as everything had been, he had the strangest peace he'd ever experienced.

He loved Heidi enough to willingly die for her. No matter if her brother had been one of the Yankees who raided his family's plantation or not. Even if the man had been the one to shoot his father. None of his anger or resentment had mattered when Heidi's life was in danger. He loved her no matter what.

With God's help, he would manage to forgive her brother. He grinned at his reflection in the wash stand mirror. His reflection with a fine mustache he'd grown because of Heidi.

Settling so much made him feel like whistling the entire way to the Grimes's house.

Except he had to explain himself to Heidi. Ask her to forgive him. Finally, be completely truthful with her about why he'd left Georgia. Then pray more intently than he had last night that she'd love him despite how he'd hurt her. If she did, she still had to decide if she'd set aside her plans and dreams and risk spending her life with him.

*Peace I leave with you, my peace, I give unto you, not as the world giveth ...*

Jesus's words to His disciples echoed through Jethro's mind so loudly they sounded as if the Lord were standing next to him, speaking into his ear instead of his heart. His stomach growled as if to remind him how much of the morning was already gone. Time to head to the main house and see what might happen today.

After knocking once, the back door opened. Mr. Grimes, with his ear-to-ear grin, must have rested well too. "Lily just put the biscuits in the oven. I was fixin' to come knock on your door."

"Thanks. I didn't intend to sleep so late."

"I was so tired I might still be in bed if Harvey hadn't woke us all up when he got hungry." The boss stepped aside to let Jethro walk away from the door he'd closed behind him.

Heidi stood at the stove, breaking eggs into the skillet. Wearing the blue calico dress that looked almost as nice as the ruffled blue one she'd worn not long after she'd come here. Maybe today he could tell her how happy he'd been to see her pick out that color after they'd also picked up her easel at the Hawkins's store.

Andrew Bridges hadn't paid her any mind since that day. Jethro had been fooling himself and Heidi, thinking he'd run the man off as a friendly favor to her. Maybe he'd explain that to Heidi today too. If not today, another time. If she loved him enough to set aside her plans for him.

"Good morning." Mrs. Grimes smiled in Jethro's direction as she handed the stacked plates to Ella for her to set the table.

Heidi kept her back turned to him. His heart screamed in silence for her to offer him even a fleeting smile. If she'd smiled all week, she hadn't offered him one. Peace. He'd hang onto that. And pray. She'd been through so much last night. Maybe she wasn't doing any better than he had after the rustlers had endangered his life.

"We'll do chores after we eat, but that's all I intend to do today." Mr. Grimes squatted next to Harvey, who whined more than played with his toys. "Breakfast's almost ready, son. We all know when you're hungry, you're hungry all over."

When Mrs. Grimes took the biscuits out of the oven, her husband set Harvey in his highchair. Heidi put the eggs and bacon on platters without saying a word. Jethro had never thought he'd wish to hear Heidi talking then take a breath and say even more.

After Mr. Grimes blessed the food, Jethro watched Heidi as best he could without staring at her so much she'd wonder what he was up to. She hadn't put her hair up. Her tired eyes signaled she hadn't slept much last night. Her bloodied lip was still swollen. He hoped the bruise on her cheek wouldn't get worse.

The boss handed him the platter of eggs, turned over easy with the yolks still soft. Heidi had learned to fix them exactly the way Mr. Grimes liked them. Again, he hoped the time would come when he could tell Heidi how he liked his eggs fixed.

"I helped Aunt Heidi gather eggs. We have three new chicks and more hatching." Ella was the only one saying much.

Jethro grinned across the table at the little girl. "As well as Heidi fries chicken, more chicks is a fine thing."

Ella licked her lips. "Yes, sir."

Heidi's slight smile was the only reaction he got. He'd be happy to settle for that for now.

When Mr. Grimes scooted his chair back, Heidi rose and started stacking dirty dishes.

"After we finish chores, do you feel up to a walk, Heidi?" Jethro held his breath as he waited for her answer.

"I'd like that. Yes. A walk would be good."

Her words warmed his soul from the toes of his boots to his heart. He followed the boss outside. "Did Heidi say anything to you or the missus about how she's doing?"

Mr. Grimes halted by the well. "Not much. The way she looks, she probably didn't sleep much last night."

"I hope she didn't have nightmares that kept her awake."

"Yeah. Staring down death is hard on anyone. How are you doing?" The boss leaned against the well as if he didn't mind how long Jethro's answer might be.

"Better than I thought after yesterday. A lot better."

Mr. Grimes's eyes filled with questions. "That so?"

"Yes, sir. Figuring out I love her feels real good. We've got some things to straighten out between us. So, I'd like your prayers. Yours and Mrs. Grimes's."

"We both figured more happened between y'all than what little she told us."

"I'd rather keep that between us."

The boss nodded. "That's the way it should be with a man and woman in love. And I do believe she loves you."

Those last words made Jethro want to throw his hat up high enough to touch one of the few clouds in the sky.

"Let's get chores done so you can talk to Heidi." Mr. Grimes clapped Jethro on the back.

After they finished, Jethro took extra time to wash up. Being as presentable as possible couldn't hurt. He wanted to talk to Heidi but dreaded it at the same time, since he wasn't sure what she might or might not say after he explained himself.

---

HEIDI WENT to Ella's room to pin her hair up after she and Lily finished cleaning the kitchen. The woman staring back at her from the dresser mirror looked much too haggard for someone her age. Leaning toward the mirror, she sighed. How many times would she have to pinch her cheeks to give them a little color? If her right cheek weren't sore to the touch.

The shock of last night was wearing off some. But she still felt … How did she feel? She wasn't completely sure. Most definitely rattled. No one had ever pointed a gun at her head before. She wasn't afraid. At least not now. Toby assured her Johann would go to jail for a long time. Her lack of sleep probably explained why her mind was so muddled, why she had no energy.

Yet she wanted to go for a walk with Jethro. Needed to be with him. She'd missed not talking to him lately. Not sharing thoughts and dreams only he understood. Until he'd no longer understood. She closed her eyes, willing his painful words away. Last night, he'd risked his life for her. She needed to know why since he'd barely spoken to her the last few days.

Lily had her bread bowl and pans out when Heidi returned to the kitchen. "I'll bake today then wash and iron clothes tomorrow. The men aren't the only ones who want an easier day."

"I won't argue with that." Heidi slipped her apron over her head.

"You're welcome to sit and keep me company if you'd like."

"I can help. I'm feeling better. Besides, I plan on deserting you whenever Jethro is ready to go for a walk."

Lily measured flour into the bowl. "That will be good for both of you."

Jethro and Toby walked in as Lily set the first batch of bread to rise.

"Are you too busy to walk with me?" The hopeful look on Jethro's face matched his eager tone of voice.

"No. I've already warned Lily I'd leave her to finish the baking alone." Heidi slipped the apron over her head, then hung it on a hook.

Toby and Lily exchanged happy looks as Jethro held the back door open for Heidi. "Thank you for doing this."

"I've been looking forward to some time with you." Which she had. She hoped and prayed they could resume the friendship they'd forged. Perhaps more?

Jethro grinned as he paused a few feet from the door. "Can you bake anything without getting flour on your nose?" He reached over and lightly rubbed the tip of her nose. "All gone."

"Thank you." His simple gesture warmed her heart. He remembered the first time she'd made biscuits and ended up with flour on her nose.

"If you aren't up to a walk, we can sit on the porch."

"I'd rather not be close enough to the house for anyone to overhear us."

"Sounds good to me."

They walked side by side to the closest ridge where they could still see the house and outbuildings. Heidi halted. "I don't want to walk too far away."

"I understand." He turned to face her. "How are you doing?"

"Um ... not as bad as last night." She licked her sore lip.

"Good." He shifted from one foot to the other. Taking in a deep breath, he stared into her eyes. "I owe you an apology for what I said to you the other day. I'm so sorry for hurting you."

No matter how much she wanted to look away from, her heart wouldn't cooperate. The longer she gazed up at him, the faster her pulse raced. She'd prayed for what to say if he offered her the apology she so well deserved, but no reply came to mind as the agony he'd caused welled up anew inside her.

"Please forgive me." His eyes brimmed with tears.

She nodded, still unable to speak.

"As you said, none of what happened to me was your fault." He swallowed hard and then stared off in the distance. "When I heard that Yankee general's name ..." His voice cracked. He took in a shuddering breath. "All the bad memories I had dammed up flooded back into my mind." He closed his eyes. "As if I were there again. Hearing my mother scream. Watching my father f … fall to the ground."

"Oh, Jethro." She placed her hand on his arm. "You would have been fifteen then?"

"Yeah." His voice was so thick with emotion he sounded as if he'd choked out his reply. "I became the man of the house. My mother and I ran our plantation as best we could during a war with my one surviving brother still off fighting."

"If I remember correctly, you lost one brother during the war?"

"Right. So, Yankees killed my father and brother." He looked her way again. "The war was hard for a lot of reasons, especially for a boy barely old enough to shave, much less become the man of the house."

"I can't imagine. But a Rebel killed my brother."

His eyes widened. "Yeah. I, uh … I hadn't thought of that before."

"Which is probably the main reason my parents didn't want Lily with Harvey now that I'm thinking about it. They still privately say terrible things about the Rebels."

"So, they don't like me or Mr. Grimes either."

She shook her head. Her fingers still rested on his arm. As she started to slide them off, he placed his hand over hers.

"Holding grudges like that isn't healthy or good." He turned slightly to look straight into her eyes. "I learned that much the hard way before the Lord helped me forgive my mother and oldest brother."

"What did they do?" She clamped her free hand over her mouth. So much for not saying what she shouldn't. Again.

He took in a long shuddering breath and then another.

"I'm sorry I keep speaking before I think. I should be better at not doing that by now, but—"

He placed the fingers of his free hand on her lips. "But you're not. You *are* honest. That's one of the things I admire about you." A fleeting smile played across his face for a moment only to disappear as his eyes clouded again. "Since you've always been so honest with me, you deserve to know the truth about why I left Georgia."

"Only if you want to tell me."

"I want to. It's time."

What he meant, she wasn't sure. Perhaps he'd explain his reasoning. If not now, later. He stared off toward the house, his hand still covering hers.

"My brother came home in June of '65. We disagreed about how to run the plantation. Jeffrey didn't want to listen to anything a sixteen year-old had to say." He tightened his grip on her hand.

"The way Papa doesn't listen to me or Lily."

"Right. If our former foreman hadn't stayed with us, I doubt Mother and I would have survived. So I wanted to give Methuselah forty acres and let him and his wife farm their own land the way free people should. Jeffrey didn't. He turned my mother against me. She told me Father had willed the plantation to Jeffrey after Michael died. I left in early '66 before time to plant again."

His story explained so many of the reasons she'd wondered about why he'd left his family. Why he wasn't a talkative man. But there had to be a deeper reason than her honesty with him for telling her about something that still caused him such agony to recall or mention. If he intended to be totally truthful with her, he should tell her what compelled him to bare his soul to her as no other man had ever done. "Why is it time to tell me what I doubt you've ever told anyone else?"

"Why?" He turned to stand in front of her, facing her. Taking each of her hands in his, he gazed into her eyes. "Because last night I didn't care about who your brother fought with or where. Instead of dreading to think about shooting at a man, I'd have shot Johann without worrying about it. All I wanted was to keep you safe. No matter what."

"Even if it had cost you your life." Chills ran up and down her spine as she spoke.

"Yes." A bright smile lit up his face and shone into his sparkling green eyes. "No matter how much I've tried not to, I've fallen in love with you."

"If this is a marriage proposal, it has to be one of the strangest ones a man has ever offered a woman." Again, she blurted out her thoughts before thinking first.

"Do you love me?" The sparkle in his eyes dimmed as he waited for her reply.

She gazed up at him. He deserved the truth from her too. "Yes. And I may have tried harder not to love you than you have me."

"I doubt it." His smile spread ear to ear. "Now that has to be one of the strangest declarations of love a woman has ever made to a man."

"I suppose so." She laughed.

Gripping her hands, he lifted them to his lips then lowered them. "I would ask you to be my wife this instant, but I know and understand why you've fought not to love me. If you marry me, you need to trust me enough not to hurt you again. Plus, you'd have to give up the life you've been dreaming of living. Can you—are you—willing to do that for me?"

"What if I can't answer you right now?" She searched his face and his now sad-looking eyes. If only she could tell him what he wanted to hear from her. But she couldn't. "I do love you. But giving you the right as my husband to tell me what I should or shouldn't do. Trusting you won't betray me ..." She let her words trail off, unable to completely say what she meant.

He let out a long breath. "And that's why I won't propose yet. You need time to think and pray. A wife has rights too. Remember to mull that over." He released her hands.

"You'll wait? You're willing to give me time?"

"Yes."

"How long?" She reminded herself to breathe as she waited for an answer.

"I've learned to be patient, but I'm not sure how patient I am. Shall we go back to the house?" He turned as if he'd start without her.

"We should." They walked in silence down the ridge.

## 25

Heidi awoke the next morning with sunlight flooding through the curtains. She jumped from the empty bed without taking time to stretch. How had she slept until daylight, much less not known when Ella got up? Her little niece rarely did anything quietly.

The smell of bacon and coffee drifted into the room. Quiet voices came from the kitchen. She threw on the dress she'd worn yesterday since she hadn't done enough to get it dirty and then rushed through doing her hair.

Everyone sat at the table enjoying breakfast when she walked into the kitchen. "Why didn't you wake me?" Heidi slid into her chair, tossing out her question to whomever wanted to answer.

"You were sleeping so soundly, I couldn't bear to awaken you." Lily passed the biscuits to Heidi. "We're all glad you got the rest you needed."

"Thank you." Heidi stole a glance at Jethro sitting across from her as she buttered her biscuit. His adoring smile seemed to be aimed at and meant only for her. She doubted any other man could still look so happy to see the woman who couldn't decide if she'd accept the love he'd offered her or not. She had a lot to think and pray about.

After doing dishes, Heidi and Lily washed clothes, taking advantage of the pleasant temperature and sunshine. This close to Christmas meant they could be washing clothes in much cooler weather some days. Heidi stacked the wood to start the fire under the iron wash pot in the back yard and then carried the water from the well to heat. She was used to Lily's protests now. Like, Toby, she wanted Lily to stay well.

"As I keep saying, I'll be thoroughly spoiled by the time you leave here." Lily sorted the white clothes from the colored ones.

If she left here. But Heidi wouldn't so much as hint at that possibility to the sister who had been strongly suggesting for too long Heidi should consider marriage. Especially since they were so sure she and Jethro were meant for each other.

Laundry didn't require a lot of thought, so Heidi used the time to think and pray between talking with Lily. Jethro was a good, godly man. An incredibly patient man.

But Papa and Mama had taken their family to church on Sundays, prayed before meals, read their Bibles. They'd indulged her with art lessons her other siblings might not have ever had. Yet they'd turned on her as soon as they realized she didn't want a loveless marriage with Johann. Jethro's mother and brother had betrayed him. What if Jethro changed?

"You'll have a hole in your apron if you keep scrubbing it like that on the rub board." Lily interrupted Heidi's thoughts.

"Oh." Heidi put the apron in the rinse water.

"You must be thinking some deep thoughts."

"I am." Heidi wrung out the apron.

Lily took it from her to hang on the clothesline.

"Jethro and I had a good talk yesterday. I'm thinking and praying about some things he mentioned."

"None of us ever makes a mistake turning our concerns over to God." Lily grinned as she finished pinning the apron on the line then glanced toward Ella romping with Ruckus as Harvey tumbled to the ground in his effort to keep up with his sister and her dog. Ella dusted him off and helped him to his feet.

Heidi paused from scrubbing another apron to watch her niece and nephew play. Saturday's frost had finished turning the grass brown, but the children didn't mind. Would she one day watch her own little ones scamper across her and Jethro's lawn? If so, time to paint or draw would be harder to find than it was now. Children and a husband took a lot of time and effort.

*Dear Lord, I must be the most selfish person on this earth.* Laughing children and a loving husband couldn't compare to canvases or pencils. Yet God had given her the talent to paint and draw. Scripture said every good and perfect gift comes from God.

After Jethro's compliments on her cooking, she'd dared to dream about working in a restaurant in town. Or perhaps drawing pictures for the newspaper. Maybe sending off drawings to a magazine. So many possibilities Papa and Mama would have never allowed her to consider for even a moment. Opportunities she couldn't consider if she married no matter how good and godly Jethro was and remained. Very few women got the chance to choose what she'd been offered.

Heidi spent the rest of the week pondering and praying. She searched her Bible for answers. But none had presented themselves by Sunday. They stayed home and had their own service after breakfast.

Toby read the last few verses of Psalm thirty-seven about God being strength in time of trouble for the righteous and delivering them from the wicked. "Thank God he still does that for us today." With Ella sitting between him and Lily, he didn't go into details about Heidi and Jethro's harrowing time the past Sunday.

Heidi didn't mind. She'd had more than one nightmare this week about Johann trying to drag her away. An uneventful morning and a perfectly dull time the rest of the day would be wonderful.

Lily ended their time by leading them in Toby's favorite hymn, *Just as I Am*. The third verse about "fightings within, and fears without" spoke to her.

"Before we all scatter the way we usually do on Sunday mornings, I feel like the Lord wants me to tell y'all why this is my favorite hymn." Toby's gaze went to Heidi and then to Jethro, seated in the chair by the couch. He stood. "It's warm enough by now for the kids to play in the yard with Ella's wonderful noisy hound."

Everyone followed Toby out the front door. Ella led Harvey down the porch steps as she called for Ruckus. Lily settled into her usual chair. Toby took the other two and turned them side by side to face his and Lily's chairs.

"Jethro, Heidi, I want y'all to be where you can hear me without me talking loud enough for the kids to hear." He sat beside Lily as Heidi and Jethro seated themselves as he'd asked.

Lily reached over to Toby. Taking her hands in his, he held her gaze as he smiled into her eyes. Whatever they were silently saying to each other, only they knew. The longing for someone to know and care about her as deeply as Lily and Toby cared for each other overwhelmed Heidi.

After an almost imperceptible nod from Lily, Toby leaned toward Heidi and Jethro. "By the time the war was over, I was so mad at God I quit talking to Him. I prayed for God to save my best friend when he was wounded. Billy died." He shifted in his chair. "When I came home Ma and my younger brother, Pete, were in the family graveyard. And the woman who'd said she'd wait for me had married one of my good friends." He sucked in more than one deep breath.

Lily squeezed his hand as they exchanged another intimate gaze.

Heidi ventured a sidelong glance at Jethro. He seemed to be taking in every word Toby had said about hardship and anger.

"When my sweet Lily married me, I was mad at everybody. Keeping to myself was the only way I found any peace. At least that's what I'd decided. But she and God didn't give up on me."

"No, we didn't, dear."

The loving looks they exchanged intensified Heidi's longing to be loved. To love the way Lily so loved her husband.

"The Lord finally got my attention when Harvey came way too early. I rode off to our ridge and had a shouting match with God about why He should save our boy." He closed his eyes and gulped in air. "God showed me I was the one who turned my back on Him. He'd never left me. Like the song says, He took me back the way I was. The way I am."

"Toby came home where he belonged. We had a good talk about how much we loved each other no matter how bad things were or might get." Lily finished the words Toby seemed unable to say.

"So, you two. We're through meddling. Almost." Toby grinned at them. "Heidi, I'm sure you have a painting or drawing to finish. Gather up what you need to do that. Jethro, hitch Red to the buggy and go with Heidi. Y'all seem to think and talk to each other the best when Heidi's got a brush in her hand. Don't come back here until you've got things settled between you."

Heidi looked to Jethro, not sure how to respond.

"I'd say we'd better do as we're told." The sparkle in his eyes signaled he wasn't upset with Toby's orders.

"Good." Lily got to her feet. "I'll fix a picnic for you. As Toby said, we don't want y'all coming back anytime soon."

"Jethro, I'll help you hitch up the buggy so y'all can leave quicker."

"Yes, sir."

Toby and Jethro walked off the porch together.

Heidi went to Ella's room to get her easel and other things. She'd wanted time to finish a landscape to give to Lily and Toby for Christmas next week. Knowing what to carry to the buggy was easy. Knowing what to say to Jethro wasn't. She prayed for answers and guidance as she made her trips back and forth to the front porch with what she wanted to take.

JETHRO DROVE the buggy into the yard the way he'd done since early September. He helped Heidi load her things. After he helped her into the buggy, he reached for the reins. "I'll decide where we're going today if I may."

"Oh, uh, all right." Her wide eyes filled with question marks she didn't voice.

"Thank you. I'll explain myself later."

They rode in a comfortable, but unusual silence as he headed the buggy south. The barn and outbuildings were almost out of sight, and Heidi had barely said a word. "What painting do you want to finish?"

"A landscape I've been working on. You're going to Lily and Toby's ridge, aren't you?"

"Yes, since we have time today. Maybe you can add in longhorns or mustangs."

She clapped her hands together like a child. "I'd like that more than I can say."

He shook his head at her. "I doubt that. You've never been at a loss for words since we met."

"I'm quiet when I paint."

His breath caught at the sassy look on her face. Lord willing, she was flirting with him again. "Sometimes. But Mr. Grimes is right about our best conversations happening while you're standing in front of your easel."

"Well, yes. I suppose so. But I haven't heard you complain even though you're a man of few words."

"No, you haven't." He thanked God she seemed to be so happy to be with him. Happy enough she hadn't alluded to the day he'd watched her draw her late brother.

They alternated between times of talking and times of silence the rest of the way. She was either seriously studying the terrain or seriously thinking. He hoped the latter, since she had yet to give him the answer he must have before proposing to her.

"I'm wondering about something Toby said." She twisted to where she almost faced him.

"What is that?"

"He turned his back on God and didn't want to be with anyone. What if I've done that in a different way by thinking the only way to solve my problems with my parents is to never depend on, never need anyone again?"

"I'd say that's a possibility, something you should pray about."

"Yes, I think so." She went back to looking over the winter-browned countryside. Back to her thinking? "Jethro?"

"What?" He glanced over at her.

"Please forgive me for being so blunt, but—"

"Being blunt has never bothered you before." He laughed despite her serious expression.

"No. I suppose not. You may have turned your back on God by isolating yourself. Not physically, but by not talking to anyone. You might have pushed all the pain so deep inside you didn't let God help you finish forgiving the people who killed your father."

"I'll give it serious consideration." She made some valid points, but he had a different mission to accomplish today.

"Which means I could be right?"

"Yes, you could be. It's troubling to think about. Not you. But the idea of what I might have done. You aren't trouble."

"I'm glad to hear that, since I fear that's how you thought of me the first time we met and the first time you escorted me to paint."

"Let's say you have a way of growing on people. Especially me."

"Good." She laughed.

A short time later, he halted the buggy as they topped the ridge. "I see longhorns to the west."

"Yes!" She started to scramble from the wagon.

He placed his hand on her arm. "Not today. Please allow me to assist you."

She cocked her head as she studied him. "Why?"

"Because I'd like to treat you as the lady you are."

"Oh. I don't think I'd mind that."

"I'll ground tie Red then help you." He set the brake before getting out of the buggy. Once her feet touched the ground, he didn't rush to let go of her hand. The way she gazed at him made him wonder if she'd accept his kiss, maybe welcome it. He wouldn't kiss her again until he knew for sure she trusted him enough to give up her dreams for him.

He helped her unload the buggy. If she were to become his fiancée and one day wife, he wouldn't stand by and watch her carry everything the way he had done before. Couldn't do so. But he'd wait to explain himself for the same reason he'd wait to kiss her.

The one thing he didn't change was sitting on a stool while she set up her easel and paints. While watching her, his thoughts went back to what Mr. Grimes had said on the porch. He'd had no idea his boss had suffered so many tragedies.

Yet Mr. Grimes had finally turned back to God after almost losing Harvey. Almost losing Heidi had finally brought him to his senses. She was what mattered. Not the grudges he'd held on to for so many years. The grudges that could still end the possibility of a life with Heidi if she couldn't trust him enough.

She seemed content to let him think as she painted. He could enjoy times like this from here on out with no problem. Her light green-checked dress flattered her hair, eyes, and fair complexion. The expression of utter contentment on her face as she stared off to study the terrain then put her brush to the canvas captivated him. He didn't need a book or newspaper to entertain himself.

"You should come see better what I'm doing. I'd like your opinion about adding a cloud or two in the sky."

He rose and then walked to her side. She'd never asked for his ideas before. "Your talent is amazing. A couple of small clouds might add a nice touch."

"I think so too. Here over to the left a little, drifting across the sky." She stepped back after painting the first cloud, so absorbed in her painting she hadn't noticed Jethro still stood beside her. "Perfect. This will be one of the prettiest landscapes I've done."

"I'd rather look at the beautiful painter next to me." Jethro knelt.

She gasped and almost dropped her brush before laying it down by her paints. "Oh, my."

"Heidi Schultz, I love you with all my heart. Will you marry me?"

For one heart-rending moment, she peered silently into his eyes. Perhaps he should have waited for another day. Asked her point blank if she'd give up her dreams for him. But his patience had run out.

"Yes, Jethro Bannister, I'll spend the rest of my life with you."

He leapt to his feet then took her in his arms. They exchanged sweet kisses until they were breathless. She stepped back. He left his arms draped loosely around her waist.

"I take your yes to mean you don't mind giving up the kind of life you've wanted so badly. I'd like to know how you decided that."

"As you know ..." Her words tailed off as she ran her finger over his cheek. "I've been praying and praying since the day you asked if I could set aside my dreams for you. Blindly clinging to what I wanted meant I didn't see what God really wanted the way Toby didn't see." Her beaming smile testified to her happiness. "What I'm gaining is so much better than what I thought I'd be giving up."

"Quit talking. You've said enough for now." He crooked his finger under her chin and kissed her again.

She returned his kiss with more than one of her own before stepping back from him. "I have to breathe." Tracing his mustache with her finger, she smiled up at him. "You know my love for talking could cause you trouble the rest of your life."

"I think I can handle that kind of trouble." He pulled her into his arms again. He'd be happy to deal with sore ears the rest of his life.

Betty Woods writes heartwarming romance with a southern accent. As Heidi and Jethro discover, people make their plans but God determines our steps, Proverbs 16:9. Never be afraid to let our loving Father determine or reimagine your plans.

An incurable history buff, Betty can roam for hours through historical sites or museums. She can tell you more useless trivia about cattle trails, nineteenth century life and society than you might want to know. Watching an old western movie with someone requires keeping quiet so she doesn't ruin the movie for everyone else by pointing out historical inaccuracies.

She's been a storyteller since childhood and still has the notebooks full of her handwritten stories. Plus her first "book" written in fourth grade from her dog's point of view. Her love for writing has taken several detours over the years—marriage, children, grandchildren and even great grands. Detours she wouldn't trade for anything.

When not living in her make-believe nineteenth century world, Betty enjoys time with family. Especially family RV trips with her three adult children, grandchildren and occasionally great grands. She and her husband share their Texas home with a spoiled, well-traveled Chihuahua who goes wherever they go.

Find out more about Betty at bettywoodsbooks.com.

Facebook: bettywoodsbooks

X: @BettyWoodsWrite

# MORE FROM THE TRAILS OF THE HEART SERIES

***Love's Twisting Trail***

*Trails of the Heart—Book One*

Stampedes, wild animals, and renegade Comanches make a cattle drive dangerous for any man. The risks multiply when Charlotte Grimes goes up the trail disguised as Charlie, a fourteen-year-old boy. She promised her dying father she'd save their ranch after her brother, Tobias, mismanages their money. To keep her vow, she rides the trail with the brother she can't trust.

David Shepherd needs one more successful drive to finish buying the ranch he's prayed for. He partners with Tobias to travel safely through Indian Territory. David detests the hateful way Tobias treats his younger brother, Charlie. He could easily love the boy like the brother he's always wanted. But what does he do when he discovers Charlie's secret? What kind of woman would do what she's done?

The trail takes an unexpected twist when Charlotte falls in love with David. She's afraid to tell him of her deception. Such a God-fearing, honest gentleman is bound to despise the kind of woman who dares to wear a man's trousers and venture on a cattle drive. Since her father left her half the ranch, she intends to continue working the land like any other man after she returns to Texas. David would never accept her as she is.

Choosing between keeping her promise to her father or being with the man she loves may put Charlotte's heart in more danger than any of the hazards on the trail can.

Get your copy here:

https://scrivenings.link/lovestwistingtrail

### *Redemption's Trail*

*Trails of the Heart—Book Two*

Newly widowed with her second child due in a few months, Lily Johnson has nowhere to go until Toby Grimes, her late husband's boss, asks her to stay on as housekeeper at his ranch. Remaining in the house Mr. Grimes built for her and her husband is an answered prayer. But malicious gossips see her godsend job as a ruse for a sinful dalliance since her employer is a nice-looking, single man.

God and a lot of others turned their backs on Toby during the war, so he returns the favor by keeping to himself. Yet the need to care for and protect Lily overwhelms him. The way she tugs at his heart scares him more than going into a losing battle.

Unwilling to allow anyone to destroy a fine woman's reputation, he proposes a marriage of convenience. After much prayer, Lily accepts. Her first marriage was a love match made in heaven. The second leads down a trail only God knows. The peace she has concerning a marriage to a troubled man she doesn't love begins a walk of faith to a destination neither she, nor Toby, can guess.

Get your copy here:

https://scrivenings.link/redemptionstrail

# YOU MAY ALSO LIKE ...

Homeward Trails—by Susan Page Davis

### *The Rancher's Legacy*—Book One

Will Rogers Medallion—Copper Award Winner

Matthew Anderson and his father try to help neighbor Bill Maxwell when his ranch is attacked. On the day his daughter Rachel is to return from school back East, outlaws target the Maxwell ranch. After Rachel's world is shattered, she won't even consider the plan her father and Matt's cooked up—to see their two children marry and combine the ranches.

Meanwhile in Maine, sea captain's widow Edith Rose hires a private investigator to locate her three missing grandchildren. The children were abandoned by their father nearly twenty years ago. They've been adopted into very different families, and they're scattered across the country. Can investigator Ryland Atkins find them all while the elderly woman still lives? His first attempt is to find the boy now called

Matthew Anderson. Can Ryland survive his trip into the wild Colorado Territory and find Matt before the outlaws finish destroying a legacy?

Get your copy here:

https://scrivenings.link/therancherslegacy

***The Corporal's Codebook*—Book Two**

Jack Miller stumbles through the Civil War, winding up a telegrapher and cryptographer for the army. In the field with General Sherman in Georgia, he is captured along with his precious cipher key.

His captor, Hamilton Buckley, thinks he should have been president of the Confederacy, not Jefferson Davis. Jack doubts Buckley's sanity and longs to escape. Buckley's kindhearted niece, Marilla, might help him— but only if Jack helps her achieve her own goal.

Meanwhile, a private investigator, stymied by the difficulty of travel and communication in wartime, is trying his best to locate Jack for the grandmother he longs to see again but can barely remember.

Get your copy here:

## *The Sister's Search*—Book Three

*A young woman searches for her missing brother and finds much more awaits her —if she can escape war-torn Texas.*

Molly Weaver and her widowed mother embark on an arduous journey at the end of the Civil War. They hope to join Molly's brother Andrew on his ranch in Texas. When they arrive, Andrew is missing and squatters threaten the ranch.

Can they trust Joe, the stranger who claims to be Andrew's friend? Joe's offer to help may be a godsend—or a snare. And who is the man claiming to be Molly's father? If he's telling the truth, Molly's past is a sham, and she must learn where she really belongs.

Get your copy here:

*Stay up-to-date on your favorite books and authors with our free e-newsletters.*

ScriveningsPress.com